He promises to love, honor, and tempt her with the most scintillating desire...

"Mr. Enright, do you know where you are?"

Those expressive brows came together but, before he could answer, he began shaking. The chills were starting to come upon him, and she had nothing to use to help him fight them off.

"I need to fetch help," she said, starting to rise. "You—"

She didn't finish her sentence. With unanticipated swiftness and a strength that must have cost him everything he had, Mr. Enright grabbed her, placing a hand to the back of her neck so he could look her in the eye. "*No.*"

The single word reverberated in the air around them.

"But you need help," she said. Surprisingly, she was not afraid. "If you don't receive care, you could die here."

She watched as he processed her words, and realized he'd already accepted the possibility of death. He *knew* how ill he was.

"Please," she whispered. "It might not be too late."

"No," he repeated, the word spoken softer but just as emphatic. "No one else. Safe here." It was taking great effort for him to speak. "Secret. Keep . . . secret. Promise me."

CATHY MAXWELL

The Groom Says Yes

THE BRIDES OF WISHMORE

AVON

An Imprint of HarperCollinsPublishers

This is a work of fiction. Names, characters, places, and incidents are products of the author's imagination or are used fictitiously and are not to be construed as real. Any resemblance to actual events, locales, organizations, or persons, living or dead, is entirely coincidental.

AVON BOOKS
An Imprint of HarperCollins*Publishers*
195 Broadway
New York, New York 10007

Copyright © 2014 by Cathy Maxwell, Inc.
ISBN 978-0-06-221929-9
www.avonromance.com

First Avon Books mass market printing: October 2014

Avon Trademark Reg. U.S. Pat. Off. and in Other Countries, Marca Registrada, Hecho en U.S.A.
HarperCollins® is a registered trademark of HarperCollins Publishers.

Printed in the U.S.A.

10 9 8 7 6 5 4 3 2 1

For my wonderful, loving friend Anne Elizabeth

The
Groom Says Yes

Chapter One

September, 1817
Tolbooth Prison
Edinburgh

The minister was a slight man with thinning brown hair and was obviously uneasy at being in the presence of the "Irish Murderer." The hands holding his prayer book shook.

Frankly, Cormac Enright hated the epithet. It had been coined by the writers of the broadsheets printed almost daily during his trial. On the morrow, those filthy scribblers would line their pockets selling hundreds of papers and pamphlets detailing his execution, and Mac wished them happily to hell for their greed.

He lifted his broad shoulders from the rickety cot where he'd lain for the past several hours . . . thinking of nothing . . . thinking of everything.

The cleric, in spite of his fear, gave the air a sniff and wrinkled his nose in disgust.

Mac almost laughed. He was a trained physician. He had fought in battle and lived as rough men do, and even he had found the stench of the Tolbooth hard to take, and he was certain he reeked of it as well. The building was ancient and highly unsanitary. It was so bad, it was scheduled to be torn down in a few months. Mac's hanging was to be the last held here, and the guards had assured him he should feel honored. This was a moment in history. The crowd already gathering to watch him put to death might number in the thousands because Edinburgh did like a good hanging.

And because the woman Mac was accused of murdering, Gordana Raney, had been beautiful, young, and a popular singer around the taverns.

Mac's sole consolation was that he'd managed to keep knowledge of his title, earl of Ballin, from the leeches and the corrupt lawyers who had convicted him although, he realized, it was of little matter. He was the last of his line. There was no one left to witness the shame his foolishness had brought upon his family. Then again, of what value was a penniless title?

Aye, he'd deemed it wiser to keep quiet.

But that didn't mean the pride of five hundred years of Irish nobility didn't pound through his veins.

He raked a hand through his unruly hair. He had not been allowed to shave, to make himself presentable. His dark blue jacket was torn at the sleeves and in need of a good wash. *He* was in need of a good washing.

"If you've come to hear my confession, cleric, you will be disappointed," Mac said. He'd not spoken in days. His voice sounded rough, hoarse. "I may hang for a crime I did not commit, but I'll not confess to it. Not that anyone cares what I say."

The reverend nodded, his brow furrowed as if he had concerns of his own, then, to Mac's surprise, he said to the guard standing at the door, "Leave us."

To Mac's further amazement, the man did.

The guard's name was Harris, and he'd taken particular delight in making Mac's life hell over the past months. Now, he acted as docile as any lackey. Mac felt his guard go up.

The reverend gave his spectacles a push up his nose. "You are a big, brawny man. No one told me you were so tall."

"Will that be a problem for my execution?"

The man actually took a nervous step back, but then he stopped. "I am Reverend Kinnion. Reverend Kinnion of Kenmore," he said, his voice barely above a whisper. "I am here because there are those who wish to repent for their mistakes."

"I don't repent."

"I'm not speaking of *you*." The Reverend Kinnion shifted his weight. His manner had changed. He seemed focused, intent. "They say you don't know what really happened. That you were drunk when you killed the girl."

Aye, he'd been blind drunk that night. Sick with drink. "I wouldn't have harmed her."

"You were covered with her blood."

"I had no blood on my person—" Mac denied heatedly, then stopped and gathered himself. No good would come from alienating the last person willing to hear his side of the story, especially one watching him so intently.

Modulating his tone, Mac said, "They found a man's blood-soaked cloak on the floor of my room. They claimed it was mine. It wasn't and I don't know how it came to be there." The smell of Gordana's blood seemed to be always present with him, choking him. "I am a fool of a man, Mr.

Kinnion. I've done many things, most of them wrong. But I vow I did not harm her."

"I know you are telling the truth," the Reverend Kinnion said. He moved closer to Mac but not too close. "However, I needed to hear your denial from your own lips. A friend, a man I hold in high esteem, has asked me to do a favor. One I did not know I could carry out until this moment. My friend is not like you. He wishes no darkness on his soul."

"Who is your friend?"

The reverend hesitated. His voice grew even more hushed as he answered, "Davidson. Richard Davidson."

"That *bastard*."

"He asks your forgiveness."

Mac almost choked on the audacity of the man. "His *false* testimony put the noose around my neck. He *lied* when he claimed he saw me murder Gordana Raney. I'll forgive him in hell."

"Fair enough," the reverend countered. "Meanwhile, I shall pray that you will one day find it in your heart to grant his wish. As for right now, you and I need to leave this place."

"Leave?" Mac wasn't certain he'd heard the man correctly.

"Aye, but we haven't much time. I bribed the guard with me, Harris is his name, to look the other way as we made our escape."

"You are here to help me escape?" Mac said dumbly.

"Aye, if you will move your feet. Are you coming or not?"

Mac was across the cell in a blink. "What of the other guards?" he whispered.

"Harris said he will try to manage them, but we take our chances. He told me how to find the back entrance. The crowd that has been gathering for your hanging is by the gallows. This exit should take us away from them." He opened his prayer book. The pages had been hollowed out and a coin purse hidden there. He gave the purse to Mac. "This will pay for your passage away from Scotland. Do you understand? You are to leave and never return."

Mac nodded. He would agree to anything to leave his hellhole. He tucked the purse inside the coat he wore. "You don't happen to have a pistol in that book as well?"

The Reverend Kinnion's eyes widened at the suggestion. "I would not. And I must go first. I was the one told the way and, if something happens, and you are captured, well, I hope you understand, but I'm going to run. I hope to see my wife again."

"I pray you do," Mac answered. Moments ago, he had been in despair. Now hope surged through him, filling his being with anxious energy.

The cleric drew a shaky breath. "Very well. We shall go now."

But before he could leave, Mac grabbed his arm. He looked into the man's eyes. "I thank you for this. I'm beholden to you."

"You are not. I could not rest easy knowing you were innocent."

"Why not declare what you know? Why protect Davidson?"

"Because letting it be known he lied when he testified against you would ruin him. He is a good man, Mr. Enright. He was caught up in a situation he could not control."

"All he has to do is speak the truth."

"And that is never easy." The Reverend Kinnion changed the subject. "Down this main hall is a connecting corridor. Harris will see that it is dark. Wait for a count of ten, then follow me."

The reverend slipped out the door.

Mac listened, counting, barely hearing the other man's footsteps, then he eased out past the door and into the hall.

Everything around Mac took on importance. The pitch burning in the torches stung his nostrils. The worn soles of his boots were careful of the uneven floor, and his ears were attuned to those sounds coming from the guard post. He could hear the scrape of a chair being set on its feet, of a man's groan as he rose . . . of Harris's accented voice saying, "That reverend has been with Enright long enough. I'd best go check on them."

Damn the man. Mac didn't trust him. He would take Kinnion's bribe and turn on him.

Mac hastened his step toward the darkness of the connecting hallway—and then he heard the shout of *"Hey!"* and knew he'd been caught.

Harris had betrayed them. He'd taken the cleric's bribe but was probably planning to foil the escape and see himself a hero. *That* was the guard Mac knew.

Harris shouted again for him to halt, but he spoke to air. Mac had charged around the corner into the darkness. He heard a door open ahead and knew it was Kinnion. Heart pounding, Mac picked up his pace, his muscles screaming after months of forced inactivity. Still, he was in better shape than the guards, or so he bloody prayed.

The Tolbooth was a bit of a labyrinth. There were doorways and half floors. But Kinnion seemed to have found his way. He was well ahead of Mac, who now had to listen for the reverend's footsteps as well as the clamoring noise of his gaolers in hot pursuit.

He was upon the stairs before he realized they were there and practically tumbled to the bottom. There was another door. Mac opened it. He could no longer hear the Reverend Kinnion. He now trusted instinct.

When he'd first come to the prison, he'd tried to memorize where he was in the building and its peculiarities. He sensed there was a door to the outside close at hand. The air smelled of freedom. Sweet and fresh and tinged with a hint of salt from the sea. All he had to do was keep going forward.

The guards had reached the top of the stairs. They now started down just as a musket shot cracked the air.

The gunfire was not in the building. The sound would have reverberated.

Above him, the guards went still. "What was that?" one of them asked.

"Was it Enright?" another questioned.

Mac moved forward, his hand trailing the wall. He found the door, twisted the handle, and pushed it—*the door did not open.*

Something blocked it from the other side.

With every second counting, Mac threw his body at the door, shoving on it until he moved whatever was in the way to the side enough for him to squeeze through.

He fell out into the night, stumbling over a man's body, collapsed in front of the door.

Kinnion.

In the dim moonlight, he appeared dead, blood staining his shirt. The gunshot had attracted attention. People began running out of the darkness.

The first to come forward was a hulking brute who gave a cry when he saw Kinnion's body. Mac had been leaning down to see if Kinnion was alive and if there was anything he could do for him. The brute grabbed Mac by the collar and threw him toward the street. "Run, man. *Run.*"

The order brought Mac to awareness of how dangerous his position was. He began backing away as the large man picked up Kinnion. A crowd quickly surrounded them, apparently believing the reverend was Mac.

Mac took a step back, then another. No one had recognized him yet. He had to be bold. He had to stay calm. He moved into the shadows, forcing himself to walk, to act as if he were one of those gathered for the hanging.

Rumors were starting. It was quickly put out that the good reverend was the Irish Murderer. Someone dropped his hat on the ground, and Mac picked it up, pulling the wide brim down over his eyes to hide his face.

Guards came out of a door close to Mac, but their attention was not focused on him. They ran right past him. His hopes began to build.

The bullet that had struck Kinnion had probably been meant for Mac. Even the escape might have been a trap. But this was not the time to pause and reflect.

Mac did know one thing—he would not be leaving Scotland. Not until he'd had a conversation with Richard Davidson.

The decision was *not* wise—but then, when had the Irish ever let wisdom and prudence interfere with bull-nosed stubbornness?

Of course, he didn't know where to find Davidson. He knew the man was from the country, but he knew little else. However, Davidson had a friend, the good Reverend Kinnion of Kenmore. *Kenmore.* The name had the sound of a village to it, and Mac would find Kenmore if he had to travel to the end of Hades.

And so he did. He began walking west, walking into Scotland.

He found a stream to bathe in. The water was so cold, his skin turned blue, but a good washing made him feel human again.

A bit before dawn, he was offered a ride on a passing driver's wagon. Mac didn't ask the driver if he'd heard of the Irish Murderer, and the man didn't speak of the Old Tolbooth escape. This gave Mac hope that his story was not known very far outside the city and that his Scot's accent was passable.

He concocted a story about his being a sailor recently returned. This explained his scruffy appearance.

The Scots were hospitable. Not as open as the Irish, but they were not as dour as he'd been led to believe. A yeoman lent Mac his shaving kit. The dull razor served well enough, and Mac began to feel a bit like his old self.

Each day, each hour, Mac traveled closer to Kenmore. He was a man on a mission, and he'd not rest until he tracked down Davidson and asked why he had lied.

He was riding in a tinker's wagon when the man stopped at a crossroads, and said, "Kenmore is about two miles across that moor. Just follow the road. You'll see Loch Tay through a line of trees and know you are close."

"Thank you," Mac said, jumping down from the cart. An ache had started to form behind his eyes. He welcomed a stretch of the leg and fresh air.

However, he hadn't walked long until he realized he was experiencing the first stirrings of real illness. His step faltered. Dizziness was making it hard for him to walk. His stomach cramped. He practically fell onto the dirt road and crawled to the side, where he lost what little food he had in him.

He knew the grippe very well. Influenza was a killer amongst battlefield camps.

The world whirled around him, his insides threatened to erupt again, and for all of his great size, he had the strength of a newborn.

He managed to scramble to his feet. He tried to walk on, but it was no use. He was in danger of collapsing again—and that is when he noticed the bothy, one of the stone huts built for shepherds and wayfarers that dotted the moors across Scotland.

Here was shelter.

Mac staggered into the bothy. This one was located not far off the road. There was no door, just an opening. The floor was hard earth. He fell to it, his legs no longer able to support him.

He yanked his jacket off and curled into a fetal position, wishing he were dead, the fever rattling his bones.

Here he was, almost in sight of his one link to Davidson and unable to take even a step closer.

Instead, he hugged his sides and prayed, something he'd thought he'd forgotten how to do. But his prayer was not for healing or Divine benevolence. Oh, no, Mac prayed that he'd not depart this world until he could put his hands on Davidson's throat and choke the truth out of him.

Chapter Two

Kenmore

*F*or today's program of the Ladies' Quarterly Meeting, Mr. Iain McClain, the schoolmaster, read a poem he'd written in praise of the local mountain, Schiehallion.

Sitting in the kirk sanctuary with two dozen other women considered prominent in the valley, Sabrina Davidson noticed that he was very free with the word "breast" when describing Schiehallion's shape. He used it no less than three times. Then, when he referred to mountain's "nippled crest," Sabrina almost laughed aloud. She stifled the sound when she realized no one else seemed to think there was anything awkward or humorous about his imagery. Indeed, they clapped enthusiastically at the end of his recitation of his dreadful poem. Sabrina clapped as well, albeit less enthusiastically.

The women then, as was their custom, piled out of the church to walk across the way to the Kenmore Inn, where a delicious luncheon awaited them.

Sabrina walked in their midst, surrounded by their happy chatter . . . but acutely aware that no one was actually speaking to her. No, they talked of matters that interested them—children, household concerns, husbands—topics that didn't include Sabrina.

Not for the first time did she realize that if she stopped and let them go on, no one might notice she wasn't part of the group. It wasn't that they didn't care for her. She was the magistrate's daughter. She had a place in their society, including the fact they needed her musical skills to play the pianoforte for the local assemblies.

However, Sabrina was an outsider and would always be one. She was nine-and-twenty and unmarried. Thankfully, her father had been devoted to her late mother and would never think of disgracing her memory by remarrying. Otherwise, Sabrina might have become that most pitied of souls, an unmarried female relation.

As it was, she not only served as her father's hostess and helped him as his secretary, but she was also the earl of Tay's niece. Her position in society was secure.

Still, Sabrina had caught herself thinking about the married ladies quite a bit lately. There was a mystery to men that other women seemed to understand, and she didn't. During those years when a woman was young enough to catch a husband, Sabrina had been caring for her mother, who had battled a wasting illness, and now the time for courting had passed her by.

Lately, she wondered what she'd missed.

Perhaps her thoughts along these lines were prompted by her cousins' recent marriages. Or that after two years of mourning her mother's death, Sabrina had finally set aside her black.

It was also possible that something deeper stirred inside her, like the tiniest hint of rebellion at the thought she was only worthy if she was a wife or a mother. That her intelligence was of no value otherwise.

She'd caught their pitying glances, those looks between them that said louder than words they thought themselves superior to her.

And maybe she agreed with them . . . just a little.

She knew she couldn't reason this out herself. She needed a mentor. For that reason, she'd penned a note to Dame Agatha, one of the widows of their group, asking if she would sit with her today. The dame was well respected and appeared to enjoy her life as an independent woman. Sabrina hoped for her advice.

The innkeeper, Mr. Orrock, and his wife greeted the flock of women at the door, giving them a chance to remove their bonnets before grandly escorting them into the inn's public room. The tables had been set with silver and napkins. The women fanned out to claim their chairs.

All the tables in the room were set for four or six, except for one. It had service for two and was located in the corner by the hearth. True to his promise, Mr. Orrock had placed the "reserved" card Sabrina had designed in the middle of the table, thereby ensuring it was kept for her.

She took her seat and began pulling off her gloves as she looked around for Dame Agatha. However, before she knew what was what, Mrs. Lillian Bossley, the notorious "Widow Bossley," pulled out the chair opposite hers and plopped her ample bottom into the seat.

The aging widow was a robust woman of relatively good looks and lax morals. She had a head full of graying blonde curls and a guilelessness to her blue eyes that men seemed to admire, especially since she was quick to jump into their beds.

Last year, she had carried on a scandalous affair with Sabrina's dissolute uncle. Of course the earl did what he always did with women—he tired of her and didn't hesitate to toss her aside.

In that respect, Sabrina did feel a bit sorry for her. The gossip was that, after the earl's disgraceful abandonment, Mrs. Bossley's spirits had been very low.

However, sympathy did not mean Sabrina wished to share "the special table" with the likes of the widow.

"I'm sorry," Sabrina hastened to say, "that seat has been claimed."

"By whom?" Mrs. Bossley had the effrontery to ask.

"By Dame Agatha," Sabrina answered.

"Oh, you needn't worry," Mrs. Bossley said, waving a hand in the direction of the other tables. "Dame Agatha suggested I take this chair."

"*She did?*" Sabrina looked over to see that the diminutive matriarch had seated herself at a table with three other women. The dame smiled at Sabrina, her expression as benevolent and unrelenting as a queen's.

And since everyone else in the room was seated, Sabrina had no choice but to accept the arrangement.

The serving lad, the Orrocks' oldest son, placed soup and bread in front of them.

"May we have a pot of tea?" Mrs. Bossley asked the lad.

"Yes, mum," he murmured, and hurried away.

Mrs. Bossley considered Sabrina's stiff silence, and said, "Don't be too upset, Miss Davidson. Aggie knows I needed to speak to you on a matter of some importance. That is why she suggested I sit with you."

Aggie?

Sabrina set her gloves to the side. She could barely look at the woman. "If you wished to discuss a matter of some importance, would it not be wiser and more circumspect to call upon me in private?"

"I have attempted to do so, Miss Davidson," Mrs. Bossley answered, slathering butter on her bread. "But you have not accepted my call."

"That is not true—"

"Of course it is. I called yesterday and the day before. Mrs. Patton told me you were not at home although I am certain you were."

"I believe you are imagining things," Sabrina

countered, even as heat rose to her cheeks. She sparingly buttered her own bread. In truth, she had seen the widow approach the house and had begged Mrs. Patton, who served as cook and general housekeeper to the Davidson household, to inform Mrs. Bossley she was out. She also sensed a quietness in the chatter in the room and realized that everyone was interested in their conversation. It was as if the other women sensed something was afoot.

Sabrina's guard rose even higher.

The lad brought a pot of tea for them to share. Mrs. Bossley took it upon herself to pour them each a cup. She lifted the creamer, silently asking Sabrina if she wished a drop in hers as well.

Sabrina shook her head and picked up her spoon to sample her soup. Forcing a smile and keeping her voice too low to be overheard, she said, "If you wish to speak to me about the earl, let me assure you I have no control over my uncle's behavior, good or bad. No one does."

Of course, in Sabrina's mind, the Widow Bossley had behaved just as poorly as the earl and had probably received exactly what she deserved. Her mother had always cautioned Sabrina to not be too bold around gentlemen, and after witnessing the widow's behavior, she understood why. Perhaps in the future, Mrs. Bossley would not be so free with her favors—

"Your father has asked me to be his wife, Miss Davidson, and I have said, yes."

If the chair had fallen apart beneath Sabrina, she could not have been more surprised. She waited, spoon poised in the air, for the woman to laugh.

There was no humor in Mrs. Bossley's expression.

Sabrina put down her spoon. "I don't believe you."

"It is not a question of whether you believe me or not," Mrs. Bossley countered serenely. "It is a truth and therefore not subject to judgment. Your father has been courting me for the past three months." She held out her gloveless right hand, opening her fingers to reveal a dainty gold ring in her palm that had belonged to Sabrina's mother. It had been in the family for generations. After her death, her father had attached it to his fob chain.

"Richard gave this to me as a pledge of his troth. He asked me not to wear it until he had spoken to you."

Sabrina's gaze was riveted on the ring. This was to have been *her* ring someday, the only memento that had truly belonged to her mother and had been passed down from mother to daughter over several generations.

And her father had given it to *this* woman?

"Now that you are aware of our intentions," Mrs. Bossley continued crisply, "we can have the banns announced. However, I do have one important question."

"And that is?" Sabrina managed to say through her shock.

"Can you accept me as your stepmother?"

Sabrina felt suddenly, violently ill.

She threw down her napkin and pushed back her chair. "I need air." She didn't wait for a response but moved quickly from the room. She shoved open the inn's front door and almost fell into the road. She took several deep breaths of air, needing to regain her balance and clear her head.

What the widow had said couldn't be true. *It couldn't.*

The door behind her opened. Mrs. Bossley came outside. "We are not finished with our conversation."

"No, we are not," Sabrina agreed. There were no prying ears here. The road between the inn and Kenmore Kirk across the way was empty save for vehicles and horses and a few drivers waiting in front of the church for the ladies to finish their meals.

At last, Sabrina could speak her mind.

"You asked if I could accept you as a stepmother? The answer is no. I will *never* accept you," she said, infusing each word with as much disdain as she could muster. "Nor will my father ever marry you. If he had intended to do so, he would have told me of this himself."

"He was afraid of your reaction," Mrs. Bossley countered. "Of your childishness—"

Those were fighting words. Sabrina took a step toward the woman, ready to "childishly" throttle her.

Mrs. Bossley's chin took on a determined angle as if daring Sabrina to attack. "I *will* be your father's wife," she promised. "And be forewarned. No household can have two mistresses. My rightful place will be by his side, and if you cannot accept my position, then we shall have difficulties between us with perhaps only *one* solution."

"And what will that be? Tossing me out? You believe my father would place you over me?" Sabrina challenged. "That he would ask me to leave?"

"We are *lovers*." The widow threw out the declaration with the glee of a gambler showing his winning card.

"That can't be true."

Mrs. Bossley smiled, her confidence unnerving. "You are such an innocent."

Her words slapped Sabrina across the face.

There was a movement in the inn's windows. A curtain in the public room dropped as if someone had been peering outside and was afraid to be discovered.

"They are all watching," Mrs. Bossley said with a touch of cynicism. "We shall be the dinner discussion around many a table unless we settle this amicably between ourselves. Accept the marriage, Miss Davidson, let us walk back into the dining room as friends, and the gossips will not have anything to go on about." She offered her hand.

She was right. A feud between them would ignite the vicious tongues in the valley. Although Sabrina did not think highly of the Widow Bossley, apparently there were many who did—like Dame Agatha. Sabrina could not fathom why. The local society had so many strict standards where a woman like herself could be verbally pilloried, and yet, a blind eye could be turned on someone like Widow Bossley.

And the valley had easily accepted Sabrina's cousins because of their extraordinary beauty although one had been divorced and the other was a spoiled brat.

And *everyone* tolerated the earl's excesses.

Meanwhile, people were always quick to point out Sabrina's flaws. She was not like the other Davidsons. She was dark like her mother. Her hair was thick, with just a hint of red to it, and no one had ever called her even pretty. "They" said there was too much intelligence in her eyes, and her tongue was too quick. Yes, "they" wanted her to lead the kirk's charities and play for their dances, but she was pitied more than respected.

Something inside Sabrina snapped.

Had only minutes earlier she'd wondered if she was dissatisfied with her life? She now knew the answer. Yes.

Her own culpability filled her with anger. Furious in a way she'd never experienced before, resentment came roiling up inside her like a pot boiling over.

Ignoring the offered hand, Sabrina turned and began walking away from the inn. Her cart and pony were hitched with the others. Dumpling, a shaggy Highland beast with a flaxen mane and tail, had one back foot cocked as he slept standing in the afternoon sunlight.

But Sabrina didn't walk in that direction. Instead, without the hat or the gloves she'd left behind in the inn, she chose the road leading toward the moors.

"*Miss Davidson,*" Mrs. Bossley called, an impertinent note in her tone as if she expected Sabrina to immediately come marching back.

Sabrina wouldn't. She couldn't.

What she needed to do was to have a moment alone so that she could release this terrible anger building inside her. She had to clear her head to think. Her whole life was about to change, and it was all her father's fault.

He'd been courting the Widow Bossley and hadn't said a word to her? She couldn't believe he wanted to remarry. It was completely out of his character.

Her father had always been a cautious man, a reserved one . . . although since her mother's death, there had been times Sabrina had concerns for him, something she hadn't realized until this moment. He did not always act quite himself. However, she had never imagined he'd be open to clandestine meetings with the Widow Bossley. And asking her to marry him made Sabrina wonder if he was ready for Bedlam!

The worst was having the widow behave in such a condescending manner. She'd called Sabrina "innocent." Another way of saying naïve. Or unimportant.

However, she did speak one truth. If her father remarried, Sabrina would be subject to the widow's whims. Men were that way. They could be led.

Hot tears spilled from her eyes. She swiped at them, angry with herself for being hurt, for being afraid.

How soon men forget their grief. How quickly they move on. Bitterness threatened to consume her. She couldn't return home, not yet. She'd do and say things she would regret.

As she moved to higher ground, she left behind the trees and the silver waters of Loch Tay. She left behind civilization. Here, where the sky touched the wild moors, she had space to breathe, to cry, and to scream her anger.

Not far from the road was an abandoned bothy. When her mother had been so frighteningly ill, there had been many a time Sabrina had needed escape. She'd discovered the bothy and realized here was a place she could go to release the horror of watching her mother slowly die.

In the bothy, she could break down, rage at

God even, then dry her tears, dust herself off, and travel home with no one's being the wiser. Because of the bothy, she had smiles for her mother and soothing words for her father.

And right now, Sabrina needed its haven.

The bothy was nestled in the crook of the moor's rolling land. She picked up her step. Without hesitation, she ducked under the open doorway, strode right through the first room past the door into the second, windowless one. She stopped, facing a corner. Her face was flushed and her breathing labored from exertion and anger.

Doubling her fists, she gave vent to her outrage, speaking to the air as if to her father.

"You *can't* marry that woman. You *mustn't*. And if you think *I* shall live under the same roof with her or sit at the same table—you are wrong. Wrong, wrong, *wrong*. I shall not disgrace my mother's memory by recognizing her. Do you hear me? *I won't*."

That last felt good. And so, she repeated it.

"I. Won't. Not *ever*. You may cut me off, send me to the poorhouse, whip me with chains, but I will *not* sit at a table with the Widow Bossley. And she will never be a mother to me. Or anything else."

She could have jumped up and down she was so angry. She'd never speak these words to her father. Mrs. Bossley was right; Sabrina had no choice but to accept the marriage.

Sabrina would become an unwanted appendage in their lives, a shadow of what she'd once been. Then she would die. Alone. Unmourned. A morality tale to young girls of what happened to the unmarried—

Her thoughts broke off as the hairs on the back of her neck tingled with awareness.

She might die alone, *but she was not alone now.*

In the space of a pause, she'd heard someone else's breathing, a heavy sound as if with difficulty.

Slowly, she turned, and her heart gave a start.

A man blocked the doorway to her room. He leaned against the stone wall as if needing support to stand.

He had the disreputable appearance of a brigand or a pirate. His black hair was overlong. A beard shadowed his jaw. He was tall, lean, muscular—and deathly ill.

His eyes burned with fever, he said, "Help me. Please. Water—"

His plea broke off as he fell to the floor at her feet.

Chapter Three

Sabrina stared at the man sprawled out on the floor—and then thought to scream.

She wasn't one for hysterics. Her belated cry sounded as if she had been startled by a mouse, not a well-over-six-foot man with villainous looks.

A man who had dropped like a sack of grain . . . and didn't appear to be breathing.

Surprise gave over to curiosity.

Was he dead?

Charging up to the bothy alone now seemed like a terrible idea, especially when her only escape from the hut was blocked by his big body, although flat out on the ground, he didn't seem as frightening as he'd been a moment ago. And what sort of blackguard asked for water? Certainly not a dangerous one . . . she didn't think.

He wore dark breeches and a shirt made of what appeared to be good material. The linen was filthy now. His jacket and the neckcloth were in a heap on the floor of the other room. His boots were run-down at the heels.

Her heart slowed its beat. Common sense returned.

It was quite possible that he wasn't anyone to be alarmed over but a traveler who had taken ill and sought out the shelter of the bothy for protection.

Sabrina had learned a great deal about healing while caring for her mother. She now considered the gentleman with a critical eye before kneeling and pressing her fingers against his neck. He had a pulse, a faint one. His skin was hot to the touch, and her fingers left white print marks. The man did need water and anything else liquid she could think of to pour down his gullet and cool the fever.

He'd probably suffered chills as well. Fever and chills. She didn't want to think he could have the influenza.

There hadn't been a bout of it in the valley since the disease had claimed the life of the Menzies baby and one of the family's aged aunts as well last year. Many others had come down with the sickness, but after a period of *wishing* they were dead, they had recovered.

Usually, people Sabrina's age could weather the illness. This man should be able to fight off influenza *if* he'd been healthy enough before contracting it, and that was the question.

He was thin, too thin. He might not have been in robust health before the illness. There was a pallor to his skin she could not like, and the rattling in his chest concerned her. She knew that sound. She'd heard it in her mother before she died. He might not survive the night if something wasn't done for him quickly.

Her own problems evaporated.

"Sir, do you hear me?" Sabrina said, talking loudly and distinctly and wanting to rouse him.

He did not answer. He didn't move.

Unafraid of doing something drastic to make the man respond, she clamped her thumb and her finger around his well-shaped nose.

He appeared capable of breathing out of his mouth, but then he started coughing. Good.

She held on.

Unable to catch his breath, the man came awake with a start, his eyes opening in surprise.

"Hell-o," Sabrina said. "Who are you? What is

your name? Do you have family?" The answer to those question would be very important if he died.

His brows came together. He had definitive brows, the kind that could express emotion on their own, the kind that made a man's face interesting, appealing.

"What?" he grumbled out. "Couldn't . . . breathe."

"Of course, you couldn't. I was holding your nose." Sabrina clambered to her feet.

His scowl deepened. He'd understood her. "Me nose?"

"Your nose," she confirmed. *Me nose.* What a quaint quirk, she thought, then realized he had the hint of an accent she couldn't quite place. "Where are you from?"

He'd started looking around the bothy as if completely disoriented. She repeated her question.

However, instead of answering, he tried to help himself up, using the stones of the doorway for leverage, but he lacked strength. His arms could not give him support, and he fell back against the door between the two rooms, his expression dazed as if he didn't understand what was happening to him.

Sabrina softened her voice. "Sir, you are very ill."

Glassy brown eyes met hers. They reminded her of the color of good sherry when sunlight passed through it.

"What is your name?" she asked again.

"Enright," he said.

"Enright," she repeated, wanting to confirm what she'd heard. When he didn't correct her, she said, "Mr. Enright, do you know where you are?"

Those expressive brows came together, but before he could answer, he began shaking. The chills were starting to come upon him, and she had nothing to use to help him fight them off.

"I need to fetch help," she said, starting to rise. "You—"

She didn't finish her sentence. With unanticipated swiftness and a strength that must have cost him everything he had, Mr. Enright grabbed her, placing a hand to the back of her neck, so he could look her in the eye. "*No.*"

The single word reverberated in the air around them.

"But you need help," she said. Surprisingly, she was not afraid. "If you don't receive care, you could die here."

She watched as he processed her words and

realized he'd already accepted the possibility of death. He *knew* how ill he was.

"Please," she whispered. "It might not be too late."

"No," he repeated, the word spoken softer but just as emphatic. "No one else. Safe here." It was taking great effort for him to speak. "Secret. Keep . . . secret. Promise me."

For a second, Sabrina could imagine they were the only two people in the world. He was asking for her trust.

"If I promise, you must let me help you," Sabrina said, uncertain even as she spoke the words why she should be willing to make such an offer, and yet there it was.

Suspicion came to those hard sherry eyes.

"You aren't in a position to refuse me," she reminded him gently.

A bark of rusty laughter escaped him, as if she'd made a jest only he understood. His hand slid from her neck to rest on his thigh. He slumped against the door, a wan smile of defeat on his lips. "Suit yourself," he managed, and Sabrina felt a note of triumph.

She sat back on her heels. "I always do," she admitted. "Is there anyone I should contact for you if the worst happens? A wife, perhaps?"

He shook his head. It was all he could do. His eyes were growing heavy, and his shivering grew stronger. Sabrina stood and fetched his jacket. She placed it like a blanket around his shoulders. "I will return shortly," she promised, and left the bothy. She needed to fetch her pony cart. She could not leave Mr. Enright alone overnight. He would not survive without food, water, and good care.

And she *would* have to tell one person of his presence—her father. Certainly, Mr. Enright could understand the necessity.

Besides, she hadn't given him her promise, not actually, although she would honor his wishes to the best of her ability.

Her feet didn't slow until she reached the trees surrounding Kenmore village.

Little more than an hour had passed since she had walked out of the Kenmore Inn, but it seemed as if her confrontation with Mrs. Bossley was another lifetime ago.

The ladies of the Quarterly Meeting had apparently finished their luncheon and gone home. All the vehicles were gone. Only Dumpling remained, and he was lonely. He caught Sabrina's scent on the wind and called to her.

Sabrina had to step into the inn to collect her

hat and gloves. The Orrock lad had been watching for her and had them at the ready. She had no doubt the ladies had thoroughly thrashed out what had happened between herself and Mrs. Bossley. The look in the lad's eye told her that he'd heard a thing or two.

But Sabrina couldn't worry about what people thought of her right now. She had to save Mr. Enright's life.

She thanked the lad for his help, promised him a coin when she saw him next for his diligence, and left the inn.

Tying the ribbon of her bonnet under her chin, she crossed the road to her cart. As she approached the kirk, she caught a glimpse of a woman studying the markers in the graveyard around the church building. Because her mind was preoccupied, and since there was always someone paying respect to the deceased, Sabrina barely paid her a moment's attention.

Instead, she gave Dumpling a pat, promised him an extra bit of oats after they finished a "special" errand, and climbed into her cart. It was a lovely little vehicle made of wicker and white-painted wood. The sides were solid, and the undercarriage and wheels were a deep green that reminded her of the forest. The only door was in the rear and very narrow. She feared she'd have a time of squeezing Mr. Enright through it. She prayed he was conscious enough to help.

She sat on one of the two cushion-covered benches lining the sides of the cart, pulled on her gloves, and picked up the reins. However, before she could leave, Bertie Kinnion, the Reverend Kinnion's wife, came rushing up to her. She had been the person lingering amongst the gravestones.

Sabrina and Mrs. Kinnion were of the same age. Bertie was not an unhandsome woman, just a quiet one. She had been Dame Agatha's penniless niece until the reverend had offered for her and given her a position in the local society. It had been a good match. Everyone said the reverend was devoted to his wife and she to him.

"Miss Davidson, may I have a moment?" Mrs. Kinnion asked, placing gloved hands on the side of the cart so that Sabrina would be rude to pull away.

Holding up the reins, Sabrina gave the reverend's wife a cheery smile. "Only a moment. Father expects me."

"Yes, yes, I'm certain he does." Mrs. Kinnion did not remove her hold on the cart. "You left the luncheon abruptly. I hope all is well?"

Sabrina's cheery smile stretched her face uncomfortably. "I needed some air." Her words were true. She hadn't been able to breathe in the inn when she contemplated a life under the Widow Bossley's thumb.

Mrs. Kinnion nodded, but a frown had formed between her eyes, and she appeared as if she'd scarcely paid attention to Sabrina's response. This was unlike her.

Puzzled, Sabrina asked, "Are *you* all right?"

Mrs. Kinnion crossed her arms tightly against her chest. There was a beat of silence before she said, "My husband is missing."

"The reverend?" Sabrina asked, then felt silly because what other husband did Mrs. Kinnion have?

Instead of taking offense, Mrs. Kinnion nodded. "Everyone acts as if I know where he is, and I should. I pretend I do. He'd promised he would be home four days ago. I assumed his trip had kept him delayed; and then I feared I had misunderstood the date he'd told me he would return. His leaving was strange as it was."

"Where had he gone?" Sabrina asked. She hadn't even heard that the reverend had been traveling. Usually, as an important member of the church, her father would have known. Or the gossips would have ferreted out his absence.

"Edinburgh. His uncle is a church vicar there. He sent a letter saying he needed my husband for a matter of some urgency."

"Well, then, why don't you write the uncle? I am certain there is a simple explanation. Travel can be so difficult. There could be a dozen different reasons for his delay." She picked up the reins again, but Mrs. Kinnion reached for the rein nearest her and clenched a fist around it.

"I know my concerns sound a bit overwrought. I have no proof something is wrong, but inside"— she pressed her free hand to her heart—"I am certain my husband is in danger. I know it. Please, I can't share my fears with anyone else. He'd be furious if I did. But he always said you have a great deal of good sense, and I must confide in someone, Miss Davidson, or I shall go mad. He's all I have, and he is very dear to me."

Sabrina lowered the reins. "I'm certain there is a simple explanation for his late return. He may have been distracted with business. A delay of several days is really nothing to worry over, especially on the roads between here and Edinburgh. Last spring, my father made that trip quite often. He experienced numerous delays—"

She stopped, struck by what she was saying. Had her father been delayed on his travels from

Edinburgh, or had he been cozily ensconced in Mrs. Bossley's bed while she thought him elsewhere? The idea revolted her, especially since he would never have tolerated such behavior in his daughter. Why did men believe they were so special anyway?

"I never knew when to expect him," Sabrina finished lamely.

Mrs. Kinnion nodded agreement, but the air around her crackled with tension.

Sabrina reached for her hand. "I have known Mr. Kinnion for a number of years. He is the most reasonable of beings. What trouble could he find?"

"Yes, you are right," Mrs. Kinnion said, but she didn't sound convinced. "I appreciate your listening to me. I am so scared something has happened to him or could happen to him, I feared I was not being rational." There was a beat of hesitation, then she confided, "I cannot return to my aunt. I can't. She is very difficult to please."

After the trick Dame Agatha had played on her today, Sabrina could well imagine, especially in light of her own possibly changing circumstances. The thought made her shudder.

"I also hate to think my husband might have had an accident and be broken and alone in a ditch or in the care of strangers," Mrs. Kinnion was saying. "He may need my support."

Her words reminded Sabrina that she needed to help Mr. Enright.

"What a dramatic mind you have," she chastised the reverend's wife. "You are believing the worst, and there is no reason to do so, not yet. Your husband is probably busy arguing theological tracts with his uncle and has lost track of time. However," she continued, "if it will reassure you, I'll ask my father to send a message to your uncle. Do you have an address?"

"Thank you, Miss Davidson, I do—and I appreciate your listening. It helps to finally express my fear out loud. I feel much better. His uncle Ebenezer Kinnion is rector at St. Jude's in Grassmarket." She hesitated, then said, "I hope my husband will forgive me for sharing his business."

"Father will be discreet," Sabrina assured her. She lifted the reins again. "Now, if you will excuse me, the hour grows late. Dumpling wants his dinner." The pony swished his tail as if agreeing.

"Of course. Thank you." Mrs. Kinnion stepped back, and Sabrina was on her way.

Dumpling was very happy to be heading home

and not at all pleased when instead of taking the road to Aberfeldy, she turned him in the direction of the moors. He even dared to grumble at her, but Sabrina was accustomed to ignoring Dumpling's grumbles. He was an opinionated pony.

Reaching the bothy, Sabrina drove the cart right up to the front door and set the brake.

Mr. Enright was leaning against the open doorway between the two rooms where she'd left him. His eyes were closed, and he appeared to be asleep, which was probably the best thing for him. She almost hated disturbing him, but she did. He needed a warm bed for the night.

Shaking his shoulder, Sabrina said, "Sir? Please wake up. I will need your help. You are too heavy for me to move you alone."

He didn't budge or indicate in any way that he heard her. He was completely drawn into himself, his face pale.

She considered her options.

Her mother had been fragile, especially toward the end, but she had still been difficult to move. A deadweight was a heavy weight.

However, Sabrina was no fragile flower. She might have the strength to drag him to the door, where Dumpling impatiently waited.

She hiked her skirts up, tucking them between

her legs to fashion breeches of sorts so that they would be out of the way. Straddling his body, she said, "I'm going to lift you, sir." She hooked her arms under his, feeling the pull of muscles along her back. If anyone came upon her at this moment, they would be in for a shock, but she didn't care. This was the only practical way to move such a big man.

Her face close to his, she said, "If you could help, I would appreciate it. There now, one, two, three, *lift*—"

He didn't move.

She repositioned her hold and put more of her back into it, the way she'd seen workmen try harder. Nothing. He didn't budge an inch.

Sabrina straightened. "You could be more help," she informed him, not even bothering to speak loud or distinctly in her "invalid" voice. "It would make this a bit easier."

Of course, he had no answer.

So, Sabrina sucked in a deep breath and used all her might. She managed to raise one of his shoulders. She tried to turn him so that she had a straight path to drag him to the front door. Determined that success would be in her reach, she tripled her effort—

The smooth soles of her leather shoes slid. Her

legs came forward and out in front of her—and she landed on top of the man with a thud.

Right on his genitalia.

If she'd received a reaction from him by holding his nose, it was nothing compared to his response to her flattening his privates.

Men were always funny about this part of their anatomy, but Mr. Enright's response was a bit excessive. He practically jumped to the ceiling, sending her tumbling off his lap, before pulling back his fist as if ready to ward off an attacker.

For a moment, Sabrina sat in shock, her skirts in complete disarray. Her gaze froze on his hand, ready to deliver a blow.

He glared at her but then seemed to take in his surroundings from the hard, cold bothy to her stocking-covered legs. Slowly his hand lowered. "What the devil were you doing?"

Thankful she wasn't about to be bashed, Sabrina scrambled to her feet, shaking out her skirts and reclaiming her modesty. "I'm trying to save your life."

His scowl deepened. "By jumping on me balls?"

Heat rushed to her cheeks at the crudity. "That was very common," she scolded.

"I'm commonly attached to them."

"You're Irish," she answered, finally placing his mysterious accent.

Those strong brows of his pulled together in bewilderment. "Who are you?" he demanded before a bout of chesty coughing swallowed his last word. He had the good manners to try to cover his mouth.

"I'm someone you are lucky to have found you. You are very ill. And if you want to feel better, you'd best find yourself in that pony cart." She pointed to the door, where an impatient Dumpling stamped and snorted his surliness.

"I'm not leaving here," he answered.

"If you stay, you could contract pneumonia, then you could have an even graver problem. You don't need to fear me, Mr. Enright—

"How do you know who I am?"

"You told me your name."

He shook his head, not believing her.

Gently, Sabrina said, "You don't remember because you are that ill. Please, sir, you must trust someone. You will not survive out here alone. And I didn't mean to be so personal. It was an accident." She held out her hand, and promised, "I will not even breathe your name to another soul if you come with me."

He stared at her as if not believing one word she'd spoken. She wondered what or who had created such distrust in him—

His body began to spasm. He turned from her, leaning over, as dry heaves racked his body. The man had nothing in his stomach. All he could do was suffer through the convulsions.

Sabrina inched closer to him to tempt him. "You need nourishing food. A good broth will help you. Without some substance and a safe, warm place to stay, you will die."

He didn't answer. He couldn't. His body collapsed as he drew in great, shuddering breaths. Sweat beaded across his brow. His eyes started to close.

Sabrina dared to place her hands under his arms. "Help me lift you," she urged quietly. "It is only a few steps to the cart. And then you may sleep."

She could feel the struggle within him. He didn't want to comply, and yet he had no choice. She attempted to help him stand and after the briefest resistance, he staggered to his feet. She slid his arm around her shoulders and directed him to the cart. He didn't try to open the narrow door into the vehicle but fell forward over the side, where he landed on the floor.

Dumpling gave a snort of surprise.

"Steady," Sabrina cautioned both of them, but Mr. Enright was beyond caring. He curled up and appeared to fall asleep.

She fetched his jacket and neckcloth, then opened the cart door and did her best to climb in without stepping on him. He took all the room on the floor of the cart. She covered him with his jacket and had no choice but to set her feet upon him as lightly as she could. She lifted the reins, and released the brake.

"Let's go, Dumpling."

The pony wasn't pleased with the idea. He knew he had no choice, but he groaned mightily to let her know he was pulling what he considered an intolerable load.

Still, once they hit the road, and Dumpling understood they were finally, truly returning home, he picked up his pace. The afternoon was growing late. Fortunately, they didn't meet anyone on the way. Sabrina didn't know how she could explain away the presence of a man under her feet.

Within three-quarters of an hour, she pulled into the yard of the stone house she shared with her father.

The two-story house was modest in appearance, nothing like the family estate of Annefield, where the earl lived, but it was a very nice house indeed. Besides the small stable and paddock, there was a good-sized garden, making it one of the finer homes in Aberfeldy. The location was choice as well. They had a view of General Wade's bridge and their closest neighbor was several hundred feet from them.

Her pup Rolf, a brown-and-white hound who was busy growing into his paws, came bounding from his post beneath the back step and gave her a happy bark of greeting. She'd rescued him as a puppy from a group of cruel boys and he was devoted to her.

Sabrina climbed out of the cart, gave Rolf an absent pat and glanced at the house. A shadow moved in the ground-floor bank of windows that looked into her father's study.

He was home, and her conversation with the Widow Bossley came roaring back.

Mr. Enright had not moved other than to cough or reposition himself as best he could in such close confines. He was a big man in a very small space. Yes, she knew a bed and nourishing food could help him, but she knew her father well enough to realize she'd have to break the news of Mr. Enright carefully. Her father could be prickly. He was not always a generous man. For example, he refused to let her pup Rolf into the house now that the dog had grown bigger and, if requests for Sabrina's time interfered with his comfort or his plans, he could be out of sorts for days.

Even knowing him as well as she did, she sometimes did not accurately anticipate his moods or responses. His courting Mrs. Bossley was a case in point.

No, Mr. Enright was better off safely tucked away in the stables while she and her father had a very honest, and certainly difficult, discussion.

Chapter Four

$\mathcal{S}$abrina planned to leave Mr. Enright in the cart while she talked to her father.

She unhitched Dumpling and gave the pony his measure of oats. She also fed her father's horse Rainer, a big-boned bay with a perpetually sour attitude. Several months ago, the earl had cut her father's living to pay gambling debts. As a consequence, her father had to let his man Emory go, and the feeding of the animals had fallen on Sabrina's shoulders.

Even with Mr. Enright's weight, she was able to easily maneuver the cart by its shafts, backing it into an empty stall. Checking him one last time before she left, she found his forehead hot to the touch, too hot. Worried, she grabbed a cup in the tack room and used it to attempt to give him a drink.

The water they pumped in the stables was icy cold. It would be good for him. However, it dribbled out of his mouth as if he had no strength to even swallow. Alarmed, she raced back to the tack room, grabbed a clean linen rag from a stack, wet it, and placed it on his brow.

"I'll return for you as soon as I've talked to Father," she promised.

Of course, he had no response.

Rolf had watched all of this with a solemn eye. He did not trust men, not even Sabrina's father, and was known to growl his feelings.

However, he seemed accepting of their unconscious guest. He'd even stood on his hind legs to look over the edge of the cart and sniff the air around Mr. Enright.

Of course, that did not mean she trusted the dog alone with their guest. "Come, Rolf. We must talk to Father."

She started for the house, but her pup didn't follow. Instead, he sat on his haunches in front of Mr. Enright's stall.

"Rolf, come," she ordered.

The dog considered her a moment, then stretched out on the ground, alert, wary, and determined not to leave his post, his manner more protective than threatening.

"So you believe he is all right then?" she asked.

Rolf actually seemed to smile.

There were many times that Sabrina fancied the dog understood humans. He appeared to follow conversations around him and could anticipate her moods. Why would he not have formed an opinion of Mr. Enright's character? If one was fanciful, and she could be, it didn't seem a stretch of the imagination.

"Well, then, keep watch," she said. "And wish me luck. You know how difficult Father can be."

Rolf's brown eyes said that he did. She left the stables.

Mrs. Patton was in the hall, throwing her shawl over her shoulders, when Sabrina entered the back door. The cook already had her wool cap on her head. Once she had the dinner made, she didn't linger unless she was needed. She was three years older than Sabrina, the wife of the local cooper's apprentice, and they had five hungry sons under the age of twelve waiting at home to be fed. Sabrina and her father could serve themselves, and the cook would clean the kitchen in the morning.

"There you are," Mrs. Patton said in cheery greeting. "Your luncheon went well?"

"Fair enough," Sabrina murmured. "How is Father?"

"In good spirits. I heard him humming."

That was unusual although he *had* been in a pleasant mood the past week. She wondered when he'd given Mrs. Bossley the ring.

"Has he had any visitors?" Sabrina wanted to know if Mrs. Bossley had come running with news of their confrontation at the luncheon.

"No, he has been alone all day. He's barely taken time to have a bite to eat."

Good. Sabrina would have a chance to talk sense into him.

"Is there any broth?" she asked the cook.

"Aye, I stewed a chicken. There should be plenty. Why?"

"We have a sick parishioner," Sabrina answered. That wasn't truly a lie. Mr. Enright was physically in the parish at this moment, and he was not well. "I thought to take some broth to him."

"*Och*, who is it?" Mrs. Patton said with a touch of alarm. "Do I know him?"

Sabrina thought fast as she removed her hat and pelisse and hung them on the hook on the wall next to her father's. "I don't actually know the name. Mrs. Kinnion told me of him. I'll deliver the broth to her."

Mrs. Patton accepted her explanation. "Well, take some fresh bread as well. I baked plenty since I won't be in on the morrow. Did you remember that?"

"Yes, you are going to Pitlochry with your husband. Don't worry about us. We shall be fine. I hope you enjoy the day."

"Thank you," Mrs. Patton said, a beaming smile of anticipation splitting her face. "I will see you then?" With a nod, she was gone.

And Sabrina was alone with her father.

She faced the study. When she used the room, she usually kept the door open, but her father liked the door closed. She didn't hear humming.

Her father had always been a distant parent, an aloof one. Her mother had been the person she'd turned to for guidance, and yet her father's wishes and dictates were always considered first. Her mother had insisted. She did not like confrontation in any form, and over the years, Sabrina had followed suit.

Then again, her mother could not have imagined her father chasing the likes of the Widow Bossley.

Sabrina knocked on the door.

"Yes?" her father's baritone voice asked, the sound abrupt.

She entered the room.

Her father sat at his desk by the window, scribbling away on a sheaf of papers, his glasses pinching his nose. He did his own copying or else gave the work to Sabrina. There was no money to pay for a secretary.

He didn't acknowledge Sabrina's presence. He often expected her to stand and wait. He'd explained once that it taught her patience and discipline.

In the past, Sabrina would have cooled her heels while studying the tomes on philosophy and law lined up on the shelves of the wall nearest her. Today was different.

"I enjoyed the Ladies' Quarterly Meeting today."

He didn't even raise a brow. "That's pleasant," he murmured as he removed the top page of his stack, one covered with his small, neat handwriting, and set it aside for the ink to dry. He dipped his nib into the ink bottle and began writing on the next page.

"I sat with someone outside of my usual acquaintance. Mrs. Bossley."

The pen stopped moving.

He began writing again. "Interesting," he said.

Sabrina frowned. "You do not act like a man in love."

The pen was placed aside.

He looked up, meeting her eye for the first time since she'd entered the room.

Sabrina understood what the widow would see in him. The Davidson men were a handsome lot, even the older ones. They were tall and had regal bearing. Drinking and hard living had damaged the uncle's looks, but her father still had a clear eye, square jaw, a sense of dignity, and most of his graying hair.

"She says you have asked her to marry you." Her tone was clipped, her feelings on the subject very apparent.

Her father's glance shifted to the door. The corners of his mouth turned grave. For a second, Sabrina could imagine him denying Mrs. Bossley's claim.

And then he nodded. "I have."

That was not the answer she wanted.

"*Why* was I completely unaware of this?" she demanded, betrayal closing her throat. "She said you have been courting her for months. In fact, everyone in the room today acted as if they knew of your liaison as well. That is, everyone but me."

He had the good grace to act discomforted. "Sabrina." One word. Her name. He said it as if it were an explanation.

It wasn't. *"Why?"*

He frowned at the stack of papers. "I didn't want to upset you. I knew you would not be happy."

"Should I be? Do you remember all of the disparaging things *you* said about her when she was carrying on madly with my uncle?" She leaned her hands on his desk. "You were so disapproving, Father, and now, I learn, *from her*, that the two of you will *marry*? Do you know what she asked me? She wanted to know if I was going to give her any difficulties. She made it quite clear that she expected to be the mistress of *this* household."

For a second, their eyes met, then he looked away. He didn't speak. He didn't answer her.

"How could you, Father? How could you replace my mother with this woman? You know *what she is.*"

His face turned red. He came to his feet. *"You* don't know her. If you did, you would not be so harsh in your judgment."

"I haven't had time to judge her. I've rarely even thought of her. This is all a surprise to me."

He came around the desk. "I know this may seem sudden to you, but *I've* thought it out. This is what I want. I want to marry Lillian."

Sabrina couldn't believe what she was hearing.

"If it was what you truly wanted, why did you not tell me you were courting her? Why has it been a secret?"

"I was trying to be sensitive to you," he said. "You seemed so distraught after your mother died."

"So did you, Father."

"I was—" His voice broke off on the last word. His gaze dropped to the floor. He took a step away, and Sabrina pressed, believing he was listening to her, that he would reconsider what she was certain was a hasty decision.

"We both feel her loss," she said. "It hasn't been that long since she left us. Not quite two years. I'm surprised you think to remarry so quickly—"

"Quickly?" he echoed. He looked up. "Two years is comparable to a decade for a man my age. Furthermore, Millie was sick a long time, Sabrina. Longer than you knew. I have been without a wife for decades, and I was loyal. Most men would not have been."

"I understand the sacrifices you made, Father," she said, her words terse. "Mother's illness was not easy for any of us."

"Except, I'm a man, Sabrina. A man has needs."

"*Needs?*"

He raised a hand. "You wouldn't understand—"

"Oh, I do understand," she answered. Years of grief and mourning held tightly in her chest were suddenly unleashed with anger. "Contrary to what Mrs. Bossley thinks, I am *not* naïve. I know what attraction she holds for you. And I know how long Mother was ill. I had been at her beck and call since she first took to her bed. I spent day and night with her. She never asked you for anything other than fifteen minutes of your time each afternoon. I tended her, I bathed her, I fed her, I gave her all that I had, and now you are telling me I don't understand? And because of what you believe *you* want, what is due *you*, I must grovel to the notorious Widow Bossley? Really, Father, if you were going to call on someone, could you not have had higher standards?"

"She is a good woman," he began in his paramour's defense, but Sabrina would have none of it. His affair with Mrs. Bossley had released a simmering cauldron of resentment inside her.

"She is the *earthiest* of creatures. She flaunted her liaison with my uncle. She bragged she would be his next countess. Why you would call on such a feather-brained creature, I understand. You do have *needs*—" She had to draw out that last word, she couldn't help herself, and she was growing more agitated and less wise as she spoke. "But you gave her Mother's ring. Mrs. Bossley can have everything else in this house but that was mine. It belonged to *me*."

"Actually, it belonged to me. It is *my* property."

The coldness in his voice whipped around her. His manner had changed. He went from being somewhat self-conscious to the man who could hold others' fates in his hands. "Your only purpose here," he continued, "is to do what I expect of you."

There had been a time when Sabrina could have been cowed into submission.

That time was past. She'd given up too much. She'd sacrificed. She'd done what had been needed.

Her hands clenched into fists at her side, she gathered all the Davidson pride in her being. "I am not chattel. I have a purpose and a right to an opinion."

"You do not."

If he had struck her, he could not have hurt her more deeply than with those three words.

Her mind reeled. She had believed her father felt some indebtedness toward her if not paternal acceptance. She had not considered herself an unwitting slave with no will of her own. She understood that as a daughter of the house she had no rights under the law, but she had trusted that her father saw her as a person with intelligence.

As if realizing he'd hurt her, he tempered his tone to say, "You are wrong about Lillian. She is a sensitive soul. She understands loss. She knows how I feel."

That statement stunned Sabrina.

He continued, "I admit, I had thought the worst of her, but after listening to her story, to her concerns—"

Probably while considering her ample bosom, Sabrina couldn't help thinking.

"—I came to know her in a way that was not based upon gossip and innuendo. You should appreciate that, Sabrina. You are always railing about the gossips in the valley. You, yourself, would champion Lillian if you knew what I know about her."

"You and the Widow Bossley are sharing a bed. You are lovers."

The blunt statement came out of Sabrina's mouth before she could question its wisdom. And once it was out, she'd not call it back. After all, if he had no respect for her, why was she tiptoeing around him?

It also felt good to speak forthrightly to him. "You can dress it up, Father, but the understanding she offers is as old as what Circe presented to shipwrecked sailors."

His mouth dropped open at her effrontery, but he recovered enough to say almost primly, "I am shocked by your attitude, Daughter."

"I am shocked by your behavior," she shot back. "So, when you told me you had business around the valley or you were traveling to Edinburgh, you were actually calling on 'Lillian,' correct?"

A look crossed his face, one she couldn't read.

She pressed. "You have proudly built your reputation on honesty. And yet you were not honest with me."

He clasped his hands behind his back, his shoulders rigid, unyielding, his jaw set. There was nothing he could say in his defense.

Sabrina attempted to appeal to whatever love he had for her. "And what is to become of me, Father? Where is my place in this new household you are creating?"

There was a heavy beat of silence, then he said, "As my wife, I will expect Lillian to receive all that is due to her."

Her heart dropped . . . because now she understood. She felt quite ridiculous actually. Any authority Sabrina believed she had carried had been an illusion. Male that he was, her father would let

Mrs. Bossley take her mother's place and also determine what was best for Sabrina.

Her life stretched bleakly in front of her as a long, lonely road.

And there was nothing more for her. Charitable works and playing the pianoforte for other people to dance were how she would be remembered if anyone thought of her at all.

She turned to the door. There wasn't anything left to say. She felt empty, abandoned . . . she thought of Mr. Enright.

Now was probably the best time to mention their guest. She'd wait a bit. However, she had made a promise to Mrs. Kinnion.

"One other matter," she said softly, unable to meet his eye. "Mrs. Kinnion is concerned for her husband's welfare."

"His welfare?" Her father's interest sharpened dramatically as if he was relieved with a change of subject.

"He went to Edinburgh on business. He should have returned days ago, but she hasn't heard a word from him."

"She hasn't?" her father said.

"Did you know he was gone? The deacon spoke at services last week, but I had not realized Mr. Kinnion was traveling."

"Yes, I had some knowledge of his trip," her father responded, sounding distracted.

"Well, he's only late returning a few days," Sabrina emphasized. "Still, his wife is concerned. Mr. Kinnion went to visit his uncle, who is the rector at St. Jude's Kirk in Edinburgh's Grassmarket. I said you might be willing to send a note to the uncle just to inquire that all is as it should be. I hope that was all right?"

He frowned at her now as if she had grown two heads, and he couldn't comprehend a word she was saying. But then he seemed to recover, and murmured, "Of course, of course. St. Jude's."

"Ebenezer Kinnion is his uncle's name. Would you like me to write it down for you?"

He dismissed her with a curt wave of his hand. "I know him."

Sabrina frowned. Mrs. Kinnion's request seemed to have grabbed hold of her father's mind. He stood as if uncertain of which way to turn and what to do. "Father, is something the matter?"

He gave a start, then barked, "Why do you say that?"

Sabrina blinked at his abruptness. "The Reverend Kinnion's absence seems to have upset you."

For a second, her father appeared shamefaced, then he fired back with a burst of anger, "You say the man is missing and that his wife is worried. Why would I not be concerned? He is my friend. Or has my offer for Mrs. Bossley so completely tainted your opinion of me that you can't believe anything good of me?"

Sabrina held a hand up as if to ward him off. "I meant no insult. I just, well—" She broke off. She couldn't very well chastise him for caring more for a friend than he did his own daughter. Not if she wanted peace. After all was said and done, her mother had taught her well. Her father's needs were to be considered first, and she had already pushed him to his limit—for now. Sabrina knew she'd revisit the topic of Mrs. Bossley with him. She could not afford to lose this battle.

"I'm also worried," she finished lamely.

But he was no longer paying attention to her. Instead, he had moved over to his desk and sat in his chair, but he did not pick up his pen. No, he just stared at the stack of papers with unseeing eyes as if he was working something out in his mind.

Sabrina lingered by the door. "Father?"

His head jerked up. "Go on about your tasks," he ordered, sounding preoccupied. "I'm fine." He picked up his pen and began fiddling with his papers.

The curt dismissal did not set well with Sabrina, not after the argument. He would probably explain everything to Mrs. Bossley.

And then she remembered that she had her own secret. Mr. Enright. She would talk to her father about him later, after dinner, when he'd had a glass of whisky and mellowed a bit. Mr. Enright would be content for the moment, provided she served him a portion of Mrs. Patton's chicken broth.

"I need to see to supper," she said.

Her father didn't reply. He acted as if he hadn't heard her.

Sabrina didn't understand his mood, but then, to be honest, since her mother's death, there were times the two of them acted like strangers. Her best course was to prepare their meal and see to her patient.

She marched into the kitchen and crossed to the fire, where Mrs. Patton had left several pots hanging on hooks. The bread baked for the day was cooling on a good-sized trestle table that took up the center of the kitchen. It was here Sabrina and her father ate instead of the dining room. There was a pantry in the far corner, and the chairs for the table were lined up against the wall.

The broth was scalding hot. It should have been removed from the fire's heat some time ago. Sabrina picked up a cloth and lifted the pot off the hook. She'd just set it on a marble slab on the hearth to cool when she heard the back door slam shut.

She listened, and she didn't hear another sound. Had her father left? She went to the hall. No one had come in, and the study door was open. The room was empty.

Her first panicked thought was that her father had gone out to the stables for whatever reason and would discover Mr. Enright. She dashed to the door.

She was right. He'd just gone through the garden gate and was taking long strides toward the stables.

Sabrina flew out the door. She hurried down the step, scampering as fast as she could with any dignity toward the stable, her mind awhirl with a plausible story about Mr. Enright's presence, and that is when she came to a halt.

She couldn't tell her father she'd just come across the man in a bothy and brought him home. In the mood her father was in right now, he would never let the man in the house. She could tell him Mr. Enright was a friend of someone she'd come across today and that person had asked the Davidsons to keep their friend for a bit.

That wouldn't work either.

Her father might ask the name of the person. And then what would she say—?

Her father came riding Rainer out of the stables at a high gallop. He even slapped his reins against the bay's sides, urging him to go faster. The horse was happy to oblige. Mud and stones were kicked up into the air as his huge hooves dug in and surged forward.

"*Wait.*" Sabrina ran to the gate, wanting to know where he was going, but her father didn't stop. Indeed, he acted as if he didn't see her. In a blink of an eye, he galloped across the bridge into Aberfeldy and was gone from view . . . heading in the direction of Borlick—home of the Widow Bossley.

Sabrina stared after him, stunned by his abrupt abandonment.

He hadn't said a word to her about leaving. Her father had never done that before.

And if she had needed a demonstration of exactly where she fell in his affection when compared with the widow, she had received it.

Within the half hour, her father and Mrs. Bossley would be cozying up together and giggling over how "innocent" his daughter was.

Sabrina reached down, grabbed a handful of stones, dirt, and new grass and tossed them at the road her father had just taken. She was furious and feeling more than a little betrayed. She *hated* her life.

Caring for her mother had not been easy, but at least she'd had a purpose and reason for being.

Now, she had nothing. Even her cousins had married and gone off on their own. Why had the Almighty given her a keen mind and common sense if all she was supposed to do was arrange flowers and dust tabletops—?

A frantic whimper interrupted her temper tantrum.

Rolf had come out into the stable yard. He stood in indecision, as if wanting to cross to her but afraid to leave the building.

He whimpered again.

"What is it?" she asked, walking toward him.

He disappeared inside the stable, then returned to stick his head out to be certain she still followed, and her thoughts went immediately to Mr. Enright. She lifted her skirts and began running.

Satisfied she understood the urgency, Rolf ran ahead to the pony cart. He whimpered, pacing as if anxious she check on her patient.

Mr. Enright was curled up in the bottom of the

cart, sprawled exactly as she had left him, but he was quiet. Too quiet. And his skin had the look and texture of wax.

He didn't even move when Rolf jumped against the cart, making it rock to and fro—and Sabrina's immediate thought was that he was dead.

Chapter Five

$\mathscr{P}$anic propelled Sabrina into the cart.

The vehicle bounced beneath her as she scrambled over the bench so that she could check him closely. Dumpling, always curious and in the stall next door, put his head over the wall as if he had something to say about the goings-on in the stable. Rolf whined and paced as if he thought he should be doing something.

Mr. Enright's skin was still hot, but that did not always mean life. Fever had so consumed old Mrs. McDavid that her skin had been heated to the touch for a good fifteen minutes after her death.

Sabrina searched for his pulse in the vein along his neck and listened hard for sounds of his breathing.

His heart beat—and then Rolf jumped right on top of him. The dog had leaped right into the cart, landing on top of the man's waist and shoulders. He stuck his cold, black nose right into the crook of his neck.

Mr. Enright jerked as the dog's weight squeezed the air through his lungs. He gasped as if needing more air and unable to receive it—*but he was alive*. Albeit just barely.

"Move, Rolf," Sabrina ordered, shoving her dog out of the cart with both hands. Rolf didn't take offense at being dumped to the ground. He sat up, his tail wagging as if he understood he'd performed a good service.

Her patient had settled back into his fetal position, his breathing labored but strong, as if he'd momentarily given up but now continued the struggle to survive.

His dark hair was pressed against his head in damp rings. Shadows emphasized the hollows of his face. If she didn't act quickly, she could lose him.

"I'm moving you," she said to him. "I'm taking you into the house." She started climbing out of the cart as she spoke. "When we reach the back step, I will need your help. I can't move you alone, and no one else is here."

Her father would not approve. She should have spoken to him, but it was too late now, and she wasn't about to keep Mr. Enright a moment longer out here in the stables. He needed good care.

Besides, her father was already so annoyed with her, he'd charged out of the house. Carting home a sick stranger would be just one more thing about her that irritated him.

"He and Mrs. Bossley can discuss this transgression as well," she muttered under her breath as she picked the cart up by the shafts and began pulling it out of the stall. It wasn't difficult to pull, just awkward, and she decided to see if she could guide it all the way to the back door without dealing with Dumpling.

For his part, the pony watched her efforts with interest, as if wondering if she found being hitched to the cart as much of a chore as he did.

Rolf trotted along beside her.

The dog's interest in Mr. Enright's well-being was very curious to Sabrina. She could only surmise that the man must be a halfway-decent sort if Rolf gave his approval. She hoped that was true. After all, she knew nothing about Mr. Enright. Why, he could be some brigand.

But he didn't seem to be such a character. If anything, he struck her as a man who'd had a measure of bad luck. There were telltale signs, from the good leather of his boots with their run-down heels to the quality linen of his filthy and sweat-stained shirt. He needed some kindness.

Offering kindness could help her as well.

The cart's height fit perfectly the top back step. She propped the door open.

Now came the hard part, physically moving him. She'd opened the cart door. All he had to do was step from the vehicle into the house. Simple really . . . if one were conscious.

"Mr. Enright," Sabrina called, shaking his shoulder. "Mr. Enright, you must rouse yourself. *Please.* I can't take you inside without your help."

He didn't budge. There was no movement. Not even the flicker of an eyelash.

She could ask for help from a neighbor, but for some reason, she was reluctant to do so. Perhaps because of the promise Mr. Enright had extracted from her. Perhaps because she felt her father should be informed first before she mentioned her patient to others.

Or perhaps because of her own stubbornness. Sabrina had rarely asked for assistance when she was tending her mother. She didn't like to bother others, and, yes, her pride was involved as well. She was independent by nature. Doing a task herself was easier than letting others pry into her business.

She rushed up to her bedroom and pulled the counterpane off her bed. She took it downstairs and spread it on the floor by the door.

"Mr. Enright," she called again, this time shoving his shoulder since he hadn't reacted to her gentle shaking, "I need your help."

Nothing. No response at all.

"Please, Mr. Enright."

He seemed to settle in deeper.

Finally, she took a lesson from Rolf. She took both hands and all of her weight and pounced on him.

Mr. Enright woke, his glassy eyes opening.

"Stand up," she ordered, as she lifted his arm and placed it around her shoulder. This man was solid. Weak but muscular. "Please, stand," she encouraged, and to her blessed relief, he did.

He unfolded himself and with her aid, stood in the rickety cart. For a second, they wobbled, then she pushed him forward. He grabbed the side of the door and stepped inside the house. She jumped after him.

"You can lie on the blanket," she said. "I'll be able to drag you to the stairs."

Mr. Enright half turned to her and stared as if trying to make sense out of what she was saying, then he began a lurching walk down the hall.

Sabrina was ecstatic. This was better than she had hoped. They managed to reach the stairs. "All right," she said. "Let us climb them. One at a time."

He shot her a look that said he thought her quite mad and sat on the stairs, like a stubborn toddler who could not take one step more. He leaned his shoulder against the wall.

For a second, she debated leaving him here. She looked around the rooms off the hall. The dining room was one of the smallest rooms in the house, and the table, chairs, and sideboard took up any floor space that could accommodate a man of his size. Nor would he fit in the tight space between the foot of the stairs and the front door.

She could fashion a comfortable bed for him on the floor of the sitting room. Her pianoforte was in one corner, and there were chairs for conversation by the front window, but they could be moved. However, Sabrina didn't want her father to walk in the door and see Mr. Enright until after she'd had a chance to explain his presence.

So, how to guide him up the stairs and to the back bedroom that was reserved for guests?

Mr. Enright solved her conundrum by turning on his own and half crawling, half climbing the stairs. She had to step lively to catch up with him.

Nor was he truly conscious. A part of him was acting on instinct. He trusted her because he had no choice. He could not fend for himself.

At the top of the stairs, he didn't walk down the hall toward the guest bedroom by the attic door but turned sharply to the right and trudged into her own bedroom. He fell facedown upon her bed.

Sabrina stood in the doorway, relief mixing with dismay. She had not had the difficulty she had anticipated carrying him up the stairs. However, he had chosen *her* bed. He could not stay there, and yet he appeared to have lost consciousness again.

She walked to the bed. This room was her sanctuary, the one place in the house that was hers alone. The bed was a simple four-poster and could certainly bear Mr. Enright's weight. However, she was very particular about the pillows and the sheets. Mrs. Patton and her father always accused her of being fussy about wanting her sheets clean and fresh. She liked plump pillows, too. She added feathers as she found them to the three pillows until they were just the way she liked them, and she did not share. Especially with someone who had his boots on her sheets.

As if he read her thoughts, Mr. Enright rubbed his hairy face against the smooth pillowcase Sabrina had sewn and embroidered herself. He snuggled in deeper.

And Sabrina's frustration rose to the top. "You can't stay here."

He didn't move. He probably hadn't heard her. However, if he could climb the stairs, then he could rouse himself to march down the hall.

"*Come*," she ordered, reaching for his arm to drag him out of the bed.

He didn't move.

Worse, the fever had hold of him again. If anything, he was hotter to the touch than he had been before.

Sheets could be cleaned, but she was not going to let this man die in her bed. Oh, no.

She flew across the room to her washstand and poured water into the basin. The water had been sitting all day and was just the right temperature. She carried the bowl over to the bed and set it on the nightstand before leaving to collect clean cloths from the linen press in the hall.

Sabrina began to do what she could to cool him down. She pressed compresses to his forehead and his chest beneath his shirt. She had a good supply of herbs and ointments in her mother's medicinal chest. She prepared an herbal poultice that contained eucalyptus leaves to clear the lungs and bound it to his chest.

She removed his boots. They were not difficult to pull off. Mr. Enright had obviously lost weight during his illness or perhaps before. This alarmed her more than anything, that and the pasty color of his skin. He might not have the resources to see him through his fever.

She turned to rush downstairs for the broth she'd left cooling in the kitchen and was surprised to see Rolf standing in the bedroom doorway. The back door must still be open. The dog watched with an anxious eye.

"He is not well, is he?" she said.

Rolfe did not wag his tail.

When she went downstairs for the broth, Rolf walked into her bedroom and sat beside the bed. He had been there many times before. When he was a small pup, she'd let him sleep with her. She was not happy with her father's dictate that the dog stay outside, and she certainly was not going to order Rolf out now.

A few minutes later, she returned with a tray holding a large bowl of good broth and a spoon.

Sabrina had ladled food into many a patient, starting with her mother. The doctor from Pitlochry had claimed her mother would have died much earlier in her life if not for Sabrina's care.

She now followed her usual procedure. She sat on the bed, picking up Mr. Enright's huge head and resting it in her lap. "Eat," she encouraged him. "Come along now, swallow."

Of course, he did not obey, and she feared he was already too close to death to be saved.

Mac didn't know where he was.

He had been traveling, no, floating actually, through cavernlike halls with arched white doors lining the walls. The halls were connected with stone steps, two steps here, four there, and the path, the only direction he could go, seemed to lead deeper and deeper into a place he did not understand.

The sound of rushing water roared in his ears. A part of him thought if he could find a river or stream, then perhaps he could escape the darkness.

The darkness.

Oh, yes, it was dark, but the doors were a brilliant white. They didn't just stand out in the shadows of this place, they glowed.

He moved past them, unable or unwilling to touch

them. They had no handles, and they reminded him of the priests' cubbies he'd once seen in an ancient monastery. Cells they were . . . and then he was in a cell.

The Old Tolbooth . . . and outside, beyond the building's ancient walls, came calls for his execution. Disembodied voices shouted for his head on a pike. They were witnesses to his death, and he realized he was ready to give them what they wanted. He was tired. Done. Spent. Life had become a sorry burden, and for the first time in all his struggles, Mac was bloody exhausted from trying to hang on.

He was once again on the wrong side—always on the wrong side. Then again, he was Irish, it was his nature to rebel . . . but not any longer. He wanted peace—

"More. You must drink more."

The command was clear, the woman's voice distinct.

He looked around the cell. She was not there. He was still alone, and yet, he heard her again.

"Another bit," she ordered. "A bit more. Please, do you understand me? You are making me angry, sir. If you don't eat, you'll die. Now, please, try."

She was a bossy bit.

And yet, her voice was melodic and warm and concerned. Anxious even. He saw himself open his mouth, wanting, yearning for the tenderness that only a woman could offer.

Did they know how strong they were? How they

could make a difference in the way a man saw the world?

Mac had a fondness for women, all of them—young, old, feisty, and calm. They intrigued him. They teased him, and he enjoyed teasing them back. They were poetry and song in his life, but they were not meaningful. No woman had been meaningful after Moira. He wouldn't allow it. Moira had taken too much from him—

"Mr. Enright, another spoonful. Now."

Instead of obeying, he tried to open his eyes. It took superhuman effort. He hadn't realized they were closed. It was as if he was lost in the depth of a dream—

Light hurt his eyes, and his vision was not clear. Nor were his senses operating the way he expected. The analytical part of his brain, the physician in him, immediately registered how ill he was. His chest was heavy and his breathing labored. He wanted to fall back into that peaceful obscurity.

Still, he needed to see her face.

"You are awake," she said, a sense of wonder in her voice.

He struggled to focus, and slowly, her features came into view.

She was an angel. He should have known.

And angels were just as lovely as his gram had claimed they'd be.

Her hair was sable rich, thick and curling. Strands of it hung around her face as if it had become unpinned.

She had crystal blue eyes and clear, creamy skin. There were freckles, the very faintest ones across her nose.

His angel smiled at him, but a tear escaped from her eye. "You must live," she told him. "You must fight hard."

Yes, he had to fight hard. The Irish always fought hard. There was no easy path for them. His angel should know that.

Mac wanted to reach up and touch her cheek, but he lacked strength. Indeed, his body was weighed down, his long legs stretched out. His gram had always called his legs his "long jacks."

"Hurry your long jacks," she would admonish him and his brother, urging them to quickly do her bidding. She'd feared laziness in either of them. She'd said their father had enough for the whole family.

And Mac had wanted to please her. She'd been the one to tell him the story of his country, of the myths and legends. "You have an angel watching over you, Cormac," she had told him. "Listen to her."

An angel.

Here she was. His Irish angel . . . and Mac felt himself murmur the words although he said them too softly for her to hear.

She leaned closer. "What?"

He wanted to repeat himself, but he couldn't. He was drifting away again. He had to think to breathe. He would tell her later.

Mac returned to the hallway. That was good. He never wanted to see the inside of a prison cell again.

The hall was deep, under the earth. He understood that now. Earlier it had been unbearably hot. Now, he was chilled, shivering.

Needing to find warmth, he approached one of the doors. He pressed his hand upon it, marveling at the glow of light.

The door swung open and there was his gram.

She was not alone. A girl sat at a spinning wheel turning coarse wool into a silken cord. His gram stood over the lass, surveying her work.

Gram smiled, and, in her forthright manner, said, "Come here, Cormac. Come tell me what you've been doing. I hear you've had adventures."

Mac moved forward, not feeling of the earth but not a part of this place either. Not yet. He put his arms out to give his gram a loving hug, for some reason expecting them to go through her, but they didn't. She was solid. Real.

She nodded as if she understood his thoughts. "Come on, lad. Tell me a story. Make it a good one."

He did as bid . . . and found himself telling her about the first time he'd met Gordana Raney and how the girl had begged him to take her with him. She had been afraid of a man she would not name. He'd forgotten that. He'd been deep into his cups at the moment and so hadn't recalled until this moment with Gram. Gordana had told him she didn't want to be "owned." He'd laughed and asked if she meant like a slave and her answer had been "Worse."

"How could I have forgotten that?" Mac asked his gram.

"There are many things that lurk deep within us that we never remember," his gram answered. "Many things behind all of those doors out there . . ."

*H*er patient was shaking so hard with the chills the bed shook. Sabrina piled every blanket she could find upon him, including the counterpane she'd carried downstairs and the one off of her father's bed. She lit the fire in her hearth, something she rarely did.

Finally, she'd added her own body heat, stretching out beside him . . . only then did he start to calm down.

And she fell asleep.

When she woke, it was well into the middle of the night. The room was dark save for the glowing embers from the fire, the door still open.

Mr. Enright slept, his chest barely moving. Rolf, too, slept. He lay across the doorway and snored gently.

Disoriented, Sabrina sat up and almost fell off the bed when she realized where she was, and how neatly she had tucked herself in beside Mr. Enright's long body. She should have been more circumspect.

And she shouldn't have found his presence so comfortable.

Embarrassed, she stood and pushed her heavy hair back. Her pins were all hopelessly lost and her best dress wrinkled. She added some more fuel to the hearth and checked her patient.

He was hot again, but not as burning to the touch as he'd been earlier. Good. Still, he had deep circles under his eyes, and his skin lacked color and healthiness. She removed a few blankets, then realized, she needed to return one to her father.

By this hour, he must be home. She was surprised he had not noticed her door open, but she was thankful as well. Sometimes, he could be very absentminded, and so might not have noticed she had a man in her bed . . . although that didn't seem plausible.

She decided she'd best explain before he discovered her with Mr. Enright. She also should shoo Rolf out of the house before he was discovered.

Lighting a candle off of the fire, she sought out her father. "Come, Rolf," she ordered. "We need to scoot out of here before Father discovers you."

Rolf rose and stretched as if he understood.

Sabrina walked to her father's room, ready to knock on the door and explain why his bed didn't have a blanket, but the door was still open. She held her candle high to take in the details of the room.

Now she understood why her father had not woken her. He wasn't here. His bed was still made.

For a second, she couldn't think.

Her father had never not come home except when he was away on business matters.

If he had wanted to make it clear to her that he had chosen Mrs. Bossley over his daughter, he could have chosen no better way than to not come home.

Sabrina dropped the blanket and backed away from the door. The hour had to be close to midnight. He was not returning. She knew it. He'd ridden off without a word to her as if she did not matter in his life.

Perhaps he'd been waylaid, wherever he was? She overheard women complaining about their menfolk coming home late after hours spent in the public houses. Could her father have stopped for a drink and been distracted by his friends?

"Why must I think he is with Mrs. Bossley?" Sabrina said to Rolf.

The dog yawned as if pointing out she was silly to believe otherwise.

"He could have had an accident," Sabrina suggested, and began to worry. She thought about Mrs. Kinnion and her fears. Sabrina now understood and did a good job of convincing herself that her father must be in danger.

She put the blanket on his bed and went downstairs. She had closed the back door earlier when she'd fetched her counterpane. She should move the cart back to the stables, but that task could wait for morning. Instead, she ate a bite of the dinner Mrs. Patton had left for them, then went into the sitting room to wait for her father. She distracted herself by practicing on her pianoforte. She'd not put Rolf out. The dog's presence comforted her, and he seemed pleased to be there.

After another hour had passed, Sabrina ladled more broth into Mr. Enright, closed her bedroom door, and returned to her lonely watch, perched on the upholstered chair nearest the front door in the sitting room.

And there, as the first birds began chirping it was morning, she fell into the dreamless sleep of exhaustion.

*S*abrina woke to realize her head was tilted back and her mouth open. Her throat hurt from dryness. She sat up abruptly and realized she had fallen asleep in the sitting-room chair.

The morning was almost gone. Hazy sunlight streamed through the windows. She wondered why Mrs. Patton had not woken her, then remembered the cook would not be in today. Rolf was watching, his tail wagging. He looked hungry.

She rose from the chair and went upstairs. The door to her father's room was still ajar. He'd not returned.

Mr. Enright was better, his breathing easier, but he slept as if exhausted. In the morning light, his huge body appeared odd in her very feminine room, with its soft hues of greens, blues, and snowy white muslin.

He also looked entirely peaceful while she felt

cranky over her father's disappearance and achy from a night spent in a chair. Even her eyes felt gritty—

Rolf barked, a reminder that he still hadn't been fed. Dumpling must be impatient for his breakfast as well.

Sabrina combed her hair back with her hands and tied it in a knot at the nape of her neck. "One moment, Rolf. Let me polish my teeth and wash my face, and I'll see to you."

She pulled her serviceable brown day dress from its hook in the wardrobe and went to the guest room to change. About fifteen minutes later, she headed down the stairs, feeling almost presentable. Rolf padded ahead of her, anxious for his breakfast. She needed to feed Rolf, move the cart from the back door, then see to Dumpling.

Then she would consider the matter of having a complete stranger in her bed and no relative to provide a proper chaperone.

Or did that matter anymore?

After all, they called her the Spinster Davidson because they assumed she would never marry, and she probably wouldn't. Mr. Enright was a patient. Nothing more; nothing less. It had been years since she'd needed a chaperone.

And if her father was too busy cavorting with

the Widow Bossley to worry about appearances, well, she had to do what she had to do.

Indeed, just let him say something. Any contriteness Sabrina had felt over their argument yesterday was now gone. It was rude of her father to leave without a word, and so she would tell him—

A knock on the front door interrupted her dark thoughts.

Sabrina frowned. She was not expecting a guest.

She crossed to a front window and looked out.

Dame Agatha stood on her front step. She was dressed for calling in a dove gray dress, gloves, and hat. Even the feather in the hat was gray. Her driver walked the horses on the road in front of the house.

The dame had never condescended to pay a call on the Davidson household, and Sabrina was not going to let her cool her heels on the front step. She opened the door.

Dame Agatha had been gazing across the lawn in the direction of the bridge. She now turned and smiled, the expression slightly acerbic, like her personality. "Good morning, Miss Davidson. I hope it is not too early to call." She didn't wait for a response but walked right through the door and into the sitting room, pausing in the front hall long enough to notice Rolf and comment, "A dog? I don't let dogs in my house."

"Some people do, some don't," Sabrina responded, and shooed the hungry Rolf out the front door. She followed Dame Agatha. "I am so happy for your visit. May I offer you refreshment? Mrs. Patton is not here today, but I'm certain there are scones in the pantry and sweet butter, and I can put on water to boil. Or would you prefer sherry—?"

"This early in the day?" the dame asked, interrupting her. "Please, Miss Davidson, my constitution would not allow it."

"Of course, how silly of me—"

"And this is not a social call," the dame continued, standing as if she were posing for a portrait titled *Haughty Lady Beside Pianoforte*. "I wish to talk of what happened yesterday."

Sabrina stiffened. "Are you speaking of the Ladies' Quarterly Meeting?"

"And your leaving in an unexpected, hurried manner."

This was not a conversation Sabrina wanted.

"Unfortunately, Dame Agatha, now is not a good time for a visit, social or not. You will excuse me, please?" Sabrina moved to the door to open it and hurry her guest out as quickly as she had Rolf; however, the dame's next words stopped her in her tracks.

"You will accept Lillian Bossley as your step-mother and you will do it gracefully."

Slowly, Sabrina faced her. "And if I don't?"

"Then life might become lonely for you in this valley, Miss Davidson," Dame Agatha said. "Very lonely."

Chapter Six

A flare of temper, wild and almost uncontrollable, shot through Sabrina.

Her father and Mrs. Bossley were sending Dame Agatha to threaten her. There could be no other explanation.

Her father was ensconced in his lady's *boudoir*, and Sabrina was expected to accept the situation and pretend to like it? To push all her natural and right sensibilities aside for his pleasure?

He'd always held her to a high standard. He'd chastised her to not be like her cousins, the earl's daughters. Aileen had scandalized London when she'd been divorced, and Tara was known for her vanity and for being headstrong.

Sabrina had been expected to be a paragon, and

her father hadn't given a care for what such loyalty, such devotion had cost her.

Her smile grew brittle. "I don't see how this is your affair," she informed the dame.

The older woman blinked, as if startled by Sabrina's bluntness. And why should she not be? Always before, Sabrina had kept her tongue in check.

However, this was different. *This* was *her* life.

So Sabrina stood her ground, head high, shoulders back.

Unfortunately, Dame Agatha was doing the same. And she had a great deal more experience at it.

"You must understand, *Miss* Davidson, that Lilly and I are old friends. She is a good person."

Sabrina remained quiet. She knew the dame would not like her response.

Dame Agatha crossed to the door as if she considered the battle won. "Your father and my friend *will* marry. If you keep your wits about you and behave, then all will be well."

"And what if I kick up a fuss? What if I speak my mind?" Speech gave her courage. "Mrs. Bossley has informed me that I might find myself in a very difficult place in the household. I am thinking that no matter what I do, there won't be enough room under this roof for both of us."

"You are strong-willed women," Dame Agatha agreed. "Unfortunately, you are the unmarried one."

"And someone to be pitied?"

"Or foisted off onto other relatives unless you can find a willing but awkward gentleman to marry you." The dame's words were a direct reference to Mrs. Kinnion, and Sabrina's temper was outraged, especially since she didn't want to be considered in the same class.

"I was my mother's caretaker. I believe I have earned my keep *and* my father's respect."

Dame Agatha waved a dismissive hand. "Oh, yes, that is true, but life moves on. It is a sad fact. You have nothing to win, girl, by being difficult," she explained, her tone not unkind. "Your father and Lilly are in love. People will be sympathetic to them. They will even forgive all the times that Lilly has been, well, shall we say, a bit too ahead of herself."

"Which is a good reason for my father to avoid her. He would expect the same of me if our positions were reversed."

"Ah, but love has its ways," Dame Agatha said. "If you'd ever been in love, you would know."

"Who says I have not been in love?" Sabrina countered. "Why does everyone assume I have no experience in life? Years ago, a young man Daniel Burnett was visiting the parish, and he asked my father's permission to call on me."

"And?"

"And Father said no. He said Burnett wasn't the proper sort. Ironic, isn't it?"

Dame Agatha made an impatient sound. "Men are different from women. Your father was looking after your welfare."

"Well, I am looking after his. It is too soon for father to remarry."

"You would say that of anyone he chose." Dame Agatha's voice had softened. "I understand that this will not be easy for you, especially in light of the many financial difficulties you've had—" She held up a hand to stop the protest Sabrina was about to utter. "Don't pretend. We all know that your uncle has your father under his thumb, and we sympathize, which is another reason a match between Lilly and your father is good. Lilly's husband left her very well-off."

"So we overlook her transgressions?"

"Your father wishes to do so." Dame Agatha took a step toward her. "You are a proud woman, Miss Davidson. So proud, you've put up a wall between yourself and others."

This statement sent Sabrina stuttering. "A wall?

Why, I'm out and about more than any other woman in this valley."

"Oh, yes, doing your charity work. You are so busy offering advice here and giving your time that you haven't given a thought to living your own life. You act as if you are afraid to consider your wants and needs. However, if you don't change, Miss Davidson, you are in danger of being alone forever."

Her words struck a deep, uncomfortable chord inside Sabrina. "You speak as if I have power over my fate. I don't. You must understand, my mother was very ill—"

"For a very long time," Dame Agatha chimed in. "I know, I know, and I am sorry for it. Her life was not what she'd wished. However, and I'm sorry if this offends you, I believe it was wrong for your parents to ask such a sacrifice of you. You should not have been asked to give up your prospects to care for your mother."

"Who else would have cared for her? Father?" Sabrina asked, her throat suddenly tight. Dame Agatha sounded as if she had not approved.

The dame pounced on the suggestion. "Aye, he could have hired someone and let his daughter have the chance at a full life. Instead, he expected you to give up your opportunities. And here you are. How old are you, my dear?"

"*Too* old," Sabrina managed to whisper, her whole sense of herself shaken. Never once had she questioned what her parents had expected of her, until now. "You don't sound as if you admire my father," she responded.

"I see his faults. Lillian does as well, so I've reconciled myself to this marriage, and you should, too. *Live*, Miss Davidson. Take hold of your own life."

But that was easier said than done in the cloister of the valley where everyone had expectations of her.

Or had she cloistered herself?

Honesty ran deep in Sabrina. There was a challenge to Dame Agatha's words, a challenge that hit upon Sabrina's fears, her doubts. She thought of Mrs. Kinnion, who had been in the uncomfortable position of being at the dame's beck and call . . .

"Is this the same lecture you gave the reverend's wife?"

If the dame heard the challenge in Sabrina's tone, she didn't take offense. "Bertie was born to be a church mouse. I despaired of ever making her discontent with her lot in life. She'd have hidden out under my care forever. But I believe she is happy now."

And she was. Everyone knew that the Kinnions had a good marriage, and Sabrina was surprised with the knowledge that Dame Agatha had been deliberately contrite to her niece.

Or that being content was not to be desired.

"I am not hiding," Sabrina said in her defense. "I have never been the sort to attract attention. I'm not like my cousins."

"*Pffftttt*," Dame Agatha said, rejecting Sabrina's protest with that obnoxious sound. "You are a handsome woman. You could have had lads. I've watched many a time as the local boys have worked up their courage at the dances to ask you for a turn around the floor, but you hide behind your music."

"I have not noticed anyone looking at me."

"Because you don't allow yourself to be *vulnerable*." Dame Agatha pressed her gloved hand against her heart. "Is it that you fear what others think of you and your choices? Or are you one of those women who expect a man to be perfect? I'll warn you now, there isn't a one of them that is. They all have their peculiarities. You may scorn Lilly, but she is always open and willing. She has been hurt from time to time. The earl of Tay is a randy fool, to my way of thinking, but I also know he lost the opportunity to have a woman in his life who would have been good for him."

"If my uncle used her, it is because she allowed him to do so."

"It happens," Dame Agatha replied with a shrug. "But if Lilly followed your line of reasoning and hid behind her pride—"

"I'm not that proud—"

"Oh, but you are, Miss Davidson. You are. And if Lilly had been like you, then she wouldn't have met a man who does appreciate her—your father."

Sabrina wanted to reject her argument, but a new thought caught her off guard. She hadn't been that upset all those years ago when her father had denied Mr. Burnett permission to call on her. She did have enough spirit that she would have challenged him, however Mr. Burnett hadn't intrigued her, not the way Mr. Enright interested her—

Immediately, she wanted to strike such an idea from her mind. The idea that she could be attracted to him was ridiculous. They had barely spoken to each other. He was ill, a soul in need of care.

And *another* bit of *charity* to keep her mind off of living her life?

For the first time, Sabrina realized that she'd adopted the hurt her mother had confided she'd felt when her husband had spared his wife only fifteen minutes each day. Her mother had believed she had become an encumbrance, a duty, an obligation, and she was. The thought had filled her with guilt.

And now, Sabrina realized, she had spent her life trying to prove that she could earn her worth, that she had a meaningful place in her father's life.

Dear God, Dame Agatha was right.

"I see I have given you a thing or two to consider," Dame Agatha said. "It is fine with me if you wish to remain alone. I do, and I'm happy for it. My husband made the earl of Tay appear a saint. I live a good life, but I live fully. I'm not worried what others believe of me." She moved into the hall and placed her gloved hand on the door handle. "Give your blessing to a marriage between Mrs. Bossley and your father, Miss Davidson. You will find in Lillian a special friend, and I think you need one."

On those last words, she opened the door and let herself out.

Slowly, Sabrina sank into the closest sitting-room chair. With the dame's departure, the room, indeed the whole house, seemed to have lost an energy, a vitality. Sabrina looked over at the sherry decanter, tempted to pour herself a full glass.

What if the dame was even partly right?

What if Sabrina released herself from the task of worrying about others? And always doing the right thing?

Her heart skipped a panicked beat. Did she know herself well enough to know what *she* wanted? She'd never once thought to be anyone other than who she was.

Outside, their visitor gone, Rolf barked, reminding her that he had not been fed. There was a bone in the pantry with his name on it, and well he knew it. Sabrina imagined that Dumpling was also pawing for his breakfast as well.

She threw on an apron and started her chores, but her mind still worked on her conversation with the dame.

Introspection was something Sabrina had believed she practiced. Dame Agatha had proven her wrong. It was not introspection to just make excuses for oneself, and Sabrina realized she'd developed quite a habit of it.

Now that the lid had been taken off the kettle, so to speak, what did she want to do with this new perspective? What *could* she do? Time had passed her by. The decent lads who had once admired her were married and gone. The ones left were available for a reason. The opportunities she'd shied away from would never come her way again.

Such thoughts made her uneasy, especially when she realized that others, like Dame Agatha, had noticed.

If her father had been here, she *might* have confided in him. Sabrina usually kept her own counsel, even with her cousins. People turned to her with their problems, *not* the other way around. Her *pride*—

Her mind stopped on the word.

She would never confide in anyone. She wouldn't let anyone see her weaknesses. If she was lonely, she hid it. If she was angry, she swallowed it. If she was tired, she pressed on. If ill at ease, she faked confidence.

She would not wear her feelings for all to see because then she would be admitting she could be hurt. She'd feel exposed.

Sabrina prepared a bowl of broth for Mr. Enright. She tore a piece of bread to soak in it, reasoning he might be able to digest a bit more than liquid today, and it would be good for him. She went upstairs.

He lay on his back exactly where she had left him. He didn't appear to have moved, not even an inch. She stood in the doorway a moment and listened. To her relief, she heard the sound of a deep, even slumber. He was beginning to recover.

She felt his brow and was relieved. It was cool to her touch. His fever had broken and would not return. The danger of chills had passed. All he needed now was time to regain his strength.

Setting the bowl on the bedside table, Sabrina raised a hand as if to thank God, but, instead, was suddenly overcome with a wealth of emotion that had nothing to do with her patient.

He was going to survive. Something had finally gone right in her life . . . but now what?

Now what?

Huge, racking sobs that she could not control escaped her. She broke down completely.

There were tears for herself, for what she'd sacrificed, for what she'd lost. Some of the tears were the ones she'd held back when her mother had died. These tears had been inside her all this time. A Davidson did not show strong emotion, not over something like death. One carried on.

However, the need to grieve had been there. Always there.

And while she was crying, she might as well let

loose a bout of temper over *how easily* her father had gone on. He'd taken a mistress. The valley was not London. Tongues wagged, and eyes saw everything. By now, a good number of people probably suspected that he was staying with Mrs. Bossley. They knew Sabrina was *unimportant*.

That last word made her wince.

It also brought her to her senses and forced her to end her indulgence in tears. *Crying never solved anything.* Her mother used to say those words.

Sabrina crossed to the washbasin and splashed cold water on her face. She caught a glimpse of herself in the mirror. Her fit of tears had not enhanced her looks. Her cousin Tara always looked so fetching when she cried. Sabrina was not like her.

She blew her nose and faced her reflection. "From now on, I shall think of myself first." Her statement didn't sound convincing, even to her own ears.

"I shall think of myself *first*," she declared, her voice more determined.

Now she sounded like a fool.

Sabrina faced her patient. He'd slept through her fit. Her cousin Aileen had always claimed that a good cry eased the soul. Sabrina didn't feel "eased." She felt as if she could curl up on the bed beside Mr. Enright and sleep for a week.

Drawing a fortifying breath and releasing it, Sabrina attempted to feed him a bit of the broth, cooing encouraging words as she did so. When she had poured as much of it as she could down his throat, she rolled up his shirt and removed the herb poultice she had wrapped around his chest.

Dipping a cloth into water from the washbasin, she began washing the remnants of the ointment off of his skin. He made a face as his skin dried in the air but did not wake. The man was exhausted. She'd seen patients sleep twenty-four hours and more after overcoming the fever he had experienced. His body was repairing itself. Sleep could do more for a soul than all the leeches and medicines of the healer's art.

What was interesting was that, last night, she had been so worried about him, she had barely noticed the lean muscles of his rib cage and the hard planes across his chest. He had a scar along his side. She wondered about the story behind it.

He was also younger than she'd first imagined. A shave would transform him, and curious, she fetched her father's shaving kit. Sabrina sat on the bed close to her headboard and lifted his head to rest on her leg. She lathered his chin and jaw. She'd shaved patients a time or two before. She now ran the razor across his skin. He had a strong, noble nose and well-formed lips. It was a pleasure to watch the character in his face revealed. He was not classically handsome but had a look that would turn heads whenever he passed.

And soon, he would go on with his life.

She looked down at the peacefully sleeping Mr. Enright.

Yes, she did find him attractive. He was far more handsome than Mr. Burnett and was definitely the sort of man a woman would like to kiss.

An idea struck Sabrina. A desire.

She could hear Rolf barking outside, probably at a rabbit, but here, in this room, there were no sounds other than their breathing. She was alone with this man. He didn't even know her name and yet, she felt close to him. He'd been delivered to her care and he would survive. In a matter of days, their lives would go in different directions.

So, what would be the harm in stealing a kiss? To discover what it felt like? To pretend for just a moment that she had a sweetheart?

If she was with him, there wasn't a woman in the valley who wouldn't feel a touch of jealousy.

Sabrina looked down at the man resting on her leg. He had very kissable lips. She'd never noticed that about a man before. But then, there was a presence about Mr. Enright . . . and his lips. They were thin, masculine, tempting.

She told herself a kiss was an impulse, a bit of curiosity, that and no more . . . but she could also feel the reckless pull of desire.

Before she let doubts arise, Sabrina bent over and placed her lips over those of the sleeping man.

Chapter Seven

$\mathcal{T}$he doors were driving Mac to madness. He jogged through the cavernous tunnels, opening one glowing white door after another. His gram was no longer here. She'd left him. While he'd been talking to her, she had disappeared, her image growing fainter as she listened to his story.

She was gone. They were all gone, just as in life—his brother, his mother, Moira. And now, when he opened the cavern's glowing doors, he returned to his cell at the Old Tolbooth, the Condemned Man's Cell, with its foul smell and the rickety cot.

He'd slam one door shut and run to the next, then the next.

Sometimes, he heard the voices of his brother and Moira. She had been known for her laughter almost as much as her fresh-cheeked beauty. Beautiful Moira. The woman he had loved . . . and lost.

Occasionally, as he tore through the tunnels, Mac thought he could hear the sound of children. He knew without being told they were Lorcan and Moira's. He'd never met them.

Gone. All gone.

Overwhelming sadness settled upon him, and his only salvation was her voice. His angel.

Mac was immersed in the moment, but he also knew he dreamed.

A part of him still had reason. He'd had patients so exhausted by illness they slept as if dead. When they were well, they'd tell him of their dreams. Some even believed they had gone to another side, the place where Death resided, and returned.

Mac didn't put any faith in their words. After almost ten years of fighting Napoleon's war, he'd seen enough of Death to know there was nothing supernatural to it. What waited for both sinner and saint was emptiness, the same sadness that filled his life and had done so for a long time.

Now, as he wandered the halls, he wondered when he'd lost passion for life. That loss had been his reason for returning home, of wanting to reach out and forgive what had happened between himself, Lorcan, and Moira. Perhaps then, he'd feel a sense of purpose.

But they were all gone.

And he would have happily given himself over to Death as well if not for his angel.

He heard her cry and silently rejoiced when she'd found her spirit and began speaking to him again. The melodic lilt of her words was sweeter than music.

And she was close . . . somewhere behind one of these doors. He just couldn't find her—

Lips brushed his.

The caverns with their maze of doors disappeared. Mac was in Edinburgh in the room he'd rented, and it was night, the night Gordana Raney had joined him in his bed.

He'd not invited her. The girl had taken it upon herself to be there. He'd been drunk, almost to the point of a stupor, as he'd been most nights. He'd been lost in grief and regret. His brother's ghost haunted him.

Gordana was such a lovely lass, but she was young, and Mac didn't want the burden of using her. She had kissed him, but he hadn't wanted her. He was done with using people. He was done with anger. The time had come to leave self-pity behind. He'd made the decision that night—a drunken promise to change.

The girl had not taken his rejection happily. She'd left and, hours later, had been murdered.

And now she kissed him, the taste of her sweet.

When she pulled away, he found he craved her kiss.

Too soon, he wanted to say, and couldn't. He could not speak at all. He struggled to find his way out of the darkness, to call her back, then she kissed him again.

As Mac remembered, Gordana had been very aggressive. She might have been young, but she knew her business, and she'd wanted what he had.

In contrast, now, there was a shyness to her, as if she had liked the feeling of her lips against his and wanted to explore more. Her kiss stirred him with its gentle question, and he felt himself come roaring to life. Heat surged in his loins. He lived.

They had not killed him yet.

She started to pull away again.

Mac reached for her, hooking his hand around her neck and pulling her down to him.

There was a moment of resistance, then her lips were against his, and this time, instead of being a passive partner, Mac kissed her back.

Nor was this just any kiss. He searched for something, something hard to define, and yet, it was here in her kiss . . .

This was not Gordana. He knew that now. He kissed the angel, the woman whose kindness had kept him alive.

There was magic in this kiss. Hope.

And he was not about to let her go.

*M*r. Enright's lips were harder than hers, and yet soft at the same time.

Sabrina had meant to offer no more than a peck, the sort of kiss one gave the cheek of a relative or friend. She'd experienced no other sort. The moment she'd kissed him, she'd felt silly.

Hers had not been the sort of kiss that poets praised. They talked of hearts and earthiness and delight.

Sabrina's kiss with Mr. Enright had been more of a rubbing of lips, and not a very long rubbing at that. She tried it once, then tried again, more out of curiosity the second time, and a hope not to be disappointed because kissing, apparently, was an anemic thing. She'd prefer the camaraderie of a hug—

Her thoughts broke off in a panic as his hand captured the back of her neck.

Her heart leaped in shock that he'd moved with his own volition. Conscious thought vanished from her mind, to be replaced by embarrassment at being caught smacking her lips against his. How could she explain what she had been doing—?

The weight of his hand brought her lips back to his.

And this time, there was no simple brush of closed flesh.

This time, their mouths melded together.

Sabrina had gasped in surprise, and Mr. Enright had taken advantage of her half-open lips, bringing potency to the kiss. Making it daring.

She was receiving her first true kiss and perhaps her last.

A smart woman would take full advantage. She'd missed so many opportunities in her life. She was not going to miss this one.

Besides, she liked this kiss.

His hand exerted gentle pressure, urging her to turn her head to just the right angle where they "fit."

Oh, yes, they fit.

For a long moment, Sabrina marveled at how right this felt. It didn't seem silly at all. Well, perhaps if someone witnessed their lips locked on each other's, they might think they were amusing . . . but to Sabrina, this felt good. Completely lovely and nice.

Indeed, her whole body hummed with how lovely and nice it was. The kiss flowed through her, melting resistance until she could think of nothing but the connection between them.

She didn't even notice that Mr. Enright had repositioned himself until he drew her down onto the bed alongside him. And she let herself be drawn, even as the bedclothes made it difficult for her skirts to stay down. They gathered at her knees. She didn't care, she was too busy marveling over the fact their lips had never once parted.

Of course, Sabrina knew she should stop him. She wasn't too far gone to not realize this was an impropriety. She even made an attempt to sit up, but he placed a possessive hand on the curve of her hip, and she decided there was no harm in lingering a minute more, especially as the kiss began to change.

He leaned into her, demonstrating there was more pleasure to be had the closer they were to each other.

Her eyes closed, and Sabrina allowed herself the pleasure of the moment. She indulged her curiosity.

As she kissed him, she could imagine she was breathing his soul, and she liked the idea. She was aware of the weight and presence of his body and even the texture of his skin in a way she hadn't been while tending him.

Furthermore, he was warm in a comforting

way, and she liked the scent of his skin, spicy and manly from the shaving soap and a fragrance unique to him alone. His arm slid around her waist. He gathered her closer, and his tongue intimately touched hers.

This was more than just a mere kiss. This was an invitation, an intimate one.

And Sabrina was not repulsed.

Instead, every fiber of her being came alive. He *tasted* good. He *smelled* good. He *felt* good.

Her arm had found its way to his waist, her hand pressed against the small of his back. She experienced him not as a patient, but as man, sliding her fingers beneath his shirt. His skin was smooth except for the scar, and she traced the line of it up his side.

A throbbing need began to build in her. Was this desire? This yearning to open all of herself to him? Especially in the most intimate places?

He slid his tongue along hers again, and Sabrina wrapped herself—arms, legs, hands—around him.

And still the kiss deepened. It grew heated. He tasted her, devoured her.

Dear God, she liked this kiss.

Now she understood why the poets praised a

kiss. There was more to it than she had ever imagined.

And when Mr. Enright kissed her fully, without any reservations between them, she eagerly welcomed him, wanting more, more, and *more.*

Her full breasts flattened against the hard muscles of his chest as he leaned over her. Yes, *that* chest, the one she had eyed with admiration. His hips fit with hers.

But what robbed her of all reason, what sent her spirit on fire with delicious anticipation, was his hand upon her breast. Her *naked* breast. Sabrina had no understanding of how her dress had become unlaced, but she didn't care. She was undone, and happy for it.

If she'd had a will to set limits or think rationally, it had vanished.

She now became a new being. Had she once exercised good sense? How ridiculous of her! She liked *this.* She was light and laughter . . . and need. Oh, yes, she *needed* him.

Capturing Mr. Enright's jaw with both her hands, she kissed him with all the budding passion inside her, and he responded. He was as hungry as she was. She wallowed in these kisses, reveled in them, and their magic was only heightened when he circled her hardened nipple with his thumb.

She quivered, just as the poets had claimed she would . . . Her loins were on fire. Yes, she had loins, another one of those poetic terms used to describe lust. She'd never read the word "loins" again without recalling this exquisite heat ignited by his touch.

Deep within her, a pressure was building. The word *desire* beat through her veins.

Yes, she desired him. Right now, she couldn't live without him. "Please," she heard herself whisper against his lips. "Please, please, please."

He knew what she wanted.

His leg slid between hers. His hand raised her skirts even higher, so they were gathered around her waist. She was exposed to him, but she didn't feel vulnerable or afraid.

For the first time in her life, she felt completely alive.

Being this close to him, having his body all around her, feeling his hips resting on hers, was better than kissing.

She could feel his hardness. She wasn't naïve. She knew the differences between men and women, but she'd never experienced them—and right now Sabrina was caught up in the "experience."

His weight felt good. His touch was not gentle but demanding, insistent.

At last, their kiss broke.

His breath was hot against her ear as he whispered, "I need you."

I need you.

What perfect words.

In all of Sabrina's life, only her mother had "needed" her and solely because, as an invalid, she'd had no other choice.

But this man wasn't bound to her . . . other than through their kisses.

His lips brushed her temple. Even that simple contact gave her pleasure—

The first sweep of his hand against her most intimate parts was shocking. The touch jerked her out of the haze she'd been lulled into.

"Steady," he said. His low voice touched a deep chord connecting her body with the stimulation of his knowledgeable hand. He nuzzled her neck, kissed her ear, and she thought she could linger a moment longer. He was trying to make her happy—and succeeding.

"Sweet angel," he murmured.

Sabrina smiled. No one had ever described her

as an angel or sweet. He made her feel like one. Certainly, she no longer felt of this earth. And she'd do anything she must to be what he wanted. His lips captured hers once more. Such delicious lips. No wonder she liked kissing them.

Her hands found their way under his shirt. The buttons of his breeches were undone. She didn't know how or when that had happened, but she liked it. She now had access to the hard muscles of his abdomen and the curve of his hip. He was long and lean, and his skin felt warm and smooth beneath her palm. The scent of him made her wild with wanting.

Sabrina was no longer the woman everyone thought her. *Look at me now, Dame Agatha. I'm living fully.*

She was who she wanted to be—and if all the women in the parish had tromped into this bedroom behind her father, she could not have stopped herself from relishing the hard planes of his chest and from pressing liquid need against his hardness—

The thrust, sure, steady, and demanding in its strength, surprised her.

She'd barely registered the fact that he was inside her, when *sharp* pain tore through the magic of the moment, dousing it with reality.

His naked hips were cradled between her thighs. Her stockings had fallen although she still wore her shoes. Her skirts were around her waist.

His breeches were *not* around his waist. His hips, his buttocks were muscular and strong. All of him was strong, and she knew because she felt as if he were splitting her in two.

And there was the problem.

Sabrina had been so caught up in the wonder of discovery, she now discovered herself no longer a virgin.

The shock sent her mind reeling. Her first inclination was to run, to escape.

She started to scramble out from underneath him, but he braced his arms so they formed a wall around her. "No," he whispered, his voice ragged. "You can't leave now. Not now."

Sabrina shook her head. The pain was ebbing, but her body felt uncomfortably stretched and full of him. "I *must* leave."

"No," he said, drawing out the word as if cooing to her. "Please, I can't let you go. The damage is done. Just give yourself a moment."

He was right. There was no going back.

The will to struggle against him left her. It was her fault. She'd kissed him.

She'd orchestrated her own destruction.

He frowned as if he was truly seeing her for the first time, a question clear in the brown-gold depths of his eyes, and he said the words that completed her humiliation. "Who are you?"

She bucked her hips with all her might, attempting to throw him off while she shoved his chest away from her, but her actions brought him into her deeper.

The penetration no longer hurt. Nor did it feel awkward. Her body had grown accustomed to him.

"Don't," he whispered. "I'd not harm you. Not my angel," he added, then began speaking to her in Gaelic, gentling her. Irish Gaelic.

From the cadence of his speech, he was reciting a poem to her, and the language of it was beautiful. Some words she recognized. There were words of praise for her beauty, for her generosity, for the lady he called his love.

The tension eased inside her.

His gaze focused on her, his expression somber. He traced the line of her lower lip with the tip of his thumb—and then he kissed her.

Oh, his deadly kisses.

Her heart kicked up its beat. Her blood heated,

and she opened herself to him. She could not prevent the response, not with him so intimately joined with her. But even then, she was drawn to him.

And he was right. What was done could not be undone. He began moving, this time with new strength and focused intent. He'd given her a chance to accept him, and now that she had, he was taking full advantage.

Mr. Enright took her hand that was still pressed against his chest and moved it to the pillow above her head. He laced his fingers with hers, and went deeper—and it felt good.

Sabrina's hips rose to meet him. He kissed her brow. He kissed her nose, her eyes, the curve of her cheek. She didn't fight. She couldn't.

This was the great rite of passage for a woman. She could not say that he had cruelly ripped her virtue from her . . . or, strangely, that she regretted giving this to him. At last, she understood the mystery between men and women.

She also knew she would never forget this moment. She would recall texture of the sheets beneath her and the give of the mattress. She would remember that the air was cool but her skin hot. She would inhale the memory of the scent of them, and would have the vision of his hard, lean body with that wicked scar.

And, she decided, she would not be sorry she'd done this.

The pain was gone. In its place was the knowledge of the most incredible intimacy.

Above her, his eyes had lost their sharpness. They'd darkened with desire.

She noted that his teeth were white and even, and in spite of his illness, he was a formidable man. She'd chosen well for a lover.

A lover? Would that be true.

He was taking the utmost care of her. She was no longer afraid, not of him, and when she relaxed, her pleasure escalated until she was drowning once again in this newly learned hunger.

And hungry she was. She strove with him, without fully understanding where they were going. Instead, she trusted him. He knew what she needed.

He kissed her, this kiss so deep it seemed to turn her inside out.

Sabrina shook off his hand holding hers and threw her arms around his neck, needing to be closer to him. She hooked a leg on his hip.

Their joining took on a new intensity. She suddenly couldn't wait for him. Something drove her, something intangible.

The heat between them grew more forceful, his thrusts took on purpose. She was on fire. She could not think; she could only feel—and what she felt was beyond anything she could have ever imagined. She was reaching for what was just beyond her grasp . . .

And then she discovered *it*.

Her body tightened, opened, then seemed to implode with her release. Relentless, intense emotion poured through her.

Nothing could have prepared her for this experience. It defied all description. It was a world unto itself. *It was the universe.* She'd never imagined that such vivid, encompassing feelings could exist.

Mr. Enright buried himself in her, and she felt his release.

This was what it meant to become one.

Now, she understood. She relished the experience.

Her body felt perfectly right. Well used. Happy. Content. Completely, and utterly, satisfied . . . until she realized she knew nothing of this man other than his last name. She'd broken every rule of conduct she'd established for herself. She'd *liked* it. She'd like to do it again, and again.

Did that make her a Widow Bossley?

And what would happen to her if she became with child? Then everyone else would know what she'd done. *Everyone.* She would be the fodder of gossip for decades to come.

Sabrina lay on her bed, the one she'd slept on since childhood, her clothing in wanton disarray, her body growing cold and her mind boiling over with a hundred chaotic questions—and she wanted to scream.

He, on the other, rolled over on his side, threw a possessive arm across her body, and, with a contented sigh, fell into a deep, peaceful sleep.

Chapter Eight

Sabrina glared at the man snoozing beside her and had two impulses: one was to run and the other to double her fists and pound him.

She decided to run.

His arm was as heavy as a tree branch across her chest. His weight, which she'd easily tolerated moments ago, was now unwieldy. Using both hands, she lifted his arm, then didn't know how to place it beside his body without its being at an awkward angle. He might wake, and she didn't want that.

So, as stealthily as a thief, she eased out from under his arm, landing on her bottom on the floor.

A sharp glance assured her he had not noticed

anything amiss. He slept on as if he hadn't turned her world inside out.

Sabrina jumped to her feet, pulling her bodice up over her shoulders and shaking out her skirts to restore her modesty—and found she hated the dress she wore. She'd never wear it again. She couldn't without recalling this moment in vivid detail.

That he'd so easily and completely bypassed her good sense and judgment to claim her virtue, then had the audacity to sleep as if he didn't have a care in the world made her irrationally wish to burn the dress. She tiptoed to her wardrobe, pulled out her forest green day gown, the one she liked to save for doing charity work, and rushed from the room.

At the foot of the stairs, she stopped to take stock of her situation.

She was so thankful that Mrs. Patton was not here to witness her humiliation. Then again, if the housekeeper had been here, if her father had not left her alone with this man, well, then, things would not have gone as they had. She would not have dared to shave Mr. Enright, let alone kiss him.

Even now, her senses were full of him. His scent was on her skin, and in the most intimate places.

With an angry sound at her own culpability—because, after all, her vanity had started what had happened—she hurried to the kitchen and stoked the fire. She went outside, her movements determined. She was very conscious of muscles she'd never known had existed in places she couldn't have imagined. She pumped water into the bucket.

Rolf came bounding up to her. She threw her arms around him. "I'm such a fool, Rolf."

His wagging tail assured her he adored her no matter how far she'd fallen, but Sabrina could not let her failings rest.

As she marched into the house and put the water over the fire to heat, she flayed herself with the number of times she'd been sharply critical over the behavior of other young women, including her cousin Tara. She'd accused Tara of flaunting herself and quite frankly considered herself superior to her cousin.

Well, now, Sabrina was guilty of the same offense. She'd thrown herself at Mr. Enright. And he didn't even know her name.

She had to keep it that way. Somehow, she must manage to push him out of the house without his being the wiser to whom she was. She'd have Mrs. Patton tell him to leave or send for her father—no, wait, she couldn't do that. He'd want to know what the man was doing under his roof and one thing would lead to the other and Sabrina would confess all.

She didn't even want to think of the worst— that she could bear this man's child. God could not be that cruel. All she'd wanted was one kiss.

The family bathed in the kitchen where the fire was always burning. Sabrina pulled the tub from its storage place under the shelves of the pantry. She also kept towels and soaps in a small pail there as well. She shut the kitchen door, pushing the heavy table in front of it since there was no lock. This was a precaution against Mr. Enright's accidentally meandering around the house.

As quickly as she could, she prepared her bath. She threw her clothes to the floor, climbed into the tub, and scrubbed herself senseless. If she could wash away the last hour of her life, she would have.

But she couldn't. It had happened. She'd seen proof on her clothing.

And she became angry.

No one must ever know of this. No one.

She hugged her legs up close to her body in the tub, fantasizing over the possibility of Mr. Enright's vanishing or wandering off into the world, never to be seen or heard from again.

But whether he did or not, *she* knew what she'd done. A secret like this was a burden unless confessed. If her cousin Aileen had been in Scotland, she might have turned to her.

No, the only person she had close at hand was her father—and suddenly, she wanted him to come home. Moments ago, she'd not wanted him to know. Now, she needed his presence. She didn't like being alone with Mr. Enright and that seductive voice of his. She didn't want to face him without someone she trusted by her side.

Unfortunately, her father was with Mrs. Bossley, and she would not go to the widow's house to fetch him.

However, her uncle might retrieve him for her.

Leaving the house to search out her uncle might be a good thing. Distance always offered perspective.

With a plan of action, Sabrina dressed quickly, moved the table back where it belonged, and went into the hall for her hat and gloves. She listened a moment. She heard no sound from the upstairs, so she had to check on her patient. She must. Curiosity encouraged her to do so.

His large body overflowed her bed. He slept as if his conscience was clear. Could he not know what had happened between them and demonstrate a modicum of angst? Or pretend to share her regrets?

Disconcerted, Sabrina flew to the stables. She hitched Dumpling to the cart and set off for Annefield.

*M*ac woke with a start.

By the angle of the light coming through the window, he sensed the day was well advanced.

For a long moment, he lay still, trying to place his bearings. He didn't remember this room, and it had been years since he'd slept on such a comfortable mattress or had sheets this fresh.

His memory returned in snippets. He'd escaped from the Tolbooth. He remembered that. He'd been ill. He could recall the fatigue, the dizziness, the nausea. There had been a point when he'd been close to death's door. He felt weak but good right now. He'd had dreams, wild, nonsensical ones. He had a vague recollection of who was in those dreams. He knew he'd searched for Lorcan . . . he thought. And Moira. Gram had been present.

Then, he remembered the angel.

Intense, vague images came to his mind. Images with taste and texture. The scent of her was all around him. He could have reached for her, expecting her to be beside him, but he was alone.

Mac lifted himself up to rest on one arm and took in the furnishings of the room. The wardrobe door was ajar, and he could see frocks hanging there. The pitcher and basin on the washstand were plain but decidedly feminine in style and form, and there were bits of lace in the curtains.

Oh, yes, this was a woman's room.

"What have you done with yourself now, Mac?" he asked the world at large and, of course, received no answer. God had never been generous with him.

His stomach rumbled.

A bowl on the bedside table caught his attention. There was also a small pitcher for water and a stack rags that could be used for a number of purposes.

His memory sharpened on *her*. She had creamy skin, dark hair, and a kindness in her eye that had assured him he was safe. For once in his life, he'd allowed himself to trust someone, and she'd kept him alive.

He remembered the shepherd's hut. If he'd been left there, he probably would have come down with the croup and never survived. How the bloody hell had he arrived here?

And where was she now? Where was *he* now?

He listened for sounds of activity in the house, but all was quiet. There wasn't even a ticking of a clock.

Mac was also hungry. Ravenous. He needed to eat and drink. He reached for the small pitcher and downed the contents. There was nothing left in the bowl, and he had to find something. His body demanded sustenance.

As he sat up, ready to put his feet over the side of the bed, the blanket wrapped around him fell to the side. His breeches were undone, his shirt up to his chest.

His angel had done *more* than keep him alive . . . and those vague images became more defined. Just the thought of her had him stirring.

Oh, yes, he *did* remember. She'd been a generous lover, an intense one, open to whatever he asked of her, and he wondered where she was now? Theirs had been no ordinary coupling.

Mac rose to his feet, righting his clothing as he did so and combing his tangled hair back with his fingers. He rubbed his jaw with the back of his hand and was surprised to discover he was clean-shaven. She'd done that.

He buttoned his breeches.

His boots were on the other side of the night

table, but Mac didn't pause to put them on. He wanted to know where he was and who *she* was.

He was also interested in knowing how far he was from Kenmore in his quest to find the Reverend Kinnion, his only link to Richard Davidson.

The upstairs floor had three bedrooms. The room he'd been in had definite feminine touches, but the others were neat, clean, and lacking personality. There was a door at the end of the hall that led to attic stairs. He checked the bedrooms and found a wardrobe containing a gentleman's clothes. The wardrobe in the third bedroom had a man's jacket and two shirts, items that appeared to have not been worn recently. Perhaps someone had used the room and left these behind. Whatever the case, he now knew there was the woman and at least one man living here. No servants. He didn't see signs of one.

Mac tried one of the shirts. He'd been wearing what he'd had on for too long. He yearned for clean clothes. Unfortunately, it was too small.

He went down the stairs. His stockinged feet didn't make a sound on the treads.

The house seemed foreign to him. Nothing was familiar, a sign that he might have been more ill than even he realized when he'd been brought under this roof.

There was a dining room with a table, chairs, a sideboard, and brass candlesticks, not silver. A pianoforte took up one corner of the sitting room across the hall, and there were a few chairs, one upholstered, arranged around the musical instrument and the cold hearth.

Mac walked down the hall and discovered the kitchen. Several loaves of bread were laid out on a table in the middle of the room. Mac fell on one of them, pulling off great hunks of the loaf and stuffing them in his mouth. The bread was delicious. Then again, anything, including cabbage, his least favorite food, would have tasted of ambrosia.

He poked around the pots set around the fire in the hearth. There was what appeared to be a mutton stew there. A bit more nosing around revealed the pantry. It was well stocked. There was bacon, ham, onions, and, to his delight, meat pies. He'd finished the loaf of bread, so he helped himself to a pie, which he washed down with a jug of sweet cider.

Mac was beginning to feel himself again.

There was a bathing tub with cool water beside the hearth. A linen towel was hanging to dry over one of the cooking hooks. A bar of soap was on the hearthstone. Mac picked it up and smelled it. The scent reminded him of roses and lavender, strong, evocative perfumes . . . and the fragrance of his angel.

She'd shaved him, but he was in need of more grooming. Mac believed in regular bathing. He liked the way he felt when he bathed often, and he certainly preferred the way he smelled. As a physician, he'd observed there was a correlation between health and cleanliness, all other beliefs to the contrary.

He glanced at the door. Whoever lived here could return any moment. Or they could be gone for hours. He wasn't one to waste an opportunity.

Shutting the kitchen door, he pulled a chair from a row of them against the far wall. They probably belonged around the table, but it was easier to knead bread and make pies as delicious as the one he'd gobbled down if the chairs were not in the way.

He propped the chair against the door. It wouldn't stop someone from coming in but would give him time to shout a warning or defend himself, whichever the case might be.

The temperature of the water was fine with him. He'd bathed in colder. He didn't even mind the scent of the soap.

Mac unbuttoned his breeches, shucked off his pants—and froze.

He'd assumed he'd had sex when he'd woken with his breeches undone and his little friend spent.

What he hadn't realized, until this moment, was that the woman he'd so completely enjoyed had been a virgin.

The signs were there.

Mac frowned. He wasn't one to deflower the innocent. He rebuttoned himself, moved the chair, and went upstairs to reexamine the bed. On the sheets, he discovered more signs of her virginity.

What the devil was he involved in? It was as if she had taken advantage of him but to what purpose?

And he wasn't certain he minded.

He returned to the kitchen and tore off his clothes, not even bothering with the door. He climbed into the cold water, lathered the flower-scented soap, and washed himself thoroughly and completely from the top of his head to the bottom of his feet.

Sensible men did not pluck virgins. There was a price for such foolishness, especially when the man didn't know who the woman was. He didn't think she could be the wife of the house and still be intact, but if she was the daughter, well, things could become complicated.

And if there was one thing a man wanted for murder didn't want, it was more complications.

Just the thought of all that could go wrong made him dunk his head underwater. Still, he wasn't just anyone any longer. He was an earl although he didn't feel worthy of being one. And, of course, if there was a child, he would do the honorable thing.

But first, he'd wait to meet the lady.

Mac climbed out of the tub and dressed quickly. He combed his hair with his fingers before helping himself to another cup of cider which he carried as he opened the door and went out into the hall. There was another room, a study with legal papers stacked on the desk. He set his cup down and started going through them, anxious for any clue as to the owner of the house—and then he saw the name on the signature line.

"Richard Davidson."

For a second, he was stunned. His enemy, the man who could answer the question "Why," was either here or close at hand . . . and all Mac had to do was wait.

*T*he earl of Tay let Sabrina cool her heels for two hours before he entered the Morning Room, where Ingold, the Tay butler, had asked her to wait along with some light refreshments.

Her uncle did not look well.

The earl of Tay had once cut an imposing figure. Now, he seemed a seedy one.

His florid cheeks were at odds with the pasty skin of his neck and hands. His hair was grayer. He had a decided paunch and a stumble to his gait. He was still wearing his dressing gown over a shirt and breeches. His neckcloth had a large stain on it.

"You are *drunk*," Sabrina said in weary surprise, watching her uncle head to a side table boasting several bottles of port.

"The day is advanced," her uncle mumbled. He toasted her with a full glass, before saying, "Most of what I feel is from last night." He downed the glass and poured another.

"Wait," Sabrina ordered, moving to place a hand on his arm and prevent him from consuming another drink before she spoke. "I need your help."

He stared at her through watery eyes. "Eh?"

Her first inclination was to slap sense into him. Instead, she forced a smile. "I need for you to call on Mrs. Bossley and tell Father he must return home."

"Eh?"

Sabrina could feel her false smile stretch tighter. Her uncle tried to raise his arm to bring his glass to his lips. She held it down. "Father. Needs. You."

"Not if he is with Mrs. Bossley," the earl answered, sounding very lucid. He pivoted, escaping Sabrina's grasp, and took a sip of his drink. "He's probably very happy. He'll return home by and by."

"But he is making a spectacle of himself," Sabrina said, as if it should be obvious—and momentarily forgetting to whom she was speaking.

He reminded her by saying, "Good for him. At our age, it is a mark of honor to be considered a spectacle. I hope Lilly shows him a good time." He paused, eyed Sabrina, and added, "You might consider making a bit of a spectacle yourself, lass. You are too serious for your own good."

If he'd known what a "spectacle" she'd made of herself already this day, he might not be so cavalier. And it was on the tip of her tongue to inform him. She'd had a good roll with a man whom, for all she knew, could be a common criminal. *Yes,* she had! And she'd let him have her in broad daylight, which, from her limited understanding, was practically unchristian.

But she held her tongue because her uncle might applaud such behavior.

Instead, with an exasperated sound, she turned on her heel and stormed out of the house, refusing to waste one more minute of her time conversing with a drunkard.

Dumpling was not happy to see her. The Annefield stables were the pony's favorite place to visit since they treated him so well. Sabrina gave the stable lad a coin out of her meager purse and took the reins, snapping them to send Dumpling pulling the cart down the drive.

Her mind was in a tizzy. She had few options.

Calling on Mrs. Bossley was out of the question. Her father had made his choice, a fact reemphasized when she returned home and saw that her father's horse was still not in his stall. Sabrina could only pray her father came to his senses soon. Then again, the earl of Tay was not going to serve as a proper role model.

Or maybe the earl had, and for that reason her father had deserted his family and all of his responsibilities.

Whatever was going on, she realized she had little power over his decisions.

Instead, she was going to have to take care of

herself. The thought was daunting, and invigorating in a way she'd not imagined. In the process of unhitching Dumpling, Sabrina paused a moment, evaluating this new realization.

She would take care of *herself.*

The idea had never crossed her mind. She'd been more or less adrift in life, doing what was expected, anticipating others' needs, not ever considering what made her happy. But what if she took Dame Agatha and even her uncle's advice and changed? What if she decided what she would and wouldn't do?

Sabrina had never imagined her life beyond the boundaries of her family.

She scooped out oats for Dumpling and came to a decision. "I'll do my charity work and help those who value my healing skills, but I want to live for myself. And," she added, leaning into the stall so that Dumpling could see she was very serious, "I won't feel guilty for what happened this afternoon." She rocked back on her feet. "No, I won't," she repeated. She would become like those Frenchwomen she'd heard about who ran salons and were valued for their intelligence.

Maybe she would leave the valley. There was a thought to make her stomach churn with fear. However, there was a world beyond the parish and she'd experienced none of it. She'd been too busy feeling sorry for herself, just as Dame Agatha had suggested.

A thoughtful Sabrina started for the house with a length of rope in her hand. Evening had fallen. The moon was pale in the sky. No lights shone from the windows. Either Mr. Enright had left—which she hoped. Or, he had not regained consciousness, and she was going to tie him up. She didn't know what she would do with him after that, but she'd improvise. It would be easiest if she could ask him to leave, and he did so without fuss.

Rolf bounded from his post by the step to greet her, and she gave the dog a hug. His presence by the house told her Mr. Enright was probably still her guest. She liked to think Rolf was a good watchdog. She interpreted his wagging tail as a sign all was fine, and yet, an unsettling feeling tickled the hair at the back of her neck. An awareness that perhaps she should be cautious.

Sabrina wasn't one for signs, but the other day in the bothy, her senses had rightly warned her . . . and now, once again, she had a recognition of something she could not define.

She opened the back door, holding the coil of rope ready so she could use it as a weapon. The hall was dark. No one stirred. "Go inside," she told the dog.

His shiny eyes looked doubtful in the moonlight.

"Don't worry. Father isn't here." And he wouldn't be.

Rolf went inside. She watched his shadow move down the hall. He didn't sound an alarm, pausing first by the study door, convincing himself that his master was not home, then moving on to the kitchen, his favorite room in the house.

Meanwhile, Sabrina's stomach rumbled. She'd barely touched the bread-and-butter sandwiches at Annefield. She could heat the stew Mrs. Patton had made and kept warm on the hearth or grab one of the meat pies always kept in the pantry for light meals. A glass of cider would taste good as well.

Then she'd have the energy to decide what to do with Mr. Enright.

Sabrina bravely walked into the house, her rope at the ready. She didn't have to feel her way. She knew it even in the dark. Without bothering to remove her bonnet, she walked into the kitchen, set her rope aside, and placed a log on the dying fire in the hearth. Flames rose. The tub was where she'd left it. She would have to drag it to the door and pour the water out. She pulled off her driving gloves and placed them on the table before reaching for a taper on the mantel and lighting it off the growing fire. Warmth and light filled the room.

She started to carry the lit taper to a candle, when, once again, she sensed all was not as it should be. Rolf sat on his haunches by the table, ready for a treat. He didn't seem unusually alert.

"Father?"

Her voice echoed in the darkness. It was silly to think he was there. His horse was not in his stall, and he would have lit the lamp in his study or candles in the kitchen.

She blew out the taper and placed it on the table. With catlike feet, she moved out into the hall. Her eyes adjusted to the darkness. No one was there.

The door to her father's study was halfway open. She couldn't remember how it had been when she'd left. She placed her palm on the cool wood and slowly pushed the door open.

Moonlight flowed through the windows onto her father's desk. The pen and papers were exactly how he'd left them several days ago. Sabrina couldn't remember the angle of his chair behind his desk, but all seemed as it should be.

Everything was quiet save for Rolf's panting. He stood by the kitchen door, waiting hopefully.

She released her breath. Her mind was playing tricks on her. There was no sound from upstairs. Her imagination was being overactive.

With the intention of returning to the kitchen, Sabrina started to pivot, and that is when a man's figure stepped out from behind the door. Strong arms came down around her.

"Don't struggle. Don't fight," said a deep voice with the hint of an accent she immediately recognized.

"Mr. Enright?" she said.

He spun her around, his expression as shocked as she felt. "Angel?" he whispered, and then blurted out in disbelief, *"Who are you to Davidson?"*

There was anger in his voice. Malice.

Her very good common sense—*finally*—reared its head, and she realized she was being attacked in her own home. This man should not be in her father's study. She started to scream.

A hard hand was clamped over her mouth.

"Quiet, will you," he said. "I'll not harm you if you will be quiet."

Harm her?

Sabrina decided now was a good time to begin taking care of herself.

She stomped on the toe of his boot with the heel of her sensible shoes. She put all her weight into

the action and was rewarded with a very satisfying Irish grunt. His hold loosened. She pushed
him away from her and would have taken off running except he grabbed her arm.

"I'm not going to hurt you," he claimed. "I want
Davidson."

"My father?" The words rushed out of her in
alarm. Mr. Enright had been lying in wait for her
father? And he believed she found that reassur-
ing?

As magistrate, her father had made enemies—
and apparently she had allowed one of them to
have his way with her. To think, she'd nursed
this man back to health, and, on some level, had
grown to trust him. But she shouldn't have. He
was a viper.

In fairness, he seemed equally shocked. "Your
father? *I deflowered Davidson's daughter?"* He didn't
wait for her answer but muttered, "This is not
good. Not good at all."

He was right, and to show him how right he
was, she curled her fingers into claws and attacked.

Chapter Nine

*M*ac didn't know what startled him most—that his angel was Davidson's daughter, or the ferocity of her attack.

Instead of running like any sensible woman should, she charged him without fear. Her eyes in the moonlight were alive with outrage, and as she surged forward, she reminded him of nothing less than a banshee, those demons of Irish lore.

He stepped back, bumping into the doorframe, then moving into the hall. She followed, ready to scratch the skin off of him.

Her dog had caught onto the melee and began barking and running around them. Mac almost tripped over the animal. The dog snapped his teeth and tried to grab his coat.

Mac didn't feel he could fight back, but he did want her to stop hurting him. A time or two she landed a blow or a scratch that was not pleasant.

He kept retreating, leading her toward the kitchen, where there would be more space for him to maneuver than in the narrow hall. She ruthlessly went after him.

Inside the larger room, Mac ducked under her arms and reached for her waist. Using his superior strength, he easily lifted her off the floor and upended her over his shoulder. She kicked her legs wildly and attempted to reach around him in the most unladylike way possible to strike a blow.

He had to admire her. She was protecting her father. His business with her sire was deadly serious—however, she had changed the game.

Mac owed her his life. He might have survived his illness without her care but it would have taken longer for him to recover . . . and, while holding her struggling body against his, he realized that making love to her had done more to restore his spirit than any amount of nursing could have achieved.

This woman had true passion. Even now, he felt himself respond to her in spite of her wanting to rip the ears off of his head.

So she must stop this nonsense. He needed to find her father, and she was a distraction.

He set her on her feet with a thud and whirled her around before she could react. He grabbed both her arms below the shoulders and held her captive. He was ready to order her to behave . . . but the words died in his throat.

The fire from the hearth filled the kitchen with golden, flickering light. The bonnet she'd been wearing had come undone and fallen to the floor somewhere in their struggles. Her hair tumbled down around her shoulders in thick, round curls. Her eyes sparkled with defiance and, yes, fear. Luminous eyes that told him she was afraid but she'd not run.

Eyes that could bring a man to his knees.

"I don't want to fight," he said. "Not with you."

And because he couldn't help himself, and because it was what he desired, he kissed her.

It was the reasonable action in an unreasonable situation.

Nor was this kiss a common one. He couldn't remember the last time he'd kissed a woman out of true, yearning desire and not to just to meet earthy needs.

There was also a question in his kiss as well. She had given to him what should have been her gift to a lover. He wanted to know why, to understand, and the mystery of her, combined with the tightening in his loins, was a potent mix.

The world faded away. He didn't even register the dog's barking.

Miss Davidson resisted. Oh, yes, she did. Her reaction was what he had anticipated. She was going to deny him. Her lips were hard and unyielding, but her body no longer strained away from him. Instead, she had gone still, unwilling to surrender and, yet, no longer ready to fight. He sensed her internal struggle. She was as attracted to him as he found himself to her. It was there in the kiss. A brush of the lips, and the energy between them changed even though she kept hers tightly closed. She was determined not to yield, and yet she didn't shy from him either.

This woman was a challenge and, right now, he didn't care what her relationship was to Richard Davidson. She attracted him. He wanted her to touch him. He wanted it very much—

Thwack.

The sound accompanied the force of a broomstick across his shoulders. "*Unhand her,*" a woman's voice ordered.

Such was the power of the kiss, it took Mac a second to feel any pain. He raised an arm to defend himself, but he didn't want to let his lips leave Miss Davidson's—until he was whacked with the broomstick a second time. This time across the back of his ribs and with more force.

He released Miss Davidson and faced his attacker, an older woman of indeterminate age. She had graying blonde curls beneath a jaunty flower bonnet. The same sort of flowery pattern was repeated in her violet-and-blue dress. Lace gloves covered her hands holding the broomstick.

His first thought was to Miss Davidson's safety. This woman was obviously mad.

He reached to keep his captive protectively behind him, but she had already scampered away.

"Who are you?" he demanded of his new opponent.

Her response was to swing the broomstick with an impressive show of strength. It whooshed through the air, smacking him hard on the other side of his ribs.

Just as he winced from that pain, a good-sized pottery mug whizzed by his head.

He was under attack.

Miss Davidson had fled his arms only to begin pulling cups and bowls off the cupboard beside her. She threw them at him with all her might.

And then there was the dog barking.

Mac knew when to run.

Unfortunately, the flower lady blocked his escape to the door.

He leaped across the table, uncertain how he was going to extricate himself from this complication. He raised his hands to sue for peace.

Miss Davidson threw another cup. It hit him in the shoulder.

"All right," he said, his temper growing. "Let's talk about this—"

The flower lady swooshed the air with her broomstick.

Mac ducked in time to save his head.

He straightened, ready to grab that broomstick from her and break it in half—when he realized the women were no longer paying attention to him.

Instead, Miss Davidson, her hand in the air ready to lob a soup bowl in his direction, stared at her compatriot in openmouthed surprise. *"What* are *you* doing here, Mrs. Bossley?"

The flower lady had swung so hard, she'd stumbled a step, sending her bonnet down over her eyes. She pushed it back with her arm. "Helping *you*." She spit the words out with equally fevered disdain.

"I don't need help."

"Apparently you do."

Miss Davidson's chin lifted. "Remove yourself from this house right this minute."

"I will not," came the staunch reply.

Mac shifted his weight, uncertain to trust this turn of events. Were they so angry at each other that they had forgotten about him?

He didn't think that was a possibility. Women were very canny about being able to perform more than one task at a time.

However, they eyed each other with the air of avowed enemies.

And the dog had stopped barking. He stood between the two women, his tail wagging.

The unwelcome Mrs. Bossley brought her broom to rest on the floor. "I must see the magistrate," she announced stiffly. "Once I've seen him, *then* I will leave—but not a moment until." Her voice shook as she spoke, and Mac noticed for the first time her nose was pinched and her eyes red-rimmed from crying.

He felt rather sorry for her.

Miss Davidson didn't. "Once you've *seen* him? Haven't you been with him enough? Can you not *bear* a *moment* apart from my father?"

"*I must see him,*" Mrs. Bossley announced dramatically before throwing her broomstick to the floor, where it bounced on the wood floor. She went running out the door, shouting, *"Richard? Richard, please.* I need you, Richard. I can't bear to be without you."

Miss Davidson put down the bowl she'd been holding and charged after her. *"Where do you believe you are going?* Come back here. Come back here right now. This is not your house."

And Mac found himself alone in the kitchen.

Footsteps pounded up the stair treads.

Miss Davidson snapped unheeded orders for Mrs. Bossley to remove herself from these premises. The older woman kept calling for "Richard" in the voice of the lovelorn. The dog had followed them, barking his opinion.

Mac could leave the house now. No one was paying attention to him.

However, if he did depart, he might miss more of the entertainment, and he discovered he was enjoying himself. It had been a long time since he'd felt so engaged in life. He had no doubt that Mrs. Bossley was calling for Richard Davidson. He was curious as to why Miss Davidson was adamantly attempting to throw the woman out of her house.

"Ah, yes, the mysteries just keep growing," he murmured.

And he found he was interested in knowing which one would win. His money was on Miss Davidson, although the power behind Mrs. Bossley's broom swing was a testimony to her determination as well.

So, instead of going out the back door, he followed the hallway to where a lively battle was being fought.

Miss Davidson stood halfway up the stairs, her body stiff with outrage. "You have no right to be going through this house."

"Richard. *Richard*," Mrs. Bossley cried, sounding half-mad with anguish to the noise of doors opening and closing.

Mac leaned on the banister, resting his chin in his hand. These were two very passionate women.

Miss Davidson started up the stairs, stomping on the treads as if to promise a reckoning once she placed her hands on Mrs. Bossley.

She was precluded from her actions by the older woman's appearance on the top step. Mrs. Bossley had torn her bonnet from her head. She held it in one hand by the ribbons while her other hand rested on her temple as if her head was splitting with pain. She weaved back and forth as she begged, "Where is he?"

Miss Davidson pulled up short. "Where is he?"

she repeated with disbelief. "He's been with *you* since last night."

"With *me*?" Mrs. Bossley dropped her hands to her side in surprise. "Since last night?"

Miss Davidson's response was a bark of disbelief. "You don't have to pretend," she said, her words wounded and strangely affecting. "You have won. He's chosen you over his reputation, his honor, his responsibilities."

"You believe your father has been with me?" Mrs. Bossley countered, as if wishing to perfectly understand the accusation against her.

Crossing her arms tightly against her chest, Miss Davidson did not reply but studied a point on the staircase that was of interest only to her.

"He has not been with me," Mrs. Bossley said. "I haven't seen him since you and I had our little tiff at the Ladies' Quarterly Meeting."

It took a moment for Miss Davidson to process this information. Her brows came together, then her head shot up. "You have not seen Father?"

Mrs. Bossley shook her head so vigorously, several pins dropped from her hair, upsetting her style.

"Since before the luncheon?" Miss Davidson prodded.

"The night before," Mrs. Bossley added for clarification. "I was expecting him last night. You can imagine I had a few matters I wished to discuss with him. You spoke to him, didn't you?" Now Mrs. Bossley was the accuser. "You told him about our conversation."

"I did," Miss Davidson admitted stoutly, "as well I should. And then he left the house, and he hasn't returned since. Are you saying, he did not go to you?"

"That is exactly what I'm saying. I have not seen him. I expected his visit, but I've had no word or sight of him, and considering how upset you were when we spoke, I assumed he avoided me."

Miss Davidson shook her head. "Well, if he wasn't with you, and he hasn't been with me— where is he?"

It was at this point that Mac felt he could offer something to the conversation. He cleared his throat, gaining their attention, and announced, "He might be dead."

The idea had just occurred to him, but considering the events that had ruled his life, and that Davidson had helped orchestrate his escape, the possibility was real.

Both women started in surprise. Mrs. Bossley practically came tumbling down the steps to stand on the same stair tread as Miss Davidson.

"Dead?" she repeated, her hand rising to clutch her dress at her heart.

Mac rested his elbow on the newel post and nodded. The staircase was made of good sturdy wood and not ornate. In fact, everything in his house spoke of a simple, humble life, and not the home of the sort of Captain Sharp who would patronize the Rook's Nest as Davidson had done.

"Yes," he informed the women. "Richard Davidson could be dead."

Mrs. Bossley was ready to come undone. She began drawing big, shuddering breaths, but Miss Davidson had enough spirit to challenge him.

She came down a stair. "What makes you say this?"

"Because he apparently was playing with some nasty fellows," Mac answered.

"My father would not consort with anyone disreputable," she informed him.

"Did he consort with the Reverend Kinnion?" Mac asked. "Because I fear there is a strong possibility, the good reverend might also be dead."

"Dead?" Miss Davidson repeated.

"Yes, shot."

"*What* is this man talking about, Miss Davidson?" Mrs. Bossley demanded, shrilly. "*Why* is he here anyway?"

Miss Davidson shook off her companion's questions. She came all the way down the stairs so she could stand eye level with Mac. "The Reverend Kinnion has been missing for several days. Why do you believe he is dead?" she asked, her voice calm, the gaze of her blue eyes intent as they met his.

This woman was a cool player. A good one to have on one's side in a fight, but he'd learned that when she'd attempted to scratch the eyes out of his head.

And, whatever had been going on between her and Mrs. Bossley was of little consequence at this moment. She truly was concerned for her father and wanted answers.

"I heard the shot that might have killed him," Mac said. "I stumbled over his body, and he did not respond."

"Are you certain he is dead?"

"No. I started to check and was waved away by another man. I had the impression he would take care of the reverend. After all, I was trying to escape from the jail and was not in a position to linger even though the Reverend Kinnion had been helping me with my escape."

"Escape from the jail? The Reverend Kinnion?" Miss Davidson considered him a moment as if she didn't believe his story. Mac could understand her doubt.

Meanwhile, Mrs. Bossley gripped the hand railing and rocked with the drama of an actor in a Greek tragedy. "Oh, dear. Oh, Richard," she whispered. "Oh, Lord."

"Mr. Enright, *who* are you?" Miss Davidson asked.

In that moment, he had an irrational urge to kiss her again. She was just that delightful. Most soldiers lacked her single-mindedness, a trait he valued, and he couldn't help but wish to draw this moment between them out. Her directness was refreshing . . . and she had saved his life, in more ways than she could imagine, he realized. He was actually enjoying himself.

"I'm a man who came here to confront your father."

"Because . . ." she prodded.

She deserved a straight answer. He owed her that much.

"Because I'm a man wanted for murder."

Chapter Ten

$\mathscr{O}$f all the answers Sabrina could have anticipated, *that* was not one of them.

She found herself staring at him, waiting for him to deny the charge. She wanted him to laugh. "You jest."

He boldly met her eye. "I wish I did."

"And you are not teasing about my father's fate?" She couldn't say the word, *dead*. She did not want to lose another parent.

"That would mean I have a macabre sense of humor, Miss Davidson, and that is not the case. I'm not certain what has happened to Richard Davidson, but I know someone put a bullet in the Reverend Kinnion."

Sabrina feared her legs would collapse beneath

her. She reached for the newel post. Her hand
brushed his arm. He leaned forward as if to offer
support, but she pulled back, confused by the jolt
of something she feared to name that shot between them.

This was not the time to think of lust, or to trust
this man. In the kitchen, she'd almost given in to
his kiss. If he'd continued one moment more, she
feared what she would have done.

A new thought struck her, and she wanted
to bury her head in her arms. Not only had she
thrown herself in the most wanton way possible
at this man, she'd been intimate with a murderer.
Could she sink any lower?

Mrs. Bossley came charging down the stairs.
"What?" she demanded in her frantic tone. "What
did he say? I didn't hear all. I was too worried. Is
it something about Richard?"

The widow's silliness helped restore Sabrina's
courage. She needed to know what he knew.
"Were you the someone who shot the Reverend
Kinnion? Did you murder him?"

Mr. Enright frowned as if her question was ridiculous. "The good reverend was saving my life.
I'd not harm him. Nor do I wish to harm your
father. But I must find him. He is the only one who
can give me the answers I need. Whoever shot the

reverend may be searching for him as well. That person may have found him, and that is why he has disappeared."

Panic choked her. "How do you know this?"

"It stands to reason. And, for the record, even though you haven't asked, and I do believe it is an important question—let me state, I have not 'murdered' anyone."

"*Murder?*" Mrs. Bossley cried out as if she'd been trying to make sense of the conversation and had just heard the relevant word. "Murder?"

Sabrina sank to the step, overwhelmed by the turn of events. Why had she gone to the bothy that day? Why had she let this silly goose, the Widow Bossley, upset her? If she had stayed at the luncheon, then perhaps, none of this would have happened. Her father would be at home, she would still retain her virtue and dignity . . .

Of course, there would always be the widow, waiting for her father to marry her. But then he might not have ever managed to have the courage to tell his daughter about Mrs. Bossley. The "what-ifs" swirled in her head.

Sabrina now understood how people lost their sanity.

"*I said* I have *not* murdered anyone," Mr. Enright was repeating to Mrs. Bossley, with no small amount of irritation.

"Why would someone say you did if they didn't have suspicions?" the widow challenged. "Where there is smoke, there is fire. That is what I've always believed."

"Well, there is no smoke, and there is no fire," Mr. Enright shot back.

Sabrina raised her head. "Would you tell us the truth if you had? Are murderers honest?"

"Yes," he said. "What do I gain in lying to you? I have killed people—"

Mrs. Bossley cut him off with a shout of alarm. "Killed people?" she repeated, then released a gut-filled cry. *"My Richard.* My poor Riiicccch-harddd—"

"Stop that nonsense," Mr. Enright ordered, his voice ringing in the stairway and echoing Sabrina's sentiments. The woman was giving her a headache with her carrying on. He confronted Sabrina. "You can trust me. I fought in the war. I was a colonel in the Irish Regiment. I could give you my references, but my circumstances are a bit havey-cavey right now, what with the sentence for hanging and how there might be a price on my head."

A price on his head? And they wanted to hang him?

"I can imagine it is difficult," Sabrina muttered. But it certainly wasn't as difficult as realizing she'd allowed a condemned man to have his way with her.

Oh, the gossips in the valley would have a hey day with this story.

He sensed her turmoil. Leaning forward, he placed his hands on either side of the step where she sat, his eyes level with hers, those sherry brown eyes that had first sparked her interest in him. "You *must* trust me."

"Why?"

"Because I'm all you have," he said in that warm accent. "Do you expect *her* to help you?" he asked, nodding toward the anxious Mrs. Bossley.

"Help what?" the widow demanded.

"Find Father," Sabrina answered, frustrated by the woman's rattlebrained worry.

"Of course I'll help," Mrs. Bossley was quick to say.

"He is not looking for your help," Sabrina replied. She had no desire to partner with the widow. "He is looking for mine."

"But I will help anyway," Mrs. Bossley insisted. "I must."

Sabrina ignored her. Instead, she challenged

Mr. Enright. "Why do I need your help? You may be behind his disappearance."

He did not balk at the accusation but actually smiled. "You know where I was when he disappeared. In my condition, do you believe I could have played a hand in it without your knowledge?"

"Your knowledge?" Mrs. Bossley repeated. "What does that mean?"

Mr. Enright answered for Sabrina. "It means I understand what serious trouble her father might be in."

"Perhaps it would be wiser to use the law instead of you," Sabrina countered. It would not be wise to be beholden to this man.

"Your father is the law," Mr. Enright pointed out. "Who acts when he is not here?"

"The earl," Mrs. Bossley answered.

"Which means we might as well not have anyone," Sabrina said, her tone bitter, and she knew she had no choice but to accept Mr. Enright's help. "It would probably take a week to make my uncle comprehend the danger of the situation. Besides, if father is in trouble, and his disappearance strongly points in that direction, then he would not want his circumstances to be bandied about."

"No, he wouldn't," Mrs. Bossley echoed. "We

need Mr. Enright's help," she told Sabrina. "He is a military man. And that is something. But I want to know, sir, why do people believe you are a murderer?"

"That is a good question," Sabrina agreed with no small amount of sarcasm. "Mr. Enright, do you have an answer?"

"I do," he said, straightening. "But you may not enjoy what I have to say."

"The only way we'll know is if you tell us," Sabrina said.

The line of his mouth flattened. He obviously did not like her attitude, but she would not apologize.

She didn't want him to believe her gullible, in spite of what had happened between them earlier.

He turned his attention in the direction of the kitchen. "I will tell all," he said, "but I must eat first. I'm starving." He didn't wait for her comment but started down the hall. Rolf had come down the stairs and now fell into step beside him, his nails making a prancing sound on the floor.

Mrs. Bossley leaned over the railing, watching him leave with some concern. "What did he say?" she asked, as if uncertain she understood.

"That he is hungry," Sabrina answered. "And he is jolly well not going to answer any questions until his belly is full." She stood. "Come, let us hear his tale."

"*Should* we trust him?"

"Rolf doesn't like men, but he appears to accept Mr. Enright. However, should we trust him? Absolutely not," Sabrina replied grimly, aware that she had no choice. He already carried a very big secret of hers.

A damaging one.

"For right now, we'll play his game." Sabrina rose to her feet and started down the hall, her shoulders back, her pride around her. Mrs. Bossley hesitated a moment, then came trotting behind her.

In the kitchen, Mr. Enright had picked up the broom and was sweeping up the broken pottery pieces. He chewed on a hunk of bread he had torn off from the loaf that had been on the table until he'd taken his leap across it. Rolf was chewing, too. Apparently, Mr. Enright had shared his bread with a very happy dog before placing what was left on the table.

The pottery pieces swept into a pile in the corner, he set the broom aside and easily carried the tub of water out of the kitchen. What usually gave Sabrina fits, he did easily. He tossed the water out into the yard.

Sabrina stored the soaps away. Mrs. Bossley sniffed the air. "Are these your soaps?" she asked.

"Yes."

Mrs. Bossley took another sniff just as Mr. Enright walked by. Sabrina did as well and realized Mr. Enright carried the scent of her soaps. She didn't think anything of it other than that the man had obviously bathed, which was not a bad thing.

However, Mrs. Bossley raised a quizzical eyebrow. She looked from Mr. Enright to Sabrina and back again.

Sabrina frowned. She didn't know what conclusions the widow was forming in her hen-headed mind, but she didn't trust her.

Mr. Enright lifted the lid on the pot warming on the hearth. He inhaled with satisfaction. "This is what I've been needing."

"It should be mutton stew," Sabrina said. She took a taper from the kitchen mantel, lit it off the fire, then used it to light candles around the kitchen. She set one of the candlesticks on the table.

Sabrina fetched three bowls from the cupboard. "Mrs. Bossley, the spoons and a knife are in that bin on the cupboard. Mr. Enright, will you bring the pot of stew to the table?"

Mrs. Bossley proved, for once, that she could be

less than contrary by doing as bid—or so Sabrina had thought. She changed her mind when she surveyed the table settings. "Where is the knife?" Mrs. Bossley had only brought over spoons.

"Do you think it is wise?" Mrs. Bossley shot a pointed glance in Mr. Enright's direction. He was taking the chairs from against the wall and placing them around the table for seating.

Sabrina had fetched a small crock of butter from the pantry for their bread. She now silently agreed with the widow and pushed the butter to the side.

Of course, he'd noticed their whispering. "I'm not a murderer," he grumbled.

"But you are accused of murder," Sabrina stated.

He grunted his frustration.

Their dinner was ready.

"Shall we?" Sabrina said, indicating that she and Mrs. Bossley would sit on one side of the table. Mr. Convicted Murderer could stay on the other. He had the good manners to wait until the ladies had taken their seats before sitting himself. Indeed, he had impeccable manners.

Also, to her surprise, Rolf chose Mr. Enright's side of the table. She frowned at her hound and picked up the serving spoon.

Playing the hostess, she passed Mrs. Bossley her portion of the stew, but as she handed Mr. Enright his bowl, she said, "Very well, sir, you have food, and we haven't gone screaming down the road. Now, tell us, whom did you murder?"

Chapter Eleven

$\mathcal{M}$ac understood he was on trial here and that Miss Davidson would be a harsher judge than the one who had sentenced him.

For the past hour, she had behaved like a marionette on very tight strings. She might want to give the impression she was in control of her emotions, but her hands shook slightly—and it had to do with the unspoken between them, with what had happened in her bed. He could almost feel her fears. And he knew why.

Miss Davidson was of that class of women who believed they must do everything right and proper. No mistakes allowed. She gritted her teeth as if reminding herself to be brave. She feared being vulnerable. She feared being human.

He understood women like her because he'd been raised around them. He had been the male version until his brother and sweetheart's betrayal and years in the military and learning how bloody hard it was just to live, let alone be constantly honorable. Experience had knocked that nonsense out of him.

And sooner or later, he and she needed to discuss their situation. She was a magistrate's daughter. He could imagine she had some prestige in this country society. What if it became known she had consorted with the likes of him?

Or, more exactly, what *she thought he was*?

For the first since he'd learned of his brother's death and his inheritance, Mac wanted to use the title, earl of Ballin. He wanted to toss it out and watch her reaction. Would it ease her mind? Or would she still regret what had passed between them . . . because he didn't.

He'd been lost in the depth of exhaustion and illness. His body had been battered, beaten, and weakened. And then her kiss had reminded him of something he'd forgotten over those long months in the Old Tolbooth—that there was magic in a woman's touch. From the ancient sirens to the kiss Miss Davidson had bestowed, they all, every feminine one of them, had a gift that could restore a man's soul.

When she'd so passionately given herself to him, the sweet, blessed headiness, the *power* of his release had made him feel whole again. He'd slept better in those few hours after having made love to her than he had in years.

She'd healed him, and her sweet body had restored his will to push forward. The despair, the grief, the sorrow that had dogged him for so long had vanished and been replaced by a very intense interest in *her*.

So, perhaps he did owe her something . . . like his story.

"I was accused of murdering Gordana Raney," he started. "She was a young lass in Edinburgh with the voice of a songbird, and she was very popular. She chose to sing for her living instead of earning it in unsavory ways, but she was with a rough crowd. After all, they were the ones who had the money." He tasted the soup. It was warm, unseasoned, and manna from heaven could not have tasted better. "Is there something to drink?"

"Yes," Mrs. Bossley echoed. "I could do with some whisky. It would settle my nerves." Half of her hair was pinned; the other half was down around her shoulders. She reminded Mac of nothing more than a scarecrow that had been blown in the wind.

Miss Davidson looked at both of them with impatience, and with more than a hint of contempt toward the older woman. She did not like Mrs. Bossley. She obviously did not approve of a liaison between the older woman and her father.

Pulling her own unpinned and slightly wild, dark hair over her shoulder, Miss Davidson rose from the table. "Whisky for you both?"

Mac shook his head. "Not for me. I swore off whisky when they yanked me from my bed after a night of drinking too much of it and accused me of murder. Do you have wine? And if not, I'll be pleased with water."

His hostess arched an eyebrow, a silent warning that for this trouble, his story had better be good.

"Excuse me," Mrs. Bossley said to Mac as she leaned forward. "But let us start from the beginning. What is your name?"

"Cormac Enright."

"And you are Irish," Mrs. Bossley said, her nostrils twitching with a slight hint of disapproval.

"Proudly so."

Mrs. Bossley considered him a moment, then

with the right touch of slyness, said, "I knew an Irish lad once. He was a charmer."

"Tell us a lad you *haven't* 'known,'" Miss Davidson murmured as she placed a dram of amber liquid in front of Mrs. Bossley and another beside her own plate. Mac received water although he could see a corked wine bottle on the cupboard shelf. He sighed and toasted her before taking a sip.

"On with your story," Miss Davidson said, seating herself and crossing her arms tightly against her chest. She had not touched her meal, and she did not touch her glass.

"Gordana was well-known around a gaming den called the Rook's Nest. That is where I met her. Have you ever heard of it?"

"I've never been to Edinburgh," Miss Davidson said.

Mrs. Bossley answered, "I have, many a time."

"And did you patronize the Rook's Nest?" Miss Davidson asked an edge to her tone.

"Of course not," the older woman answered but then smiled as she delivered a piece of information that would repay Miss Davidson for her feline testiness, "But your father did."

Miss Davidson's reaction was swift. "*A gaming hell?* My father would *not* patronize such a place."

"Well, he did," Mrs. Bossley said simply.

"Yes, he did," Mac echoed. "He testified during my trial to it."

Miss Davidson sat back, her arms dropping to her side, her expression stunned. "And when did he supposedly do this? He rarely travels to Edinburgh, and only on matters of a legal nature."

"The trial was in May," Mac said.

"He wasn't in Edinburgh in May."

"He was," Mrs. Bossley chimed in.

Miss Davidson turned in her seat to face the woman. "How do you know this?"

"Because he told me," Mrs. Bossley answered. "He said he had to go to court in Edinburgh. He was quite worried about it. When he returned, I asked if all was well. He didn't want to discuss the matter or his business, and that was, I believe, the last time he's been to Edinburgh. Of course, before then, he and the earl traveled there several times."

A small frown line formed between Miss Davidson's brows. "I didn't know this."

"Well, he wasn't in the valley. Where did he tell you he was?" Mrs. Bossley wondered. "Sometimes he was gone for several days. And in May, he was there for almost a week."

"He traveled to Perth quite a bit. Another magistrate in that area, Sir James, was quite ill. Father would go and help the man by fulfilling some of his duties."

"Well, he may have *stopped* at Perth," Mrs. Bossley said. "Is it not on the way to Edinburgh?"

"But why would he not tell me the truth?" Miss Davidson shook her head as if it did not all make sense. "And why would he go to a gaming hell with the earl? My uncle has ruined this family with his gambling. That is the last place Father would take him."

"Who is the earl we are discussing?" Mac prodded.

"The earl of Tay is my uncle," Miss Davidson informed him.

Mac tucked this piece of information away. The earl of Tay had been sitting in the front row of his trial.

Miss Davidson reached for her whisky and took a sip. "I don't understand why Father would not say something to me," she repeated.

"I didn't understand why he didn't speak to you about *me*," Mrs. Bossley answered. "In spite of his best intentions, Richard was apparently very good at secrets." She pulled the loaf of bread over to her and looked around for a knife to cut it. "I thought you knew about us," she said to Miss

Davidson. "When I found out you didn't, I knew it was not right. That's one of the reasons I had to take you aside the other day. I had given him an ultimatum. I said, 'Richard, you have a week to tell your daughter that we are to marry. I won't wait any longer.' After he didn't say anything to you for two more weeks, then, as you know, I carried through with my promise—I took matters into my own hands." She rose from the table and crossed to where the cutlery was kept and fetched a knife. She pointed it at Mac. "Leave this alone."

He shrugged. He was more interested in Miss Davidson's reaction to this news that her father might not be the moral paragon she had thought him than he was to being insulted over a knife.

Miss Davidson's lips were pressed together as if holding words back. He sensed she wanted to lash out at Mrs. Bossley but knew she couldn't. Instead, she raised troubled blue eyes to Mac. "What did my father testify to at your trial?"

"He was the only witness, and he said he saw me beating Gordana Raney to death."

That statement sucked the air from the room.

Mrs. Bossley spoke first. "If Richard Davidson said you are a murderer, then you are a murderer."

"I am not. He lied in court," Mac answered.

"He would not *lie* in court," Mrs. Bossley shot

back, emphasizing the words with a wave of the knife. "He might not tell the truth about seeing me, but he takes the law seriously.

"He would lie, and he did lie," Mac answered.

"But that would mean he made false accusations," Miss Davidson said, placing her hands on the table, her fingers curling into fists. "He would be perjuring himself, something my father is very much against, *and* he would be sending an innocent man to the gallows."

"Now you see *my* problem," Mac answered. "Your father is not my favorite person."

"Richard would not do what you accuse him of," Mrs. Bossley stated. "He wouldn't. We can't trust this man, Miss Davidson. We can't take his word over Richard's."

Miss Davidson heard her, but then, perhaps because of the bad blood between them, she looked to Mac. "Was there any other evidence against you?"

"They presented a cloak that they claimed was mine. It wasn't. I don't own a piece of clothing as fine as that cloak was. However, it was covered with Gordana's blood."

"And no one would believe you when you said it wasn't yours?" Miss Davidson asked.

"No. It was my word against a magistrate's and

a host of unsavory characters who swore they saw me wearing that cloak."

"You say unsavory, but is that only because they testified against you?" Miss Davidson challenged.

"I say unsavory because they were gamblers, drunks, and thieves," he answered.

"Well, that could be a matter of opinion," Mrs. Bossley said, as if her words explained something, but Miss Davidson sat quiet.

Her face was pale in the candlelight. Her dog rose from where he'd been sitting on the floor as if listening to their conversation. He nudged her hand. She gave him a scratch behind the ears, and whispered, "I don't know what to believe." She looked to Mac. "I thought I knew my father, and now, after hearing he kept so much that was important in his life from me, I feel as if I didn't know him at all."

"But that doesn't mean we should listen to this, this *Irishman*," Mrs. Bossley said. "Yes, your father should have told you about our intention to marry, but the idea of Richard's lying in court is, why, I can't even consider it."

"Except he *is* missing," Miss Davidson replied. "I thought he'd left to see you, and you expected him to come calling. Something happened to him. Perhaps we should reserve judgment against Mr. Enright, at least until we have Father here to answer questions." She looked to Mac. "But we don't know where he is."

"Aye," Mac agreed soberly. "And whoever shot the good Reverend Kinnion may have done the same to your father."

Mrs. Bossley began making frantic noises again, but Miss Davidson would have none of it. "*Silence*," she snapped.

The older woman gave a surprised start and closed her mouth.

"Are you certain the Reverend Kinnion is dead?" Miss Davidson said.

"I heard the shot. I saw him on the ground. I started to stop for him, but the sound of the pistol drew a crowd. If I was going to escape, I could not linger. He could be alive, but where is he?"

Miss Davidson thought a moment, then said, "There is no evidence that Father has been harmed. There is no body. He, too, might be alive."

"That is my hope," Mac answered. "He is the only person who can clear my name. And I believe he wants to do so. He may be the honorable man you both think him."

"Why do you say that?" Miss Davidson asked.

"The Reverend Kinnion came to my cell at the

request of your father. He said a friend with a conscience had sent him. He helped me escape, and someone had bribed the guards to look the other way. Of course, they were not so honorable. They sounded an alarm."

"My father was one of the Reverend Kinnion's benefactors."

"So is your uncle," Mrs. Bossley said. "Actually, the reverend receives his living from the earl, and Richard is merely a strong supporter of the clergy."

"My uncle wouldn't rouse himself for anyone. Unless he was personally inconvenienced, he would be happy to let Mr. Enright hang. But I'd like to think that a miscarriage of justice would weigh on my father's conscience."

"Did he seem particularly quiet or disturbed this summer?" Mac wanted to know, ready to give the man any credit.

Miss Davidson shook her head.

Mrs. Bossley looked at her with some sympathy. "I did not notice him being quiet. However, when he returned from his last trip to Edinburgh in July, he asked me if I would do him the honor of being his wife."

"That long ago?" Miss Davidson said, surprised.

"Yes," Mrs. Bossley returned stoutly. "Now you know why I was growing impatient for him to say something to you."

Miss Davidson reached for her glass and drained it. Mac began to understand the undercurrent of animosity between the women. The fairer sex could be worked up over the smallest of things.

"I'd take another dram," Mrs. Bossley confided. She'd made quick work of her whisky.

"The bottle is in the cupboard. Bring it to the table." Miss Davidson sounded as if the turn of events threatened to destroy her, but then she stirred in her chair as if thinking. "You haven't seen Father since *before* the luncheon?" She addressed this to Mrs. Bossley.

"No. As I said, I expected him last night. When he didn't come to my door, I assumed you had raised a fuss and he didn't want to upset you so he avoided me."

"We did talk. He was very firm in his decision to marry you. We had strong words. However . . ." she started, as if struck by an idea, but then her voice trailed off in memory.

"However?" Mac prodded.

"However, he acted more upset when I mentioned that the Reverend Kinnion was missing."

"You told him?" Mac pressed. "How did you know?"

"Mrs. Kinnion spoke to me after the luncheon. She hadn't heard from her husband, and she was worried. Since she felt she isn't accepted by her husband's relatives, she asked me to say something to Father. She was hoping Father would send a letter to her husband's uncle—what was his name? It was . . . Ebenezer Kinnion. She said her husband had gone to Edinburgh at his uncle's request." Miss Davidson shook her head. "The poor woman. I need to say something to her."

"Not yet," Mac advised. "We need to know more before we let her know. I wonder if his uncle had truly sent for him or if that was the excuse he gave his wife? I am assuming your father asked him to go, perhaps as a favor, but I could be wrong."

"Or you could be right." Miss Davidson held up a hand as if to sort the chain of events out in her mind. "Father and I argued about the Widow Bossley, but when we were done, he returned to his work. Like I said, he was very firm in his decision to marry her—"

"My Richard," Mrs. Bossley said, a sniffle coming to her. "Ever true."

Miss Davidson continued without comment

to her. "I started for the kitchen, but before I did, I remembered my promise to Mrs. Kinnion and passed on her request to Father. The news upset him. Before I knew what was what, he was out the door. He saddled his horse and left. I assumed to see Mrs. Bossley."

"I never saw him."

"Then where did he go?" Miss Davidson asked.

"To see Mrs. Kinnion?" Mrs. Bossley offered.

"Possibly," Miss Davidson said. "But apparently that was the last either you or I have heard from him. And he'd be home by now if he'd called on the reverend's wife. There would be no reason for him to stay the night."

"He could have gone to Edinburgh," Mac pointed out—which was one place he did not want to revisit for a while. Out here in the countryside, word of his being wanted for murder might not have gone round. However, considering how many people in Edinburgh were anxious to see him hang, he was certain there were posters there.

And there would be posters here, sooner or later. It was only a matter of time.

"What I don't understand," Miss Davidson said, "is why Father would be gambling?"

"For money," Mrs. Bossley answered.

"He never has before, and we've always needed

money. It must be something my uncle put him up to."

"Well, he won that bit of cash against Owen Campbell's horse," Mrs. Bossley said. "You know the race, the one where Owen was caught cheating?"

"Yes, against my cousin's husband—"

"*Wait,*" Mac interrupted. "Owen Campbell?"

"Yes," Miss Davidson said, confirming the name.

"He owns the Rook's Nest."

The reaction from the two women was immediate. "He owns a gaming den? That sorry worm," Mrs. Bossley said.

"He is unsavory," Miss Davidson agreed. "I'm not surprised."

"Who is he?" Mac asked, wanting to know more about Campbell.

"He is a greedy lad who grew up in these parts and supposedly made his fortune in India," Mrs. Bossley said.

"Why do you say supposedly?"

"He spends a frightful amount of money, and there are rumors that he isn't as well-heeled as he pretends," Mrs. Bossley answered.

"One doesn't have a good feeling off of him," Miss Davidson confided. "Then he tried to cheat over the horse race. He ran away before people could take their anger out on him."

"Perhaps he *didn't* make his money in India," Mrs. Bossley said triumphantly. "I told Dame Agatha a year ago I couldn't believe Owen would work hard enough to have made the money he spends in the Orient. I've known him since he was this tall." She raised a hand to the height of the table. "He was a schemer then, and he's a schemer now. Any family with sense keeps their daughters away from him."

"Although if Owen owns the Rook's Nest, I'm not surprised that my uncle would search him out. And perhaps my father was trying to protect his brother."

"Are you suggesting that your uncle could have killed Gordana Raney?" Mac wondered.

Miss Davidson shook her head. "He is as lazy as Campbell. Murder would call for far too much work for him. He might let her die from benign neglect but never because of something physical."

"She has a good point," Mrs. Bossley agreed before saying darkly, "However, murder is in the Campbell blood. The stories they tell about them. Centuries of murder."

"The stories they tell about Owen," Miss Davidson agreed.

"Would your father perjure himself for this Campbell?" Mac wanted to know.

Mrs. Bossley snorted her disbelief, but Miss Davidson was more thoughtful. "I honestly do not know." She sat a moment, the wheels of her mind working, then looked to Mac. "We have two missing men and no bodies."

He nodded.

"Beyond a gaming den, what role did the Rook's Nest play in this unfortunate young woman's murder?"

"She sang there, and her body was found in an alley close to it but also in the vicinity of other places. I was staying at the Rook. They have rooms there that go cheap."

"You *chose* bad company?" Miss Davidson said.

"He was staying where it was cheap," Mrs. Bossley observed. "Maybe he didn't have many choices."

Miss Davidson shook her head. "He's too well-spoken to not have choices. And did you not say you were a colonel, sir?"

Now it was Mac's turn to feel uncomfortable.

Her direct, clear gaze was upon him. If she had been anyone else, he would have fobbed her off. Cormac Enright didn't answer to anyone, not when he had a mind to keep his own counsel . . . except she was different.

"I studied surgery at Trinity College. I'm not completely down on my luck."

"Did you finish your studies?" Miss Davidson asked.

"I did."

"Soldier . . . surgeon," she murmured, an acerbic note to her voice. "What is left to do in your life?"

He could have added that he was an earl, but he kept silent on the matter. He brought no honor to the title.

"Hopefully a great deal," Mac answered, "if I can manage to avoid a pesky problem of the Scots wanting to hang me." He paused a moment, then for no reason that he could discern, he admitted with more honesty than he had to anyone else, "I wasn't in a good place when I arrived in Scotland."

"Why is that?" Miss Davidson asked.

He leaned toward her, shutting Mrs. Bossley's presence from his mind, speaking as if there were only the two of them. "I'd just returned from seeing my family outside of Dublin. I hadn't been home in over a decade, and when I arrived, I learned they were all gone. Dead. Typhus took them." He stared at the table a moment, then said, "I was the prodigal son, the one who went away. I'm here to tell you, not once did I fear they wouldn't be there when I decided to return. That is a twist to the story that no one should have to live."

"And you chose not to stay in Ireland?"

"There is nothing for me there. However, there is nothing for me here." He made a self-deprecating laugh at his own foolishness. "The Enrights are not wealthy. Hence, my gram quite wisely told me I needed to learn a living."

"But you didn't stay in Ireland. You chose the military."

There was a question in Miss Davidson's voice. Mac sat back in his chair. She had a sharp mind.

"I was in love with a lass named Moira O'Dea. That's why I went for my studies. I wanted to be a good husband to her." The hint of Ireland grew stronger in his voice as he spoke, as he remembered. "When I returned home, I found she had chosen my brother. They were married and one on the way, and yet no one, not even my parents or gram, dared say as much to me. I suppose they felt I would find out soon enough."

"And so you left."

He shrugged. "There was no reason to stay. I did what most other heartbroken lads do, I joined the military and went out into the world. I doctored some and fought a great deal. I was very angry."

"Are you still angry?"

Her question surprised him. He'd been angry for a long time, even after he'd come to Edinburgh. There had always been something to rage against—the powers that be, his family's deaths, the irresponsibility of his father and brother that left the family estate bankrupt . . .

"I want justice," he answered.

She nodded as if she understood what he wasn't saying.

"And the blue devils that had been chasing me before Gordana Raney died seem insignificant now. It was a harsh way to be brought to my senses, but now that I have them, I'll keep my wits about me. I will need them to win my freedom."

"And I want to find my Richard," Mrs. Bossley said, reminding him, and apparently also Miss Davidson of her presence, because, for that exchange between them, their connection had been strong enough for everything else around them to fade in importance.

"Well then," Miss Davidson said, "we need to talk to the two men involved in this who are here in Aberfeldy—my uncle and Owen Campbell."

"Which one of us will talk to them?" Mrs. Bossley said. "We can't all go. Won't that look suspicious if they have something to hide? Us, quizzing them?"

"But it would be perfectly reasonable for Miss Davidson to make inquiries after her father," Mac said. "Chances are the earl and this Campbell know he is missing. They may be looking for him as well."

"Or they may not," Miss Davidson replied. "I spoke to my uncle today. He didn't seem concerned. He suggested I check Mrs. Bossley's bed."

Mrs. Bossley smiled, unbothered by the suggestion.

Mac decided he liked the woman. She was overwrought at times, but not without just cause.

And he knew he was very attracted to Miss Davidson. Definitely intrigued.

He caught a sidelong glance Mrs. Bossley slid to him. She had read his feelings accurately as well. Yes, when she wasn't giving way to hysterics, she was a wise old bird.

"Both men could be completely innocent," Miss Davidson pointed out.

"They could," Mac agreed, but he doubted it. Miss Davidson's description of the earl of Tay had been at odds with his memory of the man. He remembered a very sober lord who had been intensely interested in how the trial had played out.

Had Richard Davidson lied to protect his brother? Brothers were known to stand up for each other. That hadn't been true of him and Lorcan, but other families were different.

Of course, he wouldn't share his suspicions with Miss Davidson, not when she was kindly doing exactly what he wanted her to do.

"You will speak to your uncle on the morrow?" Mrs. Bossley said, directing her comment to Miss Davidson.

"Of course."

"What time?"

"I learned today, the earl isn't up before one," Miss Davidson said. "So I shall go then."

Mrs. Bossley brought her hand down on the table as if brokering a deal. "Good." She rose from her chair. "I will be waiting for you at the crossroads bridge to hear your report. I'll be too anxious to cool my heels waiting here or at home. You come directly to that meeting place when you are done."

"It is on the way," Miss Davidson said, then added with a touch of confusion as the older woman moved toward the door, "Where are you going now?"

"I'm going home," Mrs. Bossley said, feeling her head and realizing her hair was unpinned. "What did I do with my hat? Oh, yes, I left it upstairs. It fell on the floor." She started out the door.

Miss Davidson jumped to her feet and called her back. "Wait. You are leaving?"

"Oh, yes," Mrs. Bossley said. "Don't you believe I should? After all, we can't let whoever has Richard think we suspect something. We must carry on as normal. Mr. Kerr is coming tomorrow to fix my back step. He is expecting me to be there, especially after I told him how anxious I was to have the work done."

"But what about Mr. Enright? You will take him with you."

Mrs. Bossley pulled back as if astounded at such a suggestion. "Of course not. We need to keep him hidden. Am I not correct, Mr. Enright?"

Mac nodded. "I don't think it wise we let whoever took your father know I'm in the area. He might see it as a threat. However, I will interview the earl of Tay with you on the morrow."

"Exactly right," Mrs. Bossley said. "Protect her. However, I can't ride with him in my vehicle all the way to Borlick. Someone will see him and make a comment, especially if he is with me,"

Mrs. Bossley said. "You know how the gossips adore keeping track of my comings and goings."

"Then what do we do with him?" Miss Davidson asked.

A smile came to Mrs. Bossley's lips, a secret smile as if she'd divined there was tension in the air around Miss Davidson and knew the reason. Nor did she seem unhappy s she answered, "Why, we leave him here. With you."

Chapter Twelve

"*H*ere?" The word exploded from Sabrina. "Absolutely not. He can't stay here."

"Why not?" Mrs. Bossley asked.

Aware that Mr. Enright appeared engrossed in every word, and having a suspicion why, Sabrina lowered her voice to say, "It would be unseemly." Certainly, the widow could see that for herself.

Or had she sensed that Sabrina had fallen from grace, that her virtue no longer mattered.

Well, she'd given in to desire once, but only because it had snuck up on her. She'd not known what to expect . . . and Mr. Enright was an attractive man. Very attractive. Something about him drew her to him. She liked looking at his strong features and the way his expressions crossed his face. She noticed the slightest movement of his fingers and the strength in them. Those fingers had unlaced her and stolen their way beneath her skirts, something she remembered all too well, and had liked far more than she should for her own good.

Yes, she'd liked their coupling, and she mustn't. He was exactly what she'd feared: The Wrong Person for Her. Her father would not approve although right now, they needed Mr. Enright to find him.

That was the common sense of the matter, and it also turned out to be the logic Mrs. Bossley used. The widow's expression grew grave. "I beg your pardon, Miss Davidson, but are you saying that protecting your reputation from gossips is more important than your father's life?"

"Well, you see—" Sabrina started, then stopped, realizing there wasn't anything she could say that would vindicate herself. Her protest wasn't just that she was a single woman—although past the prime of her life—but it was *this* man she objected to, and if she said that, then Mrs. Bossley would want to know why. And what could Sabrina say? That he'd already had her, and had her thoroughly?

Oh no. No one must ever learn what had happened between them—especially Mrs. Bossley. If they found her father, and he was well, Sabrina was fairly certain he would not change his mind about marrying the widow, and her position would be more precarious than before. Her father would protect her as his unmarried daughter but as his *soiled* unmarried daughter, well, Sabrina wasn't certain his goodwill extended that far.

"You need to shelter him," Mrs. Bossley decided as if she had been named queen.

"What about Mrs. Patton? What will she say when she sees him here and Father nowhere around?"

"Does she know Richard is missing?"

"No."

"Then you've managed to keep it a secret this long," the widow said, "you can continue in the same manner. Mr. Enright, you have a responsibility as well. Keep quiet. No one must know you are here."

"Understood," he said, his deep voice giving that one word many shadings—including that of laughter.

"Then we are agreed," Mrs. Bossley pronounced, and started down the hall, muttering about how she wondered where she had left her hat.

Sabrina whirled on Mr. Enright. She did not trust his look of amused interest. "I have no doubt you wouldn't want to stay here," she said, hissing on the word "stay." "But you can't. It isn't right, and you know it."

"I haven't said a word," he answered, but his eyes danced with a hundred different devils. Oh, yes, he was very aware of her predicament.

"You don't have to," she assured him. "I know you think you are the cat who has found the cream—but you haven't. Do you hear? What happened was a mistake between us—"

"What was a mistake?" Mrs. Bossley asked, appearing in the doorway. She held her bonnet. "I found it on the stairs. What a ninny I am. I could lose my head if it weren't fastened to my neck."

"*Nothing*," Sabrina said, forcing a smile. "Nothing was a mistake."

Mrs. Bossley pushed pins into her hair and set her bonnet on her head before starting for the back door as if all was decided. "Very well, I shall see you on the morrow. Mr. Enright, better clothes would do you good. Aren't there some old clothes of your father's in the attic, Miss Davidson? Richard tells me he once had more heft to him than he does now—"

"Mr. Enright is *not* staying here," Sabrina reiterated, following the widow to the back door. "It would not be seemly. And my father would not approve if he knew *you* told him to stay here." She threw that last out as a particularly potent threat.

That suggestion did cause Mrs. Bossley to pause, but only momentarily. "Your father will be happy when we manage to free him from wherever he is, missy," she returned. She lowered her voice to add, "And if it is your virtue you are worried about, you might rethink that. You may not have a good eye, but I do. That is a fine-looking man in any woman's book. He can do far better than you, so *I'd* make the most of it."

"He is *accused* of murder," Sabrina felt she must remind her.

"The things you worry over," the widow murmured and, on that pronouncement, she was out the door, Rolf trotting behind her as if serving as her escort. "I'll see you on the morrow," she threw over her shoulder cheerily. "Richard will be proud of us." She walked across the moonlit yard to where she'd tied up her horse and gig.

The woman was incorrigible. Sabrina was so angry at being dismissed in such a rude, cheeky manner, she swung her fists in the air in frustration.

She did not want Mr. Enright under her roof.

She did not want to *see* Mr. Enright or *talk* to Mr. Enright or *breathe* the same air as Mr. Enright.

It was fine to be around him with another person, but not alone. Suddenly, the house was small, *too small* if she wished to avoid him.

And she could feel his presence behind her.

Pivoting, she found him standing in the hall outside the kitchen. The light from the kitchen had turned his foreboding presence into a silhouette.

Well, there was no time like the moment to let one's expectations be known.

Sabrina squared her shoulders. "I don't trust you."

"You would be foolish if you did," he answered, sounding all too reasonable.

"What happened between us will not happen again."

He crossed his arms. "That sounds like a challenge, Miss Davidson."

"It isn't. It is a fact." She sounded crisp and in control of her emotions. She began walking, with the intention of moving right past him and fetching a light from the kitchen before escaping upstairs to her room. Her bedroom door did not have a lock, but she would push a dresser in front of it. If she kept her step quick, she'd be done with him.

But just as she pulled up abreast of him, he put out his arm to block her way into the kitchen. "What did happen between us earlier today?" he asked.

Sabrina's heart gave a leap. Could he not know?

"Nothing," she said, the word surprisingly easy to say. In fact, she sounded almost too happy to say it.

Brown eyes studied her, then he murmured, "Your father isn't the only liar."

Indignation bristled through her. He was right. However, no one would fault her for trying to put the disagreeable incident from her mind—except, it hadn't been disagreeable. Not completely.

Not at all, if she was honest.

Of course, parts of what had happened between them had been odd and a little unexpected. So different from animals mating. Better, and more involving.

And standing beside him right now, even with him wearing the scent of her perfumed soap, she knew why.

He was masculine in a way that made her feel feminine. She'd never been so aware of a man before. Why, she'd even noticed the laugh lines around his eyes, and she found the way his mouth moved fascinating. He was not good for her peace of mind.

"I don't answer to you, sir," she managed to say. "And if you wish to keep from having a noose around your neck, you'd best be respectful." She almost cringed when she heard those words come from her mouth. Instead of sounding firm, she sounded self-righteous.

He hadn't liked them either. His jaw tightened, and a golden glint in his eye warned her she'd best consider her tongue. He might be a convicted murderer, but he had a lord's own pride.

Then again, anger would keep a wall between them.

She decided to beat a hasty retreat. She ducked into the kitchen and picked up a candle and holder. He still stood in the hallway; however, this time, he didn't block her path when she moved past him.

Yes, anger was a good barrier between them. She said, "You will sleep down here. I'll fetch a blanket."

She charged up the stairs, holding a hand around the flame of her candle to protect it. She didn't breathe until she reached the safety of the hall. And then she released a sigh of relief. She was safe.

Mr. Enright had a strange effect on her. She didn't think clearly around him, possibly because she was so disappointed in herself. Yes, that was it. Her jangly nerves were about her doubts, her fears. But she would prefer to suffer in silence than discuss anything with him.

If he stayed downstairs, and she shut the door to her room, and maybe pushed her dresser in front of it, she could sleep peacefully—and she was tired. Sabrina felt drained of all energy. She needed a moment to regroup and reevaluate.

Of course, the mussed bedsheets were a graphic reminder of what she'd done.

Her eye fell on the razor and soap that she'd used earlier on Mr. Enright. They were an eyesore in her feminine retreat. She picked them up and marched to her father's room to return them to their rightful places on his washstand.

She turned and almost dropped the candle she held when she realized that Mr. Enright stood in the doorway.

"What are you doing here?" she demanded.

"I followed," he said.

"I gave you instructions to stay downstairs."

"I didn't want to wait," he answered.

Sabrina thought her nerve endings would sizzle

from the heat of her temper. "And so you thought to creep up behind me?"

"I didn't creep. I walked."

"I didn't hear a footstep."

"Well, maybe I'm lighter on my feet than you are."

"Especially if you don't want me to know you are there?"

He made a sound as if she spouted silliness, then he horrified her by saying, "Instead of barking at me, perhaps it might be more productive if we spoke about what happened this afternoon."

Her throat went dry, making it hard for her to whisper, "That is not necessary."

"It is. I don't want you running from me. That won't help us find your father."

"There is nothing to discuss." She couldn't imagine talking about what had happened.

"Obviously there is, or you would be more relaxed."

"You are a stranger—"

"One deeply indebted for what you did for me." He took a step forward. "Miss Davidson, I am a physician. I understand the dangers of influenza, especially since I was not of good health when I fell ill. Without you, I would have died."

"Or you might have survived," her practical nature pointed out, but heat rose to her cheeks.

"Possibly." There was a beat of silence. "We made love."

Sabrina wished the floor would open up and swallow her whole.

"There are responsibilities to it, you know," he said.

She found breathing difficult. She pretended he had vanished. Poof. Gone.

But when she glanced up, he still stood right in front of her.

"Do you understand what I'm talking about?" he pressed as if he wasn't certain she'd grasped his meaning.

"I understand," Sabrina said. She could not meet his eye. She tried, but the whole conversation was awkward to her. "I realize the possible outcomes." She was trying not to think about them. She'd panic if she found herself with child.

"I take my responsibilities seriously. Even though my circumstances are not what I'd wish them to be, there is more to me than meets the eye. I will claim any child of mine."

Sabrina nodded, her throat tight.

"I also want you to know," he continued, his

voice growing deeper as he lowered it, "that I am aware of the gift you gave me. And I value it—"

He was referring to her virginity.

She was mortified. Who could have realized that an experimental kiss could lead to such total humiliation? In fact, once she found her father, she might leave for a nunnery if such places still existed.

And she fervently prayed she wasn't with child. Because right now, *this moment*, she vowed she must never kiss another man the rest of her life. Never. Ever. It wasn't safe, apparently, especially for her because while she was feeling complete shame for what had happened between them, a part of her wouldn't mind another kiss.

Yes, that was right.

In a way she'd never imagined she could ever feel before, she had an irrational desire to kiss Mr. Enright again.

"—I am a gentleman," he was saying to her. "I understand the danger of a woman in your position being compromised. You don't need to fear that I will say something to anyone beyond this room. It will be as if it never happened."

"Never happened?" Those words caught her attention.

"I understand country society," he explained. "The gossips can be cruel."

That was true. However . . .

"But you wish to act as if it never happened?" she argued.

His head tilted as if he sensed an undercurrent between them that he didn't quite trust.

There *was* an undercurrent—one she was creating and didn't quite understand.

Only seconds before, Sabrina had been embarrassed to hear him speak about their coupling, but she hadn't expected him to wish to pretend as if it had never happened.

"How offensive." The words just flowed from her lips out into the space between them.

Mr. Enright held up his hand as if an entreaty to peace. "I only thought to reassure you."

"By letting me know I'm unimportant?" Did no one see her as a woman? Even the man who had taken her purity?

Those expressive brows of his rose, saying louder than words that he knew he was in trouble. "You are tired," he said, backing away. "It has been a trying day."

Now he was running?

"Mr. Enright, stop telling me how I feel."

"I didn't mean to do so," he quickly said.

"And understand, there will be nothing of a carnal nature between us."

"Carnal?" He said the word as if it were quaint. "Absolutely not."

"Because you don't wish it?" she asked, testing him . . . and testing herself. Her anger made her feel powerful.

He stopped his retreat, a militant gleam coming to his own eye. "Oh, I wish it. In fact, I would not mind another—" He broke off as if suddenly questioning the wisdom of what he was about to say, then tried again. "Miss Davidson, you don't have experience at these matters. I do and—"

Was it her imagination, or did he blush as he spoke? As if he was a bit embarrassed at the admission?

"—What happened between us in your bed was the natural course of things, but our reaction to each other was far from common. It was not common at all. And what I wanted you to understand is that I don't treat anything you did for me lightly."

Sabrina didn't know what to say.

His directness flustered her. It was one thing to be attracted to him. He was masculine and handsome, a deadly combination for any woman.

But she didn't want to *like* him. Liking was a more potent a force than desire.

She needed to keep the space between them. Oh, yes, she did, especially when he smiled.

He held out his hand. "I want you to trust me. I know I don't have a right to ask. My situation is difficult; however, I am not the villain they paint me."

She glanced down at the hand he offered and found she wished he had offered a kiss instead.

Such an irrational, insane thought. She was completely complicit in her own undoing. And she couldn't help wondering why she felt this strong attraction for him. Her father would not approve. Anyone with common sense would warn her from him.

"Everything is fine," she managed to say. She did not take his hand.

Protect herself. She had to protect herself from herself, because she had had a strong urge to walk right into his arms.

$\mathcal{M}$ac pulled back his hand. Her missishness was damn annoying.

She was prickly as a hedgehog, but there was a vulnerability about her as well, and he'd already tasted her passion, something he wouldn't mind experiencing again.

Why had he followed her up the stairs?

Yes, he needed to assure her that he was honorable . . . but he'd be lying to himself if he didn't admit he was hoping to breach her defenses.

She fascinated him. She was moral, she was upright, and this afternoon, she'd given him the ride of his life.

Who could blame him for wanting to see if the intense release he'd experienced with her had been because of his months of celibacy or if there was something different, magical about her.

Mac had only loved one woman in his life. She had proven to him that love was a phantom, a piece of nonsense. Moira had chosen Lorcan. She'd given herself to the brother with the title.

Over the years, especially on the eves before battles, Mac had wondered what it would have been like if he'd had a wife, if he had become the healer, the country doctor he'd set out to be. Would he have been at peace?

But life had not taken him that direction. His temper and his pride had demanded he leave Ireland. Back in those days, he'd not understood the power behind forgiveness.

However, standing in this room with Miss Davidson's presence filling his senses and an empty bed waiting to be used, Mac found himself damn hard in a way he hadn't felt in years.

Yes, he being conciliatory, but he wouldn't lie to himself. Behind his request for trust was a very real hope that she'd curl up in bed beside him and let him kiss away those faint worry lines marring her brow.

She spoke. "We need to take care of what we should be doing. For one thing, Mrs. Bossley is right, you do need new clothes. There are some things in a trunk in the attic."

"I tried on a shirt hanging in the wardrobe in the other room," he said. "It was too small. My shoulders," he added, pointing out to her how wide and strong they were. It couldn't hurt.

And she did consider his shoulders. Solemnly.

He tried not to preen.

"The shirts in the other room are Father's. They need some repairs," she said. "The ones in the attic may not be in better shape. We shall need to check closely, and if we choose them tonight, I'll have time to do repairs. This way," she ordered. The lavender-and-roses scent of her soap, the same soap he'd used, trailed in the air as she passed him on her way to the attic. He mindlessly fell into step.

He wondered if he had ever been so taken by a woman, including Moira. Even the women in France lacked Miss Davidson's simple grace.

At the attic door, she paused. "Will you go first and carry the candles? Sometimes bats find their way into the attic. I detest going up there."

"No problem," he assured her.

She reached up to feel the ledge of the doorframe and pulled down a key to unlock the door. "The clothes are in the first trunk at the top of the stairs."

"We'll see what we can cobble together," Mac replied. "I can be very resourceful."

"You will need to be," she assured him, and opened the door.

Stairs led up into the inky darkness.

Mac had to duck to pass through the door. He started climbing the stairs, holding the candles so that her path behind him would be well lit. The attic was dry but cold and dusty. He listened for sounds of bats. He, too, was not fond of them—

The door slammed behind him.

The key turned in the lock—and Mac realized he'd just fallen for the simplest trick there was.

Chapter Thirteen

Sabrina stepped back from the door, the key still in her hand. *She'd done it.* She'd locked him in. She did a happy jig at her cleverness. She was free from temptation.

The light from the candles he held outlined the gaps between the door and the doorframe. "Miss Davidson," came his deep voice with its melodic accent, "open the door."

He sounded so reasonable, she found herself smiling. That was it? *Open the door.* Sabrina laughed to herself. "I'm afraid I mustn't, Mr. Enright. I'm safer with you on the other side of the door and a lock between us."

"I have no intention of hurting you."

"Oh, you have intentions, sir," she informed

him. "But they shall not bear fruit." She couldn't believe she was saying this. It felt good to put a man in his proper place, to have a bit of power.

"You misunderstand me," he said, more steel in his voice.

For a second, she wondered if she did.

Old doubts resurfaced, but she tamped them down. "I understand you very well," she informed the door. And then, because she was an honest person, she admitted, "I also realize that your hopes in that—" She paused, needing the right word. "Your hopes in that *lascivious* direction may have been with some justification—"

"*Lascivious?*" his voice boomed from the other side of the door.

"Yes, lascivious," she echoed. "It means licentious, immoral, loose—"

"I know what *lascivious* means, Miss Davidson. I am *not* lascivious."

Sabrina found that statement strangely deflating. Had she misread him? She did not believe so.

"What I am," he continued, sounding as if he stood right in front of the door, "is a man who woke to having a woman kiss him—"

"And has *expectations* for it," she declared, triumphant. He *did* have lascivious thoughts.

"And then," he continued as if she hadn't

spoken, his voice dropping a notch lower, "she allowed me the pleasure of certain other things. Breasts, loins, and private bits."

Heat rose up her neck. It was true. She had allowed it.

"Not that I complain," he hastened to add. "I thought I'd made it very clear how appreciative I was."

And that was what had made her uncomfortable. She found she didn't like being "appreciated."

It was too tame a word.

"Like I said, I'm safer with you locked in the attic," she answered.

"Then you could say, Mac, my friend, not tonight."

"Your name is Mac?" She caught on this piece of personal information.

"From Cormac. My friends call me Mac." There was a beat, then he said, "You can call me Mr. Enright."

"I don't know why you are so upset. I *should* protect myself."

"You make it sound as if I am a lecher. Well, I am not a green lad who pouts when a lady says no, not that one ever has . . . but I don't force myself on women. And you don't need to lock me up for the night. I *hate* being locked up. I've been *locked up* enough to last a *lifetime*."

He grew more agitated as he spoke, and she believed him. If she had been locked up the way he had, she'd probably feel the same way—especially if she was innocent, although, she reminded herself, his innocence had not yet been proven. Still, it couldn't be pleasant to have people want to hang you.

She stepped toward the door. "I don't do this because of you," she admitted. "I do it for my own peace of mind. I didn't mean to tumble in your arms or take advantage of your situation—well, yes, I did, didn't I?"

It was easy to confess to a door. There was no danger, and it was good for the soul.

"What happened between us, well, I just wondered what it would be like to kiss a man. That seems to be an experience that every woman should know, and yet, I've never had the opportunity. At the age when I should have been courted, I had responsibilities. My mother was ill, and she needed me. Then, my father often had tasks and duties that required my help. And it isn't as if I begrudge them any of it. I don't. But I did lose a portion of my own life. No, I gave it up actually."

There, she'd admitted it. Dame Agatha would approve.

Sabrina paused a moment. Since she was making a clean breast of matters, she might as well divulge all. "And I hate being the 'Spinster in the Valley.' Everyone calls me such behind my back. They don't mean any harm by it. To them, the spinster is just who I am. They don't realize the loneliness in that word."

Sabrina leaned her head against the door. The cool wood felt good to her brow. "And they also believe that I am sensible. Can *you* imagine that?" She had to laugh at her own culpability. "My cousins and friends come to me for advice. They tell me I am wise, and I thought I was, until I kissed you. That's when I discovered there were many things I did not understand. Who knew a single kiss could be that powerful?"

Her question circled in the air around her.

It wasn't just the kiss. Being joined with him seemed to have opened her to a whole new experience. For a span of time, she'd lost a bit of herself in him. "I shall never judge anyone harshly again," she whispered.

She placed her hand flat on the door as if she could touch him. Her lover. "I know that what we did means very little to a man—"

"Who said that?"

His voice surprised her. She'd started to think

she was merely speaking her thoughts aloud, something she often did when she was alone.

Slightly embarrassed, she confessed, "People. I've heard it said. They all claim men aren't like women. Men are like bees that must go from flower to flower—"

"*Bees?*" There was both annoyance and humor in his voice. "Miss Davidson, you must stop talking to fools. Of course the joining of a man and woman means something. In its finest form, it is the closest any of us comes to heaven."

After what she'd experienced that afternoon, she could believe what he said.

"What is your given name?" he asked.

He wished to know?

"Sabrina." She smiled and added, "But you may call me Miss Davidson."

He answered with a sharp, short laugh.

Her father had little time for what he called her "prattle," and most people in the valley always acted alarmed when she showed any humor. Along with being the "spinster," apparently she was considered very serious as well.

But Mr. Enright interacted with her as an equal.

She now thought she was doubly wise to keep space between them.

"I'll unlock the door tomorrow after I return

from my uncle's," she promised. "I'll give you a full report of what I learn at that time. Now I warn you that you must be quiet during the day. Mrs. Patton will be here. She's the cook and house-keeper. It's best if she doesn't know you are here."

There was a beat of silence, and he asked, "Do you always try to be everything people think of you?"

"Yes, of course. Why should I not?"

She waited for a response. There wasn't any. "Did you hear what I said?" she asked.

"Go to sleep, Miss Davidson," was his reply. He didn't wait for her response. The light disappeared from under the door, and she heard his footsteps climb the attic stairs.

Sabrina stood in the dark, looking at the door as if she could see through it.

She should not trust him. He could have murdered that girl. But she didn't believe he had. Murder did not seem to be in his nature. He was the sort who would have just walked away.

However, she'd be wise to be wary. She didn't replace the key in its keeping place over the door. Instead, she took it to her room and placed it under her pillow. Undressing quickly and putting on her nightdress, she slid beneath the covers. Her fingers brushed the key . . . and she told herself she felt safe.

Her last thought before drifting off to sleep was the memory of making love to him right here in this bed.

*T*he sun had been up for hours by the time Sabrina woke. She was startled by how well she'd slept and for how long. Apparently, she had been exhausted.

Her first thought was of Mr. Enright.

Last night, locking him in the attic had been right and expedient. However, this morning, with a clearer mind, she realized she had certain responsibilities to him.

The man needed to eat and to wash. She hadn't given him water or anything last night. The thought made her feel guilty. She also needed to feed Rolf and Dumpling.

The floor was cold on her bare feet. She threw a dressing gown over her nightdress. She hadn't bothered to braid her hair before falling into bed last night, and it was a tangled mess. She also needed to polish her teeth and wash the sleep from her eyes, but she would take care of her guest's needs first. Doing so would be a form of penance for keeping him locked up.

The key was still under her pillow. She dropped it into the pocket of her gown and walked barefoot to the attic door. When she'd passed her father's room, all was as she'd left it. He had still not returned.

She knocked on the door. "Mr. Enright?"

He didn't answer, but then considering how surly he'd been last night, she was not put off. Why, he could even still be asleep.

"I'll be up in a few minutes with water and something for your breakfast." She hoped she could keep that last promise. He'd eaten all the stew and what was left of the bread for their dinner. Mrs. Patton usually had a meat pie tucked away in the pantry for those times when the magistrate was out late seeing to his duties.

As for herself, all she needed was a cup of good, strong tea before she dealt with either the issue of Mr. Enright or her father. She never thought clearly until she had her morning cup. She would put the kettle on to boil while she prepared a tray for her unwanted guest.

Going downstairs, Sabrina was just approaching the kitchen when she realized the back door was wide open.

Her heart stopped. *Had* her father returned?

The sound of a chair scraping the kitchen floor caught her attention. Someone *was* in there.

Sabrina hastened her step, then slowed as Rolf came out of the kitchen to greet her, a happy smile on his hound face.

Her father would not let the dog in. Ever.

She took one step, two steps, and peeked around the door—

A gasp of shock escaped her.

Mr. Enright stood in the kitchen, half-naked. He wore his black breeches, and his boots had been given a polish. He must have found the kit that was in the cleaning cupboard.

He was not wearing his shirt or a jacket.

Any words she might have spoken died in her throat.

She'd admired his chest before when she'd been applying the poultice, but there was something about his being hale and healthy and naked that robbed her of speech.

Mr. Enright was all hard, strong muscle. His body was lean but seemingly perfect. Oh, yes, there was the scar, and the sight of it sent heat to her cheeks because she had known it was there.

He shouldn't be tempting her in this manner.

"*Where* are your clothes?" The harshness in her

tone came from her blushing awkwardness and a morsel, well, perhaps more than a morsel, of lust. Pure, unbridled, never-before-imagined lust.

He was in the act of pouring hot water into a washbowl that was kept in the kitchen for when the occasion warranted it. Her father's shaving kit was laid out on the table. He had to have been wandering around the house, and she'd not pushed her dresser in front of her closed bedroom door. He looked up and smiled as if he knew what she was thinking, all the way to thoughts of his nakedness.

She was gaining enough knowledge of his character to notice that he had a lopsided smile when he was especially pleased with himself.

It was positively crooked right now.

"Good morning, Miss Davidson," he greeted her cheerily. "My shirt and jacket are on that chair, thank you for asking. I did manage to find a few things in the trunk. Lucky for me, they don't need an airing. But I didn't want to stain them if I make a slop of shaving, so I haven't put them on yet." He changed the subject. "I have a pot of tea steeping here. Would you care for a cup?"

She reached in her dressing-gown pocket. Yes, the key was still there. The attic door had been closed when she'd checked it just moments ago.

"I hope you don't mind, but I fed Rolf," he continued, pouring tea for her as if she had assented. "I found a bone in the pantry that appeared as if it was waiting for him."

No wonder the dog adored him . . . but then Sabrina realized that he'd given the bone to Rolf in the kitchen. The hound was now stretched out in front of the fire, gnawing away.

Her father would raise the roof if he caught the dog in the kitchen chewing on a bone. She didn't think it was such a good idea, either.

Sabrina snatched the bone from Rolf's jaws. It was a slobbery thing, and she held it away from her as she carried it down the hall, Rolf prancing at her heels. She threw the bone out into the back garden. Rolf bounded after it. She closed the door.

For a second, she stood, trying to make sense of it all—and then she grew angry. She stomped to the kitchen. *"How did you escape?"*

He was lathering his face with the soap he'd mixed in her father's shaving mug. He ran it all around his jaw with expert ease, before saying, "I climbed out the window."

"From three floors up?" she asked, incredulous.

"If that is the distance, then that is what I did," he answered.

"I don't believe you," she said. "The attic window is tiny."

He raised his brows as if what she thought was of little consequence to him. After all, he was standing in the kitchen. With practiced concentration, he began applying the sharp razor to his skin, and if Sabrina had thought it hard to think before, well, watching this most masculine of actions robbed her brain of any critical thought.

And she'd never been that way before. Then again, she'd never met anyone like Cormac Enright.

He rinsed the lather off the blade in the washbowl. "By the way, you look quite fetching this morning, Miss Davidson. There is something about bare toes peeking out from beneath the hem of a nightdress that sparks a man's imagination."

The compliment startled her—until she realized it wasn't flattery but a poke, gently said, about her own state of undress, and she was mortified. She'd been so busy between ogling him, she'd forgotten she was, for all intents and purposes, *déshabillé*—which would have been fine if they had been in a boudoir and someplace far more sophisticated than Aberfeldy, but they were not.

Sabrina began backing toward the door.

"Where are you going?" he asked. The cheeky devil. He knew she'd forgotten herself.

However, before she could answer, there was a sound of humming at the back door. It began to open. *"Mrs. Patton,"* Sabrina said in a horrified whisper.

Chapter Fourteen

To his credit, Mr. Enright understood the situation immediately. It would not be good for Sabrina to be caught with a half-naked man. The gossip would fly through the valley. She had no illusions about Mrs. Patton's loyalty. A good story was a *good* story.

Half of his face still covered with shaving cream, he pulled her back into the kitchen and stepped out into the hall. Sabrina cowered behind the kitchen wall, wondering what was to become of her.

She heard Mrs. Patton gave a short cry of surprise at the sight of a stranger in her house. From her vantage point, Sabrina could only see Mr. Enright, but she could imagine the look on the cook's face as she took in their lathered guest. Mrs. Patton had a weakness for a handsome gentleman.

"I'm so sorry," Mr. Enright said, again with that morning cheerfulness. "I didn't mean to startle you."

"Who are you?" Mrs. Patton answered with her customary forthrightness.

"Colonel Cormac Enright." He clicked his heels and gave a short bow, a polite one. "I'm a guest of Magistrate Davidson. He's already left for an appointment. I was taking advantage of the peace to shave in your kitchen. I hope that doesn't upset you."

He knew it wouldn't. He understood the power of his masculine charm.

Sabrina was also certain that he was supremely confident that the sight of his bare chest would rattle Mrs. Patton enough that she would accept anything he said, and he was right.

The cook started making a clucking sound like a hen feathering her nest. "No, no," she assured him. "You don't have anything I haven't seen before, Colonel." *Hen cluck, hen cluck, hen cluck.* "Don't let me interrupt your shaving."

"I can take it somewhere else," he offered, taking a step closer to her.

Mrs. Patton's chortling clucks grew higher, and

Sabrina could well imagine her round face giddy with pleasure as she said, "Don't be silly, Colonel."

Yes, silly, Sabrina wanted to echo. Silly, giddy, *hen*—

Mr. Enright waved his hand behind his back at her, catching her attention. He was signaling that she should make her escape. She could sneak to the stairs and the safety of her room now.

To Mrs. Patton, he said, "Tell me about that pony in the stables."

Sabrina stuck her head out into the hall and realized he was directing Mrs. Patton toward the back door. He had also positioned himself to block Mrs. Patton's view of the kitchen.

Mrs. Patton was not one to stint on talking. "A fine Highland pony Dumpling is. You'll have to ask Miss Sabrina about him. She reared him herself from a foal. A farmer had given up on him. Said he would never live, but our Miss Sabrina adores her animals, and she has a gift for healing. That pony owes her its life. I say, where is Miss Sabrina?"

Sabrina was almost to the stairs. She tried not to look back. The impulse was hard to ignore.

"I don't believe she is up yet," Mr. Enright answered. "I'm escorting her to call on her uncle the earl of Tay today."

"Escorting her?" There was a wealth of speculation in Mrs. Patton's voice.

"Yes, we have a visit planned," he answered as
if he hadn't known what he'd just done. Sabrina
had not been planning to take him with her when
she called on her uncle, but now she would. Who
knew what other suggestions would pass from
his lips to Mrs. Patton's ears if she didn't keep him
close to her all day?

"Have you had anything to eat?" Mrs. Patton
wondered.

"I made a cup of tea."

Mrs. Patton made a sound of weary forbear-
ance. "Isn't that like the magistrate?" she said.
"Here we have a guest, and he doesn't tell me. I
imagine Miss Sabrina didn't know to expect you
either."

"It was a surprise," Mr. Enright murmured.

Sabrina reached the stairs. She now lingered.
She couldn't help herself.

"Well, what can one say?" Mrs. Patton said.
"Back when Mr. Davidson still had his man
Emory working for him, I'd have an idea of what
was going to happen. Emory would put the word
in my ear. However, now it is anyone's guess what
will happen from day to day."

"What happened to Emory?" Mr. Enright

asked, and Sabrina could have groaned aloud because she knew Mrs. Patton would answer honestly.

"*Och*, the magistrate let him go," the cook said. "He couldn't afford his wages. I tell you, this is a fine family—but the earl, that is a different story. The man ruins everything he touches. He'd have Mr. Davidson and Miss Sabrina begging in the street if he had his way . . ."

Sabrina could listen to no more. She wanted to staunch the flow of words coming from Mrs. Patton's mouth, but the only way to do that was with her properly clothed presence. She flew up the stairs and dashed to her room.

Ripping off her dressing gown and nightclothes, she threw them who knows where and dove into her wardrobe for a dress. She grabbed a blue day dress with lace trim at the collar. It was the sort of thing she would usually save for Sunday services, but she wasn't being choosy at the moment.

The water in the pitcher was from the day before and cold. Sabrina didn't care. She scrubbed her face, polished her teeth, and tried to tame her heavy hair. Her fingers nimbly braided it, then she pinned it into a coil at the base of her neck.

She grabbed her driving gloves and charged

out of the room, not stopping until she reached the bottom of the step to take a deep breath. Calm. She must appear calm and serene, as if Mr. Enright were any normal guest of the house. It had been very clever of him to suggest that the magistrate had been called away on business.

The smell of frying sausages drifted from the kitchen. Mrs. Patton was enthusiastically telling Mr. Enright the history of the valley, and probably of the Davidsons.

Sabrina plastered a smile on her face and entered the room.

Mr. Enright came to his feet at her entrance. He was, thankfully, dressed.

However, Sabrina realized here was a man who looked as good in his clothes as he did without them.

The bottle green wool jacket he'd scrounged from the attic fit tight across his shoulders, but that only served to emphasize their breadth and the muscles beneath the material. He'd tied his neckcloth in a simple knot. She was now glad, in a very feminine way, that she was wearing one of her best dresses.

"Miss Sabrina, you look as if you slept well," Mrs. Patton said approvingly. "I've been feeding our guest a few sausages. Would you like one?"

"I'm not really hungry," Sabrina said. The cup of tea Mr. Enright had poured for her earlier was still on the table. Sabrina sat down in the chair beside his and took a sip. It was tepid but what she needed—

"What are you drinking?" Mrs. Patton asked, her brows raised in horror. "That cup has been sitting there. Was it yours, Colonel?"

"Um, yes," Mr. Enright said. "But I didn't drink from it. I poured it and left it on the table. I'm sorry," he apologized, covering up for Sabrina's mistake and this bit of proof she had been in the kitchen earlier.

"It is not a problem," Mrs. Patton said, none the wiser. "You can enjoy as many cups of tea as you wish, sir. As for you, Miss Sabrina, here is a clean cup and I have a fresh pot."

Chastened, Sabrina took the cup and held it out. Mr. Enright poured the tea. She was conscious of his easy grace as he leaned toward her to fill her cup. His jaw was smooth and the scent of the shaving soap clean and spicy. He'd raided her father's cache, obviously foreswearing her lavender-and-rose scent. The thought made her smile.

He smiled in return.

Their moment was interrupted as Mrs. Patton shoved the pan practically between them, forcing

Mr. Enright and Sabrina to lean away from each other. "Are you certain you wouldn't like a sausage?" the cook pressed.

It was unlike Mrs. Patton to be so forward.

"I'm certain," Sabrina said, but the cook wasn't listening to her. She'd turned, her bum practically in Sabrina's face, to coax Mr. Enright to eat the last sausage.

"I hate to see food go to waste. I imagine you are the same, Colonel."

"I am," Mr. Enright said, "but I can eat no more. Perhaps we should give Rolf a treat?"

"Aye, we could do that," Mrs. Patton agreed, something she would never have allowed if Sabrina had suggested such an idea.

"I believe we need to be on our way," Sabrina said.

"To pay your respects on the earl?" Mrs. Patton wanted to know. She started making the hen-nesting sounds again and her eyes were alight as if she had match-making on her mind.

"Yes, we are," Sabrina said, and shot the woman a look, willing her to return to her old self.. Sabrina walked briskly out of the kitchen, expecting Mr. Enright to follow if he could ever escape Mrs. Patton's clutches.

She remembered that her bonnet was in her father's office. She found the bonnet on the floor. Thankfully, it was not the worse for their struggles. She tied the ribbon under her chin and went outside.

The day was a good one. The air was clear with the autumn sun promising a warm afternoon. Sabrina decided she didn't need an outer garment. There were not many clouds in the sky, so they would not have to worry about rain.

She went to the stable and hitched Dumpling to the cart. Rolf had left his bone long enough to come see what she was doing. He padded back to his bone, which he playfully threw into the air before settling down to chew on it again.

Mr. Enright had not come out of the house yet.

In truth, Sabrina had expected him to follow her out the door.

He hadn't.

Sabrina stood out in the yard, believing she could be patient and failing miserably. She stomped to the door and opened it. "Mr. Enright, we should be leaving."

"Yes, yes," he said, laughter in his voice. "I'm coming."

"Wait, wait," Mrs. Patton said, "and here is what my youngest son said, 'I thought it was the apples.'"

Both Mrs. Patton and Mr. Enright laughed up-roariously at that statement.

Sabrina hadn't heard anything funny.

"What a scamp," Mr. Enright said. "You have your hands full with him." He came out of the kitchen.

"That I do," Mrs. Patton answered, following him. "I'll roast venison for dinner this evening. You like venison, don't you, sir?"

"I like all food," Mr. Enright answered. He placed a black hat on his head, setting the wide brim at a rakish angle. It was the type of hat an ostler would wear, and Sabrina wondered where he'd found it in the attic. He now made a dashing appearance, and Sabrina was not pleased at the way her heart seemed to skip a beat at the sight of him.

She wished to outgrow her attraction to him, not fall deeper under its spell.

"I don't have all day to stand here," she practically barked.

"I'm here," he answered. "Mrs. Patton does like to talk."

"Not usually," Sabrina lied.

He smiled, the expression relaxed—and that frustrated her as well. She didn't want to feel all mixed up inside. Feeling this way about Mr. Enright was ridiculous. If she was going to be fluttery around a man, it should be one from the valley. A suitable man. A salt-of-the-earth kind of man.

Not a condemned convict.

Then again, she wasn't taking him to see her uncle for her own amusement. She was tolerating his company for her father's sake.

Or so she nobly told herself.

"Would you like for me to drive?" he asked.

"Do you know the way?" she said, sounding more snappish than she had intended.

"No."

"Then I shall drive."

He shrugged, as if it had not been an issue one way or the other for him, and hopped into the cart. He leaned against one side and stretched his long legs out, placing the heels of his boots on the other side of the cart. He took up more than his fair share of the space, crowding her a bit.

"Are you comfortable?" she asked archly.

He smiled his satisfaction, and said, "Carry on."

She thought about refusing his order. She could tell him that she and Dumpling weren't going anywhere until he sat up straight . . . but then what good would that do except to make her look more peevish than she already did? She snapped the reins, and they were off.

Dumpling started at a smart clip, and Sabrina let him go.

Mr. Enright crossed his arms against his chest, his hat low on his head, and acted as if he was enjoying the ride.

They drove through Aberfeldy, following the winding road that led to Annefield. There were a number of people out and about. Many tipped their hats or waved to Sabrina. They all stared hard when they realized she was not alone, and that the man with her was not her father.

Oh, yes, jaws dropped open, especially the female ones.

And Sabrina found it curious that so many women could immediately notice and appreciate Mr. Enright. She, herself, was usually so busy with whatever was occupying her mind she didn't register people immediately. Not the details of them. It was humbling to realize how imperceptive she could be.

"Is your life easier that every woman who crosses your path finds you attractive?" she heard herself ask.

Out of the corner of her eye, she could see him tilt his head in her direction, his expression one of confusion. "Not everyone finds me attractive."

"I beg to differ."

"Do you find me attractive?" he asked.

Now they were on dangerous territory.

Sabrina kept her gaze on the road, but her attention was on him. "I asked out of curiosity."

"Curiosity killed the cat," he replied lightly.

"I'm afraid that was true," she agreed, without realizing what she was admitting.

He laughed. This time the sound was richer than it had been, less rusty and with more feeling.

"I wasn't being funny," Sabrina said, a bit put off.

"No, you weren't. But I find your candor, Miss Sabrina, charming."

He'd used her given name. She was torn between being afraid of his becoming too familiar and wanting him closer. She couldn't have it both ways.

She knew which one was the wisest.

"I'm just saying that life is easier for the attractive," she pressed, clinging to the idea that they were having a theoretical conversation. "My cousins Aileen and Tara are beautiful women, and life has always worked out very well for them."

"You are a beautiful woman."

Sabrina almost drove the pony cart off the side of the road.

She hoped he hadn't noticed.

"*Please*," she said, infusing in that one word her dismissal of his comment.

"Do you believe I jest?" he asked. He had brought his feet in the cart so that he could better turn toward her.

"I'm not vain," she said. "Nor am I fishing for compliments."

"I'm not paying a compliment. I'm stating a fact."

She felt heat rush to her cheeks. She wasn't beautiful, but she was flattered he had called her so.

"I'm not a fool," she protested softly. "You would just like another tryst with me."

"That I would," he admitted readily. "But that doesn't mean you aren't a lovely woman."

For a second, she was tempted to halt Dumpling and throw herself in his arms. She didn't even dare look at him in case he could read her thoughts in her eyes. He was uncanny that way. It was as if he could read her mind . . . or perhaps, his thoughts echoed hers?

Once again, dangerous ground.

"Thank you," she murmured, speaking as if he had told her she had good driving skills.

And, of course, he wasn't one to accept that. "Who convinced you that you weren't lovely?" he asked.

"A mirror," she replied.

He shook his head as if she spoke nonsense.

"You don't need to flatter me, Mr. Enright," Sabrina said, deciding this nonsensical conversation could not continue. "I'm not like other women, who feel all they have to offer are their looks. I have a mind. I read and try to improve myself all the time."

"A bluestocking," he murmured.

"Yes, I am a learned woman," she said proudly. "During my mother's illness, books sustained me. Reading refreshed my spirits. However, I do not lack social graces." She wanted that understood.

"Social graces are overrated."

"They are never overrated. Did you not have a mother? Did she not teach you that?"

There was a flash of straight white teeth. "She tried her best, my lady."

"I imagine you were a handful," Sabrina had to observe.

"I imagine you were the same," he countered.

"No, I always obeyed," she said. "Although I

admit to having an independent mind. Perhaps that has been my problem. But I do try to make good use of my life. It is not very much now, but someday it will be. Yes, it will," she tacked on, realizing how empty her words sounded.

Empty. There was a word she did not like.

"And if you could do anything you wished, be anything, what would you want?" he asked.

Sabrina shot him a dubious glance. "We don't have choices in life."

"Of course, we do. Life is nothing but choices. However first, you must answer the question, what do you want?"

She focused on the road a moment. What did she want?

"Children?" he suggested. "A husband, home, and hearth?"

She considered the matter. "Well, yes, but I also think I'd like something more."

"And what would that be?"

Sabrina shook her head. "Sometimes, it is not good to think about wants. There are things we should have and things we shouldn't."

"Thank you, Reverend Davidson," he said, laughter in his deep voice. "But what if we could?"

"What would you ask for?" she countered.

"Freedom," he said.

"I can imagine so. I would not want to hang for a crime I did not commit."

"That is true, but I was not thinking of my sentence." He studied the top of the trees lining the road a moment before saying, "I'm realizing I made my own chains. Right now, I do feel free. Free of regret, of sorrow, of grief. I made poor choices because I felt entitled."

"And you wish freedom from those feelings?"

"Yes," he said thoughtfully, swinging his gaze back to meet hers. "I don't know why life takes the turns it does or why we have the experience that we do, but I believe I'm done with doubt."

"How can we do without doubt? How would we know we were taking the right paths in life without it?"

"Perhaps we've been on the right path all along but didn't realize it," he answered. "Maybe each of us has to go through what we experience to live our lives fully."

Sabrina laughed. "You are very philosophical, Colonel."

"Thank you, Miss Davidson," he answered. "In truth, I usually am the furthest thing from a philosopher."

He reached over and took the reins from her. "May I?" She let him have them. They traveled a little ways, then he said, "Miss Davidson, don't be afraid of life. Don't hold back and don't delay."

"I have nothing to hold back or delay," she answered. "My world is very small."

"It won't be once you know what you want."

"And what of you, sir? Will you find the answers to the questions you ask?"

A slow, confident smile found its way across his face, his gaze on the road ahead. "I believe I have. For better or worse, I want my future."

Such a cryptic answer tickled Sabrina's curiosity, but before she could ask questions, they arrived at Annefield's drive. Dumpling, always ready for oats, knew where they were and picked up his pace.

So it was that they pulled into the stable yard with a bit of energy and what style one can muster when driving a pony cart. Sabrina could have directed them to the front door, but family usually went straight to the stables, then walked the path leading to the house.

The stable lads called a greeting and rushed to help her from the cart, but Mr. Enright was there. He opened the door to the cart, climbed out, then offered his hand to her.

For a second, Sabrina hesitated. When he left, and he would leave either to be hanged or to travel on with his life, she would feel *emptier.* He would move toward his future. She would stay behind.

That was an unsettling thought, one that made her sad.

She distracted herself by noticing a lad dressed in maroon-and-silver livery coming down the road from the main house. He was leading a high-stepping gray pulling a high-perched phaeton with yellow wheels. She knew the owner of the rig, and her fear hollowed her out.

Coming here today had been a mistake.

Mr. Enright immediately noticed the change in her manner. "What is the matter?" he asked.

"That rig," she said, leaning toward him so that the lad wouldn't overhear. "It belongs to Owen Campbell."

Chapter Fifteen

$\mathcal{O}$wen Campbell.

Good God, it could not be mere coincidence that Owen Campbell, owner of the Rook's Nest, where Gordana had been murdered, was calling on the earl of Tay. Especially at the time when Mac had escaped hanging, and Richard Davidson had gone missing.

Something was afoot. Mac was willing to stake his life on it.

"We should not talk to my uncle now," Miss Davidson was saying. "We need to wait until Mr. Campbell is gone—"

"Oh, no," Mac countered. "This is the perfect time. However, *you* will stay here." He'd met Campbell only once where they looked each other in the eye, but he'd observed him around the Rook. There was something about the man that Mac could not like. He seemed secretive, and he agreed with Mrs. Bossley's description of Campbell as greedy. Mac knew officers of that stripe, and he'd learned not to trust them.

Seeing a well-marked path leading through a line of beech trees to the house, Mac set off, anxious for a confrontation. He'd spent months puzzling over the whys of Gordana's death, and while he wanted to save his neck, he also wanted the mystery of her murder answered.

He had just reached the sheltering trees when a hand hooked itself around his elbow and pulled hard. He stopped, annoyed to see that Miss Davidson had not listened to his order.

"What?" he snapped.

"You will not go up there," she commanded.

"Yes, I will." He shook off her arm, but she held on, digging her heels into the path's soft ground. Impatience brought out his iron will. He whirled around. *"What* is it?"

She had not been expecting his temper. Blue eyes widened.

Mac knew his power. When he spoke in that tone of voice, even hardened soldiers knew to beware. They certainly knew to obey. He expected her to perform an about face and march smartly back to the pony cart where he'd told her to stay.

However, instead of obedience, determination lifted her chin.

He could have sworn under his breath. He was in for an argument now.

"You mustn't go there," she said. "Do you believe Campbell doesn't know who you are? You are accused of murder in an establishment he owns, and you believe he will happily ignore that the authorities wish to hang you? Wait until he leaves. Then I will take you to talk to my uncle."

Mac looked at the house, looked at her, and started walking again up the path—except she had not released her hold. The woman had the strength of a sailor in her arms. She used all of it to yank him back.

He could have roared his frustration. "I *am* going there."

"Did you not hear me?" she said as if he were a simpleton. "They will hang you. My uncle is as befuddled as they come, and he might not have an issue with you, but Owen Campbell is cut of different cloth. If he is involved in this, Mr. Enright, he'll run you through and act innocent all the while. He's capable of such."

"I'd relish crossing swords with him," Mac said.

"As for hanging? I want answers, Miss Davidson. I've spent months and most of my sanity plagued by the 'whys.' Furthermore, years on a battlefield have taught me there is only one way to engage the enemy, and that is by going forward."

"But what if Campbell had nothing to do with the girl's murder? Then you could be jeopardizing your life on a goose chase."

"It is my chase and my goose," he replied. "Now, return to the pony cart, and if you see a hanging party, *leave*."

With that order, he started up the hill again.

Of course, she didn't listen.

He hadn't gone more than a few yards before she came walking up beside him . . . and then passed him—her bonneted head high, her arms pumping.

"Miss Davidson?" he said.

She paused, her feet marching in place, her arms swinging, the brim of her bonnet bouncing. "Yes?" she answered with the hauteur of a duchess.

"The pony cart is in the stable yard." He pointed in the direction behind him.

"Are you going back there?" she asked.

"No."

"Well, then, I'm not either. Someone needs to

rescue you when you find yourself in trouble." She took off up the path.

For a moment, Mac was so angry, he couldn't move. No one, absolutely *no one*, had ever countermanded him.

Then again, he'd never met anyone as stubborn as Sabrina Davidson. "Now I understand why you aren't married," he muttered.

"What did you say, Mr. Enright?" she called over her shoulder. "I couldn't hear you."

"That is probably a good thing," he returned, and began walking up the path, lengthening his stride to catch up with hers.

Together, they presented themselves on the earl of Tay's doorstep.

The house itself was a country manor that had seen better times. Mac knew the sort. He'd grown up in just such a place. The trim needed painting and the stones repointing. He imagined it was quite drafty when winter winds blew.

Miss Davidson, headstrong lass that she was, didn't wait for him but rapped on the door.

The hinges creaked as a butler, a tall man with a stoic presence, opened the door almost immediately. He smiled with genuine warmth at Miss Davidson while, in that manner all butlers seemed to have, gave Mac a disapproving stare.

Mac returned his look with open curiosity. Something about the man stirred a memory. The butler had a long jaw, and his large shoulders had a bit of stoop to them. There had to be Viking in his ancestry.

Their paths had crossed before, but when would Mac have met a country butler?

"Miss Sabrina, good afternoon."

"Good afternoon, Ingold. I wish to see my uncle."

The butler shifted his weight as if he'd been anticipating the question and had an answer. "I'm so sorry, Miss Sabrina, but the earl is indisposed."

"Because he has a guest? We know Mr. Owen Campbell is here, but it is imperative I speak to my uncle."

"Unfortunately, that is not possible," the butler said as if he truly regretted saying those words, but he was already closing the door.

Mac leaned forward and pressed his forearm against the wood panel. "Tell your master the *earl* of Ballin requests a moment of his time."

The earl of Ballin.

For the first time in his life, Mac had used the title without remorse. It had come out of him as if he owned it. As if it were his to use.

That was freedom.

He'd not realized how much he'd held back out of guilt until this moment. But the title was his. Ballin was who he was.

And his use of the title was not about impressing anyone. It was about allowing himself the right to it.

Later, he would mull over this change of attitude, but for now, he didn't wait for the butler's response. He pushed the door hard, forcing it open.

To her credit, Miss Davidson ducked under the servant's arm and placed herself inside. "Yes, please, Ingold," she said. "My uncle *needs* to see us."

The butler wavered in indecision, then confided, "Miss Davidson, you do not want to be here. There are bad doings going on. Please go."

"We know, Ingold. Announce us. After all, the 'earl of Ballin' is here." She threw out Mac's title as if she was put out with him. He was rather pleased with himself.

"No, Miss Sabrina," Ingold answered. "It is not good. Not good at all." But he turned and walked down the hall—and that is when Mac placed where he'd seen the butler.

Ingold had been at the prison the night of his escape. He'd been the first man to run up to Kinnion after he'd been shot. Mac had not had a good look at his face because he had what he considered the more important challenge of saving his neck in mind, but he could not forget the man's gait or the way his shoulders stooped.

Kinnion was from this area. The butler? Campbell—?

"Ingold is going to my uncle's study. That is where Campbell is," Miss Davidson observed, interrupting his musing.

Mac nodded. "Let us not wait for permission. Let us join them." He placed his hat on a side table. He was tense, yet anxious, ready for battle. "Would it do any good if I suggested you wait here?" he asked as he started toward the study.

"No," Miss Davidson said, falling into step behind him. And then she whispered furiously as if he had not noticed her earlier jab, "*Earl?* You have a title? Or did you make that up?"

"I haven't made up any of my titles."

The butler had stopped to knock on a door.

Mac raised his hand to signal for her to halt. They stood partially hidden from view by a wall supporting a staircase. "But yes, I'm an earl. Surprised?"

She scrunched her nose in what he found to be the most adorable way possible. "Not truly.

Do you have any other titles of which I should be aware? You seem to run the gamut from felon to titled lord, with everything in between."

He smiled at her sarcasm. He couldn't help himself. This Scottish lass was a good ally to have on his side. "It is an empty title. No money, no land, and I've just inherited it."

Her lips parted in understanding. "Your brother's death."

"I haven't quite managed to grow comfortable with it. It seems wrong that he dies and I benefit. Where is there joy in that?"

"I can understand," she murmured, and he knew she did. She was quick. Smart. A man didn't have to spend his day explaining his thoughts to her.

A voice from inside the study had called for Ingold to leave them alone. The butler knew they followed. He wasn't blind. He looked to Mac, who nodded with a silent order for him to be persistent.

The butler knocked with more force on the door.

The study door opened. *"What?"* an angry voice snapped.

Mac could hear Ingold explaining that the earl of Ballin was insisting that he must see Tay.

"Ballin? I've never heard of a Ballin," Mac overheard another man say. He recognized the voice—Owen Campbell's.

"Stay here," Mac said to Miss Davidson, "and I mean, *stay right there.*"

He moved forward swiftly, coming to stand beside the butler, just as Campbell said, "Send him away."

"Too late," Mac said, very pleased with himself as he pushed his way past Ingold. "I'm here." He enjoyed the start of alarm on Campbell's face as he recognized who the earl of Ballin was.

The library was a large room. Shelves filled with books lined one wall, and there was a large, ornate desk by the window to take advantage of the light. At one time, the earls of Tay must have had wealth.

The current earl of Tay was sprawled out in one of the upholstered chairs in front of a cold marble hearth. He was a tall man with a decided paunch and a complexion lost to his dissipations. However, right now, his cheeks were red, as if he'd been struck repeatedly, and tear-stained.

Owen Campbell stood by the door, his leather gloves in his hands. He was not what one would call a handsome man. He combed his hair forward to hide his baldness and had a taste for military style. His jacket was the cut of a Prussian officer's, with a double row of silver buttons. His shining Hessian boots, sporting silver tassels, would have made even those vain German officers jealous for the quality of the leather.

Overall, Mac thought him a mockery of a man.

The earl recognized Mac. He gave a low groan and covered his face. "This is worse. It keeps growing worse—"

"*Quiet,*" Campbell ordered. "What the bloody hell are *you* doing here?"

"Careful of your tongue," Mac answered. "We have a lady present," he pointed out, as Miss Davidson came charging into the room, as he'd assumed she would.

"*Sabrina,*" the earl said, alarmed. "Why are you with this man?"

"She's not *listening* to me, I can tell you that," Mac informed him. "She is far from obedient. I order her to stay in one place, she does as she pleases. Do you have that problem with her as well?"

Miss Davidson shot him a look of annoyance as she hurried to her uncle's side. "Don't listen to him. He prattles—"

"Prattles?" Mac repeated, offended.

She waved him away with a gloved hand and knelt by the earl's chair. "But look at you, Uncle. You look terrible. What is the matter?"

"I need a drink," was the reply. The earl lurched to his feet and stumbled toward the decanters on a side table. "It will be all right. It will. It will—"

"You have had enough," Campbell said, and the earl stopped dead in his tracks. His reaction was so abrupt, it was almost comical. Mac wondered how Campbell had that sort of power over him.

Apparently, so did Miss Davidson. She came to her feet. "What have you been doing to him?" she demanded of Campbell.

"We were visiting," was the answer, then he countered with, "What are you doing with Enright?" He asked the question rhetorically.

"Are you surprised?" Mac asked, enjoying the moment.

"Yes. When we heard you had escaped," Campbell said, "everyone assumed you would flee the country."

"Leave Scotland?" Mac repeated. "Just when I'm having a good time?"

Campbell's smile thinned, and his eyes filled with malice. Although the man had not attended the trial, Mac sensed he'd been very interested in the outcome. "Well now, it appears we will have our hanging."

"Over my dead body," Mac had to answer.

Miss Davidson started forward, her gloved hands curled into fists. "You were beating my uncle," she charged, and she would have taken after Campbell, but Mac hooked an arm around her waist.

"Steady, my girl, steady," he warned, speaking close to her ear. He looked to Campbell. "Miss Davidson is a woman of passion. You are lucky I am here to keep her in check."

"You will *not* touch my uncle," she informed Campbell, but she wisely stayed close to Mac's protection.

Campbell's beady eyes dropped to Mac's possessive hand resting at her waist. Indeed, he seemed riveted by the sight—and Mac had a memory, something Gordana had told him.

And that's when Mac understood. It all fell into place and was so obvious, he was shocked he hadn't suspected earlier.

He looked to the earl of Tay, whose cheeks were still red, either from his drinking or from being slapped by Campbell's gloves, a humiliating gesture. Campbell had not only wanted to cause pain but to make Tay do his will, and to what purpose?

Mac was certain it wasn't information about his whereabouts. Campbell had been genuinely surprised by his appearance. So what else could Tay know that would interest Campbell?

"You know, Enright," Campbell said, "I should notify the authorities you are here."

"And spoil the game?" Mac challenged.

Instead of answering, Campbell said, "Did you know you are with a murderer, Miss Davidson?"

"Did you know I don't value your opinion at all, Mr. Campbell?" she returned.

"There is a rebuke," Mac said approvingly.

"Go ahead and think you are clever," Campbell said, taking a step toward the door. "But understand, they have a price on your head in Edinburgh, Irishman. It is a good one."

"That pleases me," Mac replied. "I'd hate to be wanted for a paltry sum."

His humor did not sit well with the Scot. "You'd best be careful. The earl is deeply in my debt. He may decide to claim that reward. Certainly, that would save Annefield."

Money. Yes, money could be the motive for Campbell's being here, but Mac didn't think so.

For his part, Tay held his glass as if it contained the meaning of life, and perhaps to him it did. He was not a well man.

"My lord," Campbell said, addressing Tay, "think upon what I said." There was no mistaking the menace in his voice. "Miss Davidson, good afternoon. Enright or earl of wherever—God, I didn't even know the Irish had titles." He laughed as he said this, and Mac could hate the man.

"Ballin," Mac said.

"Aye, Ballin," Campbell repeated as if it were of no consequence. "I hope to see you hang very soon."

"Always a pleasure spending time with you as well," Mac answered. Perhaps he would just rip the man's throat out of his body.

Campbell left, and it seemed as if a foul smell had gone with him. Mac turned to Miss Davidson, ready to say as much, but her focus was on her uncle.

"What did he mean about saving Annefield?" she demanded. "Is the estate in danger?"

The earl didn't answer. Instead, he put down his glass and shuffled for the door as if he were a shell of a man. He stopped as he came abreast of Mac. "Why couldn't you have hanged?"

"Inconvenient of me, I know," Mac replied.

The man walked out the door.

She watched her uncle, her expression stricken, and he knew her mind was churning over something.

"All right," he said, "what do you suspect?"

"He has lost Annefield." She made a sound of incomprehension. "How could he do such a thing?"

"Tay's a gambler. It is not unheard of."

"But it doesn't make sense," she countered. "My father is a good solicitor. He understood the family records. He told me that Annefield was protected. After all, my uncle has no male heir. Upon his death, the title and all that goes with it would fall to my father. Granted, my uncle has had to sell off most of the land, but the house was safe. Always safe."

"Unless there was an error that would allow the entailment to be circumvented."

She shook her head as if denying that such a thing could happen. "My father boasted that all was right."

Mac shrugged. He had a very different opinion of Richard Davidson. "We shall ask him when we find him."

"You believe he is fine and well?"

"I'm now almost certain of it. And perhaps Mr. Kinnion is also alive."

"How—?" She started, but he shushed her quietly.

"Not here," he advised, taking her arm and

leading her out of the room. Tay and Ingold were not to be found, and Mac was not surprised. The butler was a loyal man.

He picked up his hat from the hall table and directed her outside. She waited until they reached the shelter of the trees lining the stable path before shaking loose of his hold and saying impatiently, "Why do you believe my father and the reverend are alive?"

"Ingold. He was there the night of my escape. When the reverend was shot, a large man was the first to come running toward us. He had an unusual silhouette. I had bent over to see if there was something I could do for Kinnion, then I heard the sounds of people coming. Of course, I couldn't stay. However, one man came out of the darkness as if he had been waiting. I did not mistake seeing Ingold."

She listened to him, her expression somber. "So what are you saying?"

"That your uncle also helped me escape."

"For what reason?"

"Conscience. Is there a better one?"

She began walking down the path, her mind obviously working. He followed, waiting, knowing she would reach the conclusion he had.

In the stable yard, Mac helped her into the cart,

then climbed in himself, picking up the reins. Campbell and his fancy rig had already left. "Which way to meet Mrs. Bossley?" he asked, driving out of the yard.

"To the north," she answered, too subdued for his liking.

He set Dumpling off at a good clip. Once they were down the drive and on the road, he asked, "What are you thinking?"

"Nothing."

"Oh, I beg to differ," he answered. "Sabrina Davidson's mind is never dwelling on 'nothing.' "

"Very well, what is Cormac Enright's, *earl of Ballin's*, mind mulling over?"

"Are you still annoyed about the title?" he asked, puzzled. "I explained, I'm not accustomed to it. Furthermore, I received the title and a load of debts for which I had to leave the country—yes, I understand perfectly how trapped your uncle feels in his debts."

"Debts that may belong to my father as well, obviously."

"Not so obviously," he argued.

"We are family," she pointed out. "My uncle may have the title, but Annefield has been in the family for centuries. I was raised to revere it."

"Times change," Mac answered. "And sometimes people, in spite of good intentions, make mistakes. My brother didn't expect to run his inheritance into the ground."

"How did he lose it?"

"Well, there wasn't much to begin with," Mac answered. "We Enrights were always on the bad side of the political game. There is something inside of us that just can't stomach the English."

"We were always on the right side. I remember as a child how well kept Annefield was. The stables are good, but my uncle could ruin those as well, couldn't he? But he can't lose Annefield. It is all we have. It is our legacy."

Mac didn't answer. She was in an odd mood. He didn't believe it was just worry over her father that made her quiet. She acted as if a light had gone out inside her.

They were approaching the crossroads.

Mrs. Bossley's gig waited on the road while she paced, her maroon velvet cape flying around her. At the sound of their approach, she stopped and watched them, her expression anxious—

Miss Davidson reached for the reins and pulled the pony to a stop well beyond earshot of Mrs. Bossley.

She didn't look at him as she said, "I believe we must part company, and it is best to do it now."

Mac frowned his confusion. "Part company? What are you saying?"

Miss Davidson raised troubled eyes to him. "I can't help you any longer," she said. "You must go on your own."

"And your reason?" he asked, surprised by how upset her words made him. Without realizing it, he had started to think of them as allies, partners in vindicating his name.

He trusted her.

She disabused him of that notion as she said, "I can't help you clear your name, not without destroying my own family."

Chapter Sixteen

Sabrina anticipated that he would be angry at her announcement. After all, she was saying she would side with his enemies. She had not imagined he would be hurt by her defection.

And yet, she had no choice.

Her father was involved in Gordana Raney's death itself. She knew that, and so did Mr. Enright, whether he said it aloud or not. That is why he suspected her father was alive. He was protecting himself.

She did not believe her father was capable of murder, but she would not rule out her uncle. Why else would Owen Campbell have attacked him?

There were too many questions here, and she

could perceive no answer that would be for the betterment of her family.

Nor did she trust that she could in good conscience play a hand in bringing her uncle or father to justice. Not if the sentence was going to be death.

She looked away from Mr. Enright. Otherwise, she would change her mind. Yes, she felt an obvious, strong physical attraction to him, but there was also something more. Something she couldn't quite define and it had nothing to do with desire. Mr. Enright treated her as if he valued her opinion, as if he considered her a full partner in solving the mystery surrounding that young girl's death.

And she was painfully aware that she was throwing his trust away as if it didn't matter.

"I see," he said.

"I don't know if you do," she murmured, feeling guilty.

"Then explain."

Sabrina wished he would just leave, and yet she also wanted to hold on to his presence as long as possible. She also found she *needed* him to understand.

Before coming upon him in the bothy, every day of her life had been the same. Then he came along. He'd engaged her intellect, and she'd begun

to believe the compliments he gave. She was starting to feel special, pretty, womanly.

Of course, he'd had very few options in his
choice of companions. No one else had paid attention to his story except her.

But now the stakes were too high.

"I fear my father has involved himself in one of
my uncle's schemes. Your suspicions about your
escape may be correct. My father might have attempted to help free you because for an innocent
man to hang based on his false testimony would
go against everything he believed in. But I can't
betray my family. I don't even want to think of the
scandal."

*If there were no Annefield . . . if her father was no
longer the magistrate . . . then what would become of
her?*

"Leave," she told him. "Take Dumpling and the
cart and leave this place. Sell them for what you
can receive and flee the country. *Save your life.*"

Desperation colored her voice. She reached for
the door, ready to climb out, but he put his arms
around her.

"You would have me take an animal you raised
and sell him to save your uncle's worthless hide?"

"We are family," she said. "Our name is all we
have." Sabrina closed her eyes, wishing he wasn't

so close. Wishing that she didn't have to tell him to leave. Wishing she had met him under other circumstances. "I have nothing else of value to give you," she whispered. "I've given you everything, but I can't help you destroy us."

He released his hold. "Destroy? That is something you did to yourselves."

The truth of his words almost crushed her.

She didn't know why her father had involved himself in her uncle's affairs. In this moment, she didn't care about Annefield. Everyone knew her uncle was a disgrace. But they'd respected her father and, consequently, respected her.

"I think my uncle and father have done something for which they feel shame. But I don't believe they are murderers. In fact, for all I know, you *could* have killed that girl," Sabrina heard herself suggest.

Those words did the trick. His body stiffened with the rise of his temper. In the next beat, he released his hold on her and climbed out of the cart.

He began walking, jumping over the stone dike so that he could cut across the field.

Sabrina watched him leave, and she felt as if her heart were being ripped in two.

She wanted to call him back. To tell him that

she was sorry, she hadn't meant those words. She'd been rattled, afraid—but none of that was true.

As he disappeared into the forest, she realized she'd pushed him away to protect herself.

Dear God, she could barely breathe from the pain of letting him go, and it amazed her. He'd swept into her life and changed her in a way no one else could have. Now, nothing would ever be the same.

He did not look back, not once.

"Don't return," she whispered. "Be safe."

But he would not hear her words or see the regret on her face.

For a moment, she feared she would lose consciousness from giving him up, and yet, what choice had she?

He'd asked for freedom. Now, he had it. The Davidsons had done enough to destroy him.

As she picked up her horse's reins, she had a sick feeling in the pit of her stomach that she'd made the worst mistake of her life. And no amount of common sense, of telling herself she barely knew him or using any rational reasoning could erase her unease.

He'd been the one.

She recognized him now. He'd been the man she'd longed for in her life, that she'd always believed was out there.

Of course, she hadn't danced at the valley assemblies or given the local lads a bit of time—she'd been waiting for Cormac Enright, the newly minted earl of Ballin. He was "the one."

And now, she had no choice but to go on with her life.

But it would not be as barren as what it had been before. No, he'd changed her.

She drove up to where Mrs. Bossley waited.

"Where did Mr. Enright go?" the widow asked.

"He had to leave," Sabrina answered.

"To go where? I thought he was going to help us find Richard?"

"Perhaps if Mr. Enright is gone, then Father will return home. After all, there will be no reason for him to hide."

"Richard is hiding?"

"I'm not certain, but I sense my uncle knows where he is." She didn't mention Owen Campbell. "With Mr. Enright gone, Father is safe."

And all would be as it was—except she didn't know how she would react toward her father in the future. Or if she could ever forgive him for what he'd done to Cormac Enright. Her opinion of her sire had changed.

The widow placed a hand on her arm. She was apparently not fooled by Sabrina's false bravado. "What is it? Why did Mr. Enright truly leave?"

"Because I told him to do so." Sabrina had wanted to keep it all in, but there were some things that could not stay contained. "My uncle may have killed that girl. Certainly he was involved in something terrible. I could see that it weighed on his mind. And he probably owes money to Owen Campbell. He may have lost Annefield."

"But that shouldn't be your father's worry."

"If any of this involves the house, then it is part of his concern." Sabrina tried to explain to Mrs. Bossley. "My father would protect the family's legacy."

"So he would lie to a jury and see an innocent man sentenced to hang? Over a house?"

Sabrina stared at Mrs. Bossley. Annefield was everything to the Davidsons.

But was it worth a man's life?

Having one's beliefs, especially those honed since childhood, challenged was unsettling. Sabrina had never known a time when the title wasn't important. What people thought of the

Davidsons was always a serious matter. Everyone knew her uncle was a wastrel, but he was still titled. And her father and *her* standing had rested on their connection to Tay.

But things were changing. Her cousins, the earl's daughters, had gone off and married men who mattered to them. Men whose positions in society were built on something other than ceremony.

Men whom they respected and loved.

Men like Cormac Enright.

"If your father is the sort of man who would lie to condemn an innocent man," Mrs. Bossley was saying, "then I would have nothing to do with him."

"But what if Mr. Enright isn't innocent?" Sabrina had to ask.

"Do you think him capable of murder?" Mrs. Bossley wondered.

"I don't know what he is capable of. I barely know him."

And yet she *did* know him. She felt as if she'd known him forever.

Oh, dear God, what had she done?

Mrs. Bossley echoed the doubts in her heart when she said, "Seeing the two of you the other night, I sensed there was something powerful stirring between you."

"How can there be?" Sabrina wanted to know. "We are very different people."

"Aye, but sometimes, it all happens like that. And quickly." Mrs. Bossley leaned on the side of the pony cart. "Love doesn't come about because a couple is courting for a certain length of time and knows all the same people and are from the right families. Sometimes it just blossoms on its own."

"Love?" Sabrina attempted to laugh, but the sound rang false even to her own ears. Yes, she cared for Mr. Enright. Yes, she felt a connection to him. But she was a sensible woman.

Sensible enough to lust for him . . . or had her instincts known something her mind had yet to accept?

Still, Sabrina had to deny it. "Men as handsome as Mr. Enright don't profess love for women as plain as myself."

"Plain?" Mrs. Bossley repeated. "Where did you gain that idea? You are a lovely girl. A very handsome one. And any man would be lucky to have you. Besides, when love is part of what happens between a man and a woman, looks are no longer important. There is beauty in admiration."

"Men admire beautiful women."

"On the surface," Mrs. Bossley agreed, "but do not sell them short. Men have great hearts. Oh, yes, there are the shallow ones. I've met enough of them. But most men, the ones I know, the good ones, they can hold a deeper love than even women. Your father is one of those."

Sabrina made a disrespectful sound. "My father? The man who barely spent a moment's time with my mother when she was dying?"

"Well who *is* good at that?" Mrs. Bossley countered.

"*I* was," Sabrina said. "I was there. But she wanted him. She wanted her husband by her side. You need to know this, Mrs. Bossley. He was not there for her. Don't romanticize him."

"I don't, lass. But I don't hold him to high standards either. He's human. He didn't know what to do."

"He could have sat by her side."

"Watching someone he loved die? It wasn't possible for him. And you know, when the time comes, and if I go before him, he'll do the same to me, and I'll understand because I love him. We all have our strengths and weaknesses."

Mrs. Bossley straightened, pushing away from the pony cart. "Most important, I trust your father. I believe he is trying to make things right."

"Would you help Mr. Enright destroy him?"

The question seemed to catch the widow off guard. "I see now what you mean."

"Father is caught up in something dangerous."

"Or he is trying to untangle himself the best he can. He may be wrong, but if he is, I will forgive him because that is the way love is. Once I love, I will not give up."

The widow might blindly offer loyalty, but Sabrina realized, she was not cut of that same cloth. She had to love with both head and heart.

"I need to know the truth behind that girl's death," Sabrina said, "regardless of the price my family pays. I am not going to back down on this. But I was right to cut ties with Mr. Enright. Of course I was," she repeated, needing to convince herself. He had been growing too close to her and clouding her vision. She needed to be protect her family. "At least until I know what happened."

And if there was a clue as to why her father was involved with her uncle's affairs, she sensed it must be in his papers. Her father always took careful notes.

Yes, she would search for answers.

"What are you going to do now?" Mrs. Bossley asked. "Do you wish to come home with me?"

The question startled Sabrina because, for a

moment, she actually considered it. A few days ago, she would not have even looked at Mrs. Bossley let alone accept her as an ally.

But if she was going to snoop amongst her father's things, she did not need an audience. She wasn't certain what she was looking for, let alone what she would find, but some insistent little voice told her she needed to look.

"Thank you, I shall be all right. Someone should be at the house in case Father returns."

"Perhaps I should go with you?"

Sabrina looked at the petite woman with her anxious expression, and said, "You really do care for him, don't you?"

"I told you, I love him."

There was a beat of silence, then Sabrina admitted, "I think you will be very good for him." The compliment had come easily to her lips and with it, resentment and anger had fallen away.

Freedom.

Mrs. Bossley smiled her happiness. "I know I will. And, listen, my dear, there will be a place for you at our table. Always. I didn't believe so in the beginning because I didn't know you. You always seemed so distant, but I think the two of us will manage well together."

"Tell that to Dame Agatha," Sabrina said.

Laughter met those words. "I will."

Sabrina didn't linger but pointed Dumpling in the direction of home. He was happy to go. It had been another long day to him. Sabrina felt drained inside, but she was also apprehensive.

The Davidsons had secrets. Perhaps it would not be wise to poke her nose into her father's affairs. Mrs. Bossley's happiness could be short-lived, depending on what Sabrina found.

Then again, she might not act on what she learned. Or she could be trapped by whatever secret she uncovered—and yet she must face the truth.

And it was best she went alone, without Mr. Enright. It would be easier, especially if she was called upon to make a hard decision.

But her heart hurt.

And she knew the sense of loss would always be with her.

Mrs. Patton was still cooking away in the kitchen when Sabrina arrived. She had finished roasting the venison and was very proud of herself.

"Colonel Enright will like the taste of this. My own recipe," she bragged. "I soak it in milk." She looked around Sabrina. "Where is the colonel and the master?"

"Father is in Kenmore," Sabrina said, amazed at how easily the lie came to her lips. "Colonel Enright will not be joining us this evening. His business with Father has concluded."

"It has?" Mrs. Patton echoed, her voice sad. She stood a moment in silence, then said, "I was hoping he would stay. What a good man he was."

"Yes," Sabrina agreed, preparing to walk down the hall.

"I thought perhaps something special might happen between the two of you," Mrs. Patton suggested.

An overwhelming sense of loss threatened to engulf Sabrina. She tried to keep her voice light as she said, "I don't have a notion what you are talking about."

"*Och*, yes you do." Mrs. Patton wiped her hands on a towel as she approached Sabrina. "I could see it in your face. He brought out a softness in you. It wasn't there the day before, but this morning, I had a strong feeling about the two of you. I can always tell when two people will make a fine match."

"All he wanted was some business with my father," Sabrina managed to answer around the tightness in her throat.

"Yes, miss. I understand," Mrs. Patton answered, and Sabrina was afraid she did.

Sabrina escaped to her room. She caught a glimpse of herself in the mirror over her washbasin. She didn't appear softer to her eyes. She appeared sad and doubtful.

And, yes, a little afraid.

Mrs. Patton called out that she was leaving. Sabrina went out to the stairs, and said, "Thank you."

The smell of fresh bread and roasted venison, the special meal Mrs. Patton had prepared for Mr. Enright, was all through the house.

Sabrina took a moment to remove her bonnet and splash cold water on her face. She went downstairs and let Rolf in. The dog trotted right to the kitchen and, was it her imagination, but did he also search for Mr. Enright as well?

She turned and faced her father's study. This was where he kept all of his important papers. She didn't know what she was looking for, but she hoped she found it here.

Two hours later, she wasn't so certain. She'd gone through every drawer, every cupboard, and opened all the ledgers. She'd not found a reason for her father to be at the Rook's Nest or to lie about seeing Mr. Enright murder that girl.

However, she learned that her father kept the Annefield books. He carefully tracked every crop raised and stallion bred.

And then, in the last ledger she had to review, she came upon a note on the edge of one of the ledgers stating "sold to Owen Campbell."

Her father could not have meant the crops but the land.

A few pages later was another entry, "land sold to Owen Campbell."

Sabrina wondered if her uncle had sold the land or lost it at the gaming table. She'd known Owen Campbell had held a portion of Davidson land, but she had not expected so much.

The hour was not late. It was six or so in the evening but the day had grown cloudy and the house was cast in shadows. She carved off a piece of Mrs. Patton's venison, put it between two slices of bread and, picking up the lamp she'd been using in her father's office, went upstairs. She lit the fire and a lamp in her bedroom, before going to her father's.

She'd never gone through his things before. They'd both respected each other's privacy. Mrs. Patton would put away laundered items, and Sabrina had no reason to pry.

The top drawer contained his smallclothes.

The second drawer held his woolens. She found a book of poetry there. It was Shakespeare's sonnets. Sabrina opened the cover and found it was inscribed from her mother to her father.

"To my loving Richard," she had written.

For a moment, an overwhelming sense of loss threatened Sabrina. How she wished her mother were here to help guide her.

And yet, in the few minutes she'd spent with Mrs. Bossley, she'd received more advice than her mother had ever offered. In truth, her mother had been bothered by her illness. It had made her feel inadequate. She'd not been one to complain although she had relied on her daughter's constant support.

Perhaps Sabrina had learned how to suffer in silence from her. She'd rarely expected anything from her father. She had an idea that Mrs. Bossley was not so accommodating, and she found herself smiling. The widow would keep her father in line.

Still, the presence of the book in her father's personal belongings touched her deeply. It meant that he did cherish her mother's memory. She flipped through the pages of the book, remembering when she'd read Shakespeare aloud to her mother. It was then when she noticed that someone had torn up a document and placed pieces of it carefully between the pages.

She placed the book on top of the dresser and began pulling out the document. She moved the pieces around until she could read what they said. It was her father's marker for a gambling debt of two hundred pounds. That was an exorbitant amount. Her stomach clenched just at the thought of it—and the paper was signed by Owen Campbell and her father.

Mr. Enright had been correct. Her father had gambled at the Rook's Nest, and he had been losing.

So, what did finding a voucher torn up and stashed amongst her father's personal belongings mean—?

Rolf, who had been sleeping on the floor by the door, suddenly jumped to his feet and began snarling.

"What is it?" she asked.

The dog ran out in the hall. She followed, listening. She could hear nothing until, with a great crash, the front door burst open, and three men with masked faces came charging into the house.

Chapter Seventeen

She'd chosen her family and their dubious honor over him.

Mac was so deeply offended, so angry, he could have ripped the forest apart with his bare hands. As he strode through the woods, his legs eating up the ground that took him away from Miss Sabrina Davidson, he had to pause every once in a while to punch the air with his fist.

He knew he wasn't being reasonable. He also was aware that Sabrina was trying to be loyal. He had no doubt she believed her motives were pure, but he thought they were rot.

She was courageous and forthright—until her family name was threatened.

On one level, he understood. He *was* a threat to her family, but he had been from the beginning.

Of course, what angered him the most was that she didn't trust him. She didn't understand that he would do all in his power to shield her, even if it meant making an allowance for her lying father and drunkard uncle.

He would protect her.

Mac made an angry swipe at a tree limb that was in his way. He was walking with no other purpose than to cool his temper. Then he would think of where he wanted to go and what his next step should be.

Perhaps he *should* leave Scotland and forget about clearing his name. He'd find a way to leave. He had spent his money, but he was resourceful. He had skills. He could disappear into the world, which apparently was what everyone expected him to do.

They just hadn't realized how seriously he took his honor . . . as seriously as Sabrina Davidson took hers—and he stopped dead in his tracks.

Sabrina hadn't sounded proud when she'd told him that she could not help him. She'd been ashamed.

But there was something else tied up in his anger. He liked her. He'd trusted her. In fact, he might be a bit in love with her.

The realization startled him.

Love. He hadn't thought about love since Moira had taken his heart and broken it open. He'd hated love, and his opinion of it had grown worse over time.

He'd met men who could accept losing an arm or a leg with stoic determination. But let a man receive a letter from home letting him know his beloved had betrayed him, and that brave man would break down into tears. He'd lose all sense of value in himself.

Mac had understood. Oh, yes he had.

When he was younger, he had taken his medical studies seriously. After all, he'd had Moira depending on him. Once he finished, they would marry and settle into a good life. He'd loved her from the moment they'd met, when he was only twelve. Even back in those days, he'd been full of himself.

But the love Moira had claimed she'd felt for him had paled in comparison to the love she had for Lorcan. Anyone could see that was true. Anyone but Mac. He'd felt as if he'd been cheated, duped. Hearing that Moira loved another had been a humbling, painful moment in Mac's life.

When she'd told him, he'd turned and walked, just like he was doing now. He'd taken himself as far away from his family as he could, and he had nursed that anger until the day he began to miss his family and his country. He'd wanted to return home—but they were not there.

However, Sabrina was no Moira. She spoke up. She didn't hesitate in letting him know exactly what she was thinking every step of this journey, even to telling him she couldn't help destroy her family.

Mac hadn't considered that was where his quest would take him. To him, it was all about learning the truth. Gordana hadn't deserved to die the way she had. And if anyone stepped into his path, well, they would reap what they'd sown.

Sabrina's vision had been clearer than his. She'd sensed where this would lead, and she'd taken stock of the cost.

He looked back in the direction he had traveled.

Funny, but he already missed her. The two of them had fallen into step with ease. He'd liked having her by his side. She balanced him.

That morning, he'd barely been able to contain himself, waiting for her to wake and discover him about the house and not locked in the attic. He hadn't climbed out of a window. He'd actually picked the lock, a simple thing to do, but she'd accepted his story. In spite of her intelligence, she could be artlessly gullible.

And she could kiss.

The memory of her waking him with a kiss was never far from his mind, as was the feeling of being inside her. She was a half of him he'd not known he was missing—and he was walking away?

Anger, resentment, fury over the injustices of his life roiled inside of Mac, then were gone like a turbulent storm that had created havoc and dissipated. In their place was a realization that he'd been brought into the presence of something better than he could have imagined. Something *finer*, and more *wonderful*, more *brilliant* than anything he had ever experienced in his life.

Sabrina.

Of course she'd sent him away—but she had been wrong to do so. He would just have to tell her that. They had started this together and, whether she realized it or not, she needed him to see it through.

In fact, he was embarrassed that he had allowed his temper to have the best of him. He should have stoutly informed her that he would not leave until they had solved this mystery. They were a partnership, a duo.

Perhaps if he had just kissed her, they both would have seen reason.

Mac began walking back the way he had come. His step was lighter and faster. He was looking forward to his coming interview with Miss Davidson. She would protest, then he'd argue, she would refuse to listen, and this time, he would kiss her into silence.

Yes, he would kiss her, and he would do something he'd not thought he'd ever do again in his life, he would love her. Not make love to her although he wanted to do that as well.

This time, he'd be certain she knew how much he respected and valued her. He would explain that life made sense when he was around her.

She would claim they didn't know each other well. He would reply he felt as if his soul had known her forever—and kiss her, again.

Sabrina would suggest they spend some proper time courting. He would answer by kissing her.

Finally, she would accuse him of being quite mad.

He would agree—then kiss her.

He'd also say that he was not about to let her escape him. There were many women like Moira, but only one was as stubborn as Sabrina Davidson.

He hadn't traveled far when he saw a gig on the road along the woods. The driver wore a maroon cape. He stopped, wondering what Mrs. Bossley was about.

She saw him as well, and called, "Mr. Enright, I'm so glad I caught you."

Mac jumped over the narrow divide of a running stream and stepped onto the road. "Are you now?"

"I am. You appear to be walking back to Aberfeldy, or have you lost your way?"

He shifted his weight, then confessed, "I am going in the direction of Aberfeldy."

"In the direction of Miss Davidson?"

"I might be," Mac said, uncertain whether he trusted this woman.

"Does this mean you will continue to help us find my Richard?"

"Unfortunately."

"Good," she answered, not taking offense. "We need you. Would you like a ride?"

"Did Miss Davidson tell you she wanted nothing to do with me?" He had to know.

Mrs. Bossley rolled her eyes heavenward. "Women like Miss Davidson are prouder than a hen that can lay three eggs. They believe family name is all they are worth, and so they have to protect it. Now, before you believe I am being harsh on her, let me assure you, most men have the same character defect. I'm going to say something here, and there are those who would accuse me of feathering my own interests. I want to marry her father. I know you don't think much of him, but he is not such a bad man. He isn't as thoughtful as my late husband was, but he is far better than his brother the earl."

"And what do you want to tell me?"

"Miss Davidson deserves a better life than the one she has right now. In this valley, she'll grow old quickly. Everyone already believes they know her. But here you've come along, and I'm seeing another side of her. Don't leave her here alone."

Mac climbed into the gig. "Then take me to her."

A huge smile broke across Mrs. Bossley's face. With a flick of her driving whip, she set them off at a smart pace. Within the hour, they were in Aberfeldy.

Darkness was falling. There were few people out and about, and most were anxious to find their homes on this chilly evening. Mac pulled the brim of his hat low over his eyes, not wanting to be noticed.

"I'll let you off here at the bridge," Mrs. Bossley said. "It wouldn't do if Miss Davidson knew I'd come looking for you even though you were already on your way back. Good luck to you, sir. She's a stubborn lass."

"Aye, she is," Mac said, giving Mrs. Bossley a small salute.

"Tomorrow we will find Richard?" she asked.

"We can try."

She nodded. "I'd best be home. He might come looking for me there." She drove away.

Mac crossed the bridge. He could see the Davidson house. He didn't know what he was going to say to Sabrina, but he trusted that the right words would come to him. He just prayed she gave him time to say them—

A sinister shadow crossed in front of the house and blended in with the darkness. Two more figures also moved, one going around to the back of the house.

And then there was a third. The house was being attacked.

Mac began running.

*R*olf was barking madly. He bravely charged down the stairs at the men filling the hallway.

"*No, Rolf,*" Sabrina cried. But the dog didn't

listen, snapping at the two men who started up the stairs toward her. The third went running down the hall as if on a hunt.

The first man up the stairs backed away from Rolf, but the man behind him shoved him aside. He lifted a club and slammed it against the dog.

Rolf went wild. He leaped for the man, grabbing the material of his sleeve in his teeth. The man lifted Rolf and threw him over the side of the stairs.

Sabrina screamed her outrage and went running to help her pet, but the man with the torn sleeve grabbed her by the wrists.

She kicked and attempted to bite him. He was a big man. He shook her hard. "Where is the Irishman?"

Her response was to lift her knee. It didn't hit where she would have liked to kick the man, but it did land in his soft belly and caused him to grunt in pain. He did not release his hold but twisted her arm, pulling her closer to him.

"Tell me where the Irishman is, and I'll be nice to you when I have you."

She'd not thought of rape. Her mind grew frenzied. She struggled to free herself, then, as if by magic, the man released his hold. She fell to the steps, landing hard on her hip. Rolf was barking again. She wanted to tell him to stop, to save himself—and then, she saw the smaller man go rolling down the stairs where Cormac Enright with his broad shoulders and lean muscles had thrown him.

"Where is the Irishman?" Mac asked. He now had the man who had attacked her bent over the banister. *"Here's* the Irishman. What do you have for me?" He held the man by his neckcloth, which he twisted painfully around his throat. "Are you all right, Sabrina?" Cormac asked.

She nodded, too afraid to speak except to say, "Rolf, come here." The dog ignored her, running to the back of the house, where there was the sound of running feet.

"Who sent you?" Mac demanded of the man, pulling down his mask.

Before the man could answer, his two companions had regrouped and charged up the stairs to help their fellow.

"Cormac, watch out," Sabrina cried, and ran to her bedroom. She grabbed the iron poker and the shovel that leaned against the hearth and, so armed, dashed to Cormac's aid, ready for battle.

Cormac was already doing a magnificent job.

He had the advantage over the men trying to grab him. They couldn't fight more than one at a time on the stairs, and Mac was taller and stronger.

That didn't mean they weren't going to try to take him down. There was no doubt in Sabrina's mind they were there to silence Cormac for good.

"Cormac, here," she said, and came up behind him with the poker.

"Lovely," he said with satisfaction. "Stand back."

He swung the poker. It made a satisfying whipping sound as it sliced the air, then he wielded it like a sword.

Sabrina stood on the top step behind him, her shovel held high, ready to bash in the first man who made it past Mac. She yearned to give them a pounding.

The men backed away, and the one nearest the door tripped over Rolf who was making an effective nuisance of himself at the foot of the stairs. The brigand flailed his arms, reached for something to hold, and grabbed the coat of the man nearest him. That man lost his balance as well, and the two of them rolled over each other to the bottom of the stairs.

They lay there groaning.

The big man looked at his companions on the

floor, then back up to the deadly poker that was pointed at his nose.

"That leaves you all alone, mate," Cormac said. "So tell me, who sent you?"

The bully wasn't so certain of himself anymore. He glanced up at Sabrina. She shook her shovel at him, and he turned tail and ran. He was a clumsy beast. He fell over his companions, scrambled up, and ran out the door.

His friends managed to help each other to their feet even as Mac came down the stairs toward them. They, too, ran.

Mac slammed the door shut. "Stay there," he ordered Sabrina. "I'm going to investigate the rest of the house."

"Stay here?" she repeated in a daze. "I couldn't go anywhere." Her knees suddenly weak, she sank to the step and let the shovel drop.

Rolf watched Mac go down the hall. She called him. "Come here, Pup. Let me see you."

The dog lowered his head as if embarrassed he hadn't been more of a guardian to her. "You were wonderful," she said. "But are you all right?"

The dog came up the stairs and wagged his tail. She hugged him, and that was when the tears came. In fact, her whole body was trembling, and the sleeve of her dress had been torn. Her hair was also hanging halfway down her back.

Rolf laid his head in her lap.

She could hear Mac closing the back door and righting pieces of furniture that the men had knocked over. He came walking down the hall. Glancing up, he saw she was crying.

He took the stairs two at a time and knelt in front of her. "Here, now, did they hurt you?"

His dark eyes were full of compassion.

"They scared me," she admitted. "I'm so glad you came back, but why did you?"

He looked down at her as if she'd asked the strangest question in the world, then he smiled, that endearing, lopsided smile of his.

"For you," he answered. "I came back for you."

His words seemed to shimmer in the air all around her. He'd returned *for her.* Silly, awkward, provincial her.

Of course, she kissed him. She must.

And he was kissing her back.

Chapter Eighteen

$\mathcal{M}$ac fell back a step as Sabrina flung herself in his arms. She had been so brave.

Her kiss was powerful, unrestrained.

And he returned it with all the passion in his being. He could have lost her. He hated to imagine what those animals would have done to her, but she was whole and vibrant and his. He knew that now. She was his.

He began undressing her.

She offered no protest. Instead, her fingers became as busy as his own.

Clothing was pulled down over shoulders or tossed aside. Laces were undone and buttons released.

The kiss had to break for Mac to remove his

boots. It also gave him the opportunity to sweep her up in his arms and carry her into her bedroom. He went straight for the feminine, frilly bed and set her on the floor. The remaining pins in her hair fell. She looked gloriously disheveled in the lamp's golden glow. Her bodice rode low over her breasts, her shoulders bare.

His Sabrina.

Other women might stand on ceremony, but she was ruled by her passions, by her heart.

He sat on the bed and held his booted foot up. "I need help," he stated.

She laughed, surprised but trusting.

Laughter, who would have thought the sound of it belonged in the bedchamber?

She tossed her hair over one shoulder and reached for his heel.

She pulled, and the exertion caused her gown to slip lower. Sabrina stopped and looked down at her one exposed breast, the nipple rosy, hard, and tight.

Mac had never seen anything so beautiful.

She glanced at him, speculation in her eye. "You knew that would happen."

He smiled. "I hoped it would happen. Come, my darling, I have another boot." He placed it in front of her.

A pout came to her lips. She had not made any move to cover her breast, and he was delighted. Sabrina's tastes were much like his own. He enjoyed the earthiness of making love. He considered it a gift.

"Is it fair I give all?" she challenged.

He laughed. His neckcloth was on the floor beside his jacket in the hall. It was a small matter to pull his shirt over his head.

She rewarded him by pulling her arms from her sleeves. Her dress fell to the floor. Her petticoats were tied around her waist, but her chest was bare, her breasts delightfully enticing. She placed her hand on his chest, leaning her body against his, and Mac forgot about the boot.

Instead, he kissed her, his hand at her hip, smoothing over her buttock, working the ribbons of her petticoats free. His woman. *His.*

She broke the kiss, looked into his eyes, and whispered, "I am amazed that you are in my life." She ran her hand over his shoulder and down his arm. Their palms met, and fingers laced.

"I was wrong to choose Father over you. Especially after what he did." Tears welled in her eyes. "But I was afraid."

"And now?"

She made a small sound of capitulation. "It

doesn't matter. Nothing matters except that you are safe, and I am with you. We can leave Scotland. We can go anywhere. I just want to be with you."

Her faith and devotion humbled him.

The kiss he gave her was not one of just passion. He kissed in loving gratitude that she was the person she was, the *woman* she was.

It was a simple matter to finish undressing each other. He kissed her chin, her nose, her neck, her shoulder, her beautiful breasts. He rained kisses upon her. He worshipped her with kisses.

He'd never wanted a woman the way he wanted Sabrina. His desire was hard and obvious. Hungry.

"You are mine," he said, looking down at her. Her head was on the pillow, her lush, dark hair spread around her. "Do you understand? Mine. Whatever happens, we are together."

"We are together," she agreed, gifting him with a dazzling smile. Her fingers wound themselves in his hair, and she pulled him down to her.

What man could resist such an invitation?

Not Mac, not with this woman. Slowly, almost reverently, he slid deep inside her.

Sabrina arched her back and released her breath, as if she'd feared pain and was pleasantly surprised. Her body stretched to accommodate him. She smiled. He smiled down at her, and she began moving, her actions innocent and untutored. He met her where she was, and, together, they discovered their rhythm. The intensity of the night before had been no mistake. They fit well.

She whispered his name against his skin, her voice tinged with both wonder and passion. He lifted her in his arms, wanting her closer, positioning her. Muscles tightened around him intimately. The heat in her was building. He pressed deeper, anxious to give her everything she desired, forcing himself to hold back.

And yet there came a moment when he couldn't. Sabrina was so generous, so giving. Her movements quickened with her breathing . . . She whispered in his ear, *"Mac, hold me."*

Oh, God, yes.

Release was more than just an act of lust and desire. It was a blessing, a benediction, a step closer to heaven than Mac had ever been. All because of *her.*

Her arms and legs banded around him. Mac did the same. Their bodies melded together. Even their hearts matched beats.

He buried his face in her neck, his lips drinking in her skin. His weight should have been crushing her, but she did not ask him to move, and he couldn't have, even if she did.

Slowly, holding her, the world returned to center.

Cool air brushed against his skin, and he heard a sound. Looking up, Mac saw Rolf's worried gaze staring at them. The dog hovered by the side of the bed.

The sight caught Mac off guard and made him laugh.

Sabrina had been lost in her own haze of completion. One arm was still draped over Mac's shoulder while her other hand stroked his arm. Her leg was hooked over his. When he laughed, her eyes lit up. "I felt that," she said, reminding him that they were still joined, which was fine with him. He never wanted to leave her.

"What makes you laugh?" she wondered, and he nodded to the dog. She turned, reaching a hand for Rolf. She rubbed her pet's head. "It's good, Rolf. All is good." Her voice sounded drowsy, satiated.

Mac kissed her ear. "It is better than good."

She turned to him and brushed aside a lock of his hair that had fallen over his brow. "Cormac," she whispered, then smiled, as if she liked the sound of his name.

"Sabrina," he answered.

Her smile widened. "May we do that again? I'm not certain we have it quite right yet."

"Oh, we must practice often," he assured her. "Every opportunity afforded to us."

"Can we practice now?" she asked, experimentally running her fingers down his rib cage.

Mac was pleased that she wanted more. However, a man can only do so much—except he surprised himself when he felt himself stir.

His body, his soul had been waiting for her, and now that he'd found her, they weren't going to let her go.

"I believe that is an excellent idea, my lady," he said.

He heard Rolf give a dog-laden sigh and trot off to guard the door.

Both Sabrina and Mac laughed before settling into the very serious business of making love.

*T*hey had joined twice, and Sabrina found himself curious to know if they could do it again. Cormac pleased her. He knew exactly what she wanted.

Now, she understood the mysteries between men and women. No wonder Mrs. Bossley was so popular.

In that moment, Sabrina knew that she was in love.

Heart and head . . . they both came together . . . in love . . . with Cormac. She didn't question her feelings or doubt them. One didn't when one was certain.

Love was the most extraordinary feeling. It opened her heart in a way she'd not known before.

And she knew why she loved him. He'd just proven himself to her. Even after she'd sent him away, he'd come back to her. He hadn't abandoned her.

He wouldn't.

But for right now, she wanted to drift off to sleep. They had climbed beneath the covers, and she snuggled into his body heat, but he had something else on his mind.

He put his feet over the side of the bed and sat up.

Sabrina frowned her protest before sitting with him. She pushed her hair back. "What is it?"

"When I pulled down the mask of that one man, did you recognize him?"

She shook her head. "Should I have?"

"Could he have been one of your uncle's men?"

Sabrina thought a moment of the stable lads at Annefield and the other servants. "No, those were not my uncle's men. I grew up around those people. We are as close as family. I can't imagine one of them threatening me in the way that man did." A shiver of distaste went through her.

"Then someone else sent them," he said quietly. "And, frankly, there is only one other person that could be."

"Because there is only one other person who knows you are here," she agreed, coming awake

He nodded. "Owen Campbell."

"But why?" she insisted, then caught herself. They both knew. She could see Mac reaching the same conclusion. "He may have murdered Gordana Raney," she said. "Why else would he want to protect himself? But I can't imagine Campbell murdering a mere singer. He has standing. Why would he jeopardize all of that?"

"I shall ask him when I confront him." Cormac rose to his feet and reached for his breeches. "What I don't understand is why your father is involved? Your uncle is the sort that will always find himself in with a bad crowd, but is your father of the same ilk?"

"I may have found an explanation," she said, remembering her discovery and pushed aside the counterpane. She, too, rose and reached for her dress on the floor. She threw it on before going to her father's room, where the lamp still burned, and the pieces of the gambling vowel were spread out on the dresser.

Mac had followed her. He looked over her shoulder. She spread the pieces of paper out for him to see clearly.

"Father owed Owen money. And there is no possible way that we could repay this amount."

"But it has been repaid. The marker is signed and torn up," Mac said, thoughtfully pushing the pieces of paper together. "He earned it back."

"Yes," Sabrina said, "by testifying against you, perhaps?"

"And now, if your father isn't dead, then he is afraid of Owen Campbell, which he should have been from the beginning. Campbell is a nasty character. He is not going to allow your father to walk the face of this earth with his knowledge of the truth of Gordana's murder."

"Or he could. After all, Father lied under oath."

Mac shook his head. "It doesn't matter. Your father changed the terms of the agreement when he helped me escape. Campbell was beating your uncle because he wants to know where your father is. He may also be looking for the Reverend Kinnion, if he is still alive. Or Campbell may have been the one who attempted to shoot us outside the Tolbooth."

Sabrina lightly touched a scrap of paper. "At least Father did the right thing in the end." She looked up at Mac. "But what do we do now? He could be in danger."

"He *is* in danger. You saw the look on Campbell's face today. He wasn't using force with your uncle because he was pleased." He moved the pieces of paper around, and murmured, "Everything is related. There are connections, and they must make sense. Your uncle gambles, but your father doesn't."

"Yes."

"But it is your father's name on the marker."

"Perhaps he decided to do something foolish."

"Or, as we discussed, he might have had a good reason. However, the common factor is Owen Campbell. They went to the Rook's Nest for a reason."

"They know Owen."

"Yes, but not everyone who owns such an establishment would want an easy mark like the earl of Tay for a patron."

"What do you mean?" Sabrina asked.

"Tay is hard-bitten. He's lost a great deal at the

gaming tables. What did he have left to wager? Campbell would only let him play if he thought he could relieve him of his possessions."

"He already owns a good amount of land that my uncle lost."

"And perhaps your father didn't want him to lose more; but maybe he fell into the gambling pit himself."

"He's never gambled before."

"But that doesn't mean he couldn't start. This marker is from the third of May. Gordana was murdered on the tenth. To have this torn up, your father paid it in full by witnessing against me. Campbell must want to know where your father is for a reason. He sent those men after me to see me dead. That would solve one of his problems. And then your father might have been safe. But I doubt it. Only a guilty man would hide his tracks."

"Did Gordana ever mention Owen Campbell?"

"She sang at the Rook. I know she was looking for a benefactor. When she first started trailing after me, I told her I wasn't interested. She was a young girl, and I didn't have much to my name. She told me that was fine. She just needed to give the impression that she was in my care.

"Why?" Sabrina wanted to know.

"Someone was pressuring her to be in his bed.

She never told me his name. In hindsight, I can see she was afraid of him. Why else would a woman want to pretend to have a protector?"

"And the irony would be to have you accused of her murder," Sabrina observed. "But did Campbell kill her? And why?" she asked.

"Excellent questions. I will ask him when I see him, but first, I want to find your father. He knows the answer. Would he leave the country?"

"I don't believe so. He truly cares for Mrs. Bossley. And we don't have the money."

Cormac nodded as if a thought had crossed his mind. He walked toward the door.

"Where are you going?" she asked.

"You stay here. I have an idea where your father might be. Having a passing acquaintance of your family, I believe I know where any of you would go."

"Annefield?" The estate was the first thing that came to her mind. She followed him out of the bedroom and into hers.

Cormac started dressing as he confirmed her suggestion. "Yes, and if my supposition is correct, your uncle and father may not know what to do. Campbell is breathing down their necks. They are trapped as long as I'm here."

"But why wouldn't they have made their presence known when we were there? Why would Father not at least tell Mrs. Bossley?"

"Because he is afraid for his life." Cormac pulled on a boot and reached for another. "I must find him before Campbell does."

"And you are going tonight?"

Cormac nodded. "What would you do if you were hiding out? I'd come out at night, when the servants are in bed. Of course, they can't keep it up. Not forever."

"I'm going with you," Sabrina said. She began tightening the laces of her dress and reaching for her stockings.

"No," he answered. "It could be dangerous."

"Yes, it could be dangerous for you if I'm not there. You need me. Father might not trust you otherwise."

She put on her good, sensible shoes and quickly braided her hair as she followed him out the door. "I'm ready to go."

He paused. "Sabrina, I would feel better if you stayed here."

"And I would go half-mad with worry if I did. Besides, you don't know the way to Annefield," she said, and won the argument.

Well within the hour, they had secured Rolf, so

that he wouldn't run after them, and were in the pony cart on their way.

It was half past midnight. There was a moon, but occasionally it was covered in clouds. Fortunately, Dumpling was always pleased to travel to Annefield, even when roused from his night's sleep.

When they came to the entrance of the drive, Cormac tied Dumpling up and gave him hay they had brought with them. Otherwise, Dumpling would start complaining and make a racket.

Taking Sabrina's hand, Cormac led her along the trees lining the drive to the house.

All appeared quiet. There was a light in an upstairs window. "Whose is that room?" he asked.

"My uncle's."

"You stay here." He started forward. "I'm going to break into the house."

"Why don't we just knock on the door?"

"And give your father a warning? I think not." He started off, but she grabbed his arm.

"You are very certain that Father is there? If you break into the house like a thief, things may not go well."

"Yes, I am certain he is there, and, yes, I will be careful." He pressed a hard kiss on her lips, then took off before she could offer another argument.

Sabrina watched him leave. "I love you." She whispered the words. She hadn't the courage to say them to his face, and yet, they needed to be spoken.

She looked up at the light in the bedroom. She knew very little about her uncle's habits other than his taste for whisky. He'd spent a good portion of her life living in London.

In a few minutes, she saw Cormac's shadow run around to the back of the house. She wondered if he would open a door or a window. At one time, Ingold always had a footman sit in a chair in the front hall in case there were late-night guests. She didn't know if that was still true or not.

She stood. The night was cold. She crossed her arms, hugging herself and worrying.

Actually, it was more that she *told* herself she was worrying. In truth, she was very annoyed. She didn't like being left behind. Furthermore, she could probably talk to her uncle better than Cormac could.

Sabrina had just decided she needed to go to the house and join him when she noticed a shadow moving from the stable path.

At first, she thought it was Cormac returning. But then the shadow separated into four different forms moving toward the house—just as Mac had told her they had when they'd attacked her.

The front door opened, and two of the figures went inside. Another two went around the back, and Sabrina was done with waiting.

She ran toward Annefield to warn Cormac.

Chapter Nineteen

After climbing through a window, Mac found himself in the study. He carefully picked his way through the dark to the hall, then turned to the left, expecting there to be a servants' stairway.

He found it without difficulty and began quietly climbing the stairs. Hades could not be darker than the stairwell. He was careful. He didn't want to make a sound that would alert anyone to his presence.

At the top of the first flight of stairs, his fingers traced the wall and found the door. He stepped into the hall. There was only one room with light spilling out from under the door. He moved toward it.

But just as he passed the main staircase, down-stairs, the front door opened. Mac recognized the creak of the hinges. He stepped deeper into the shadows and held his breath.

His initial thought was that it was either a servant up and about, or Sabrina had decided to defy his command—again.

The sound of the small table in the front hall falling over and a distinct, male grunt caught his attention.

The servants would know where the table was—and would the love-of-his-life grunt?

That question gave him pause. Sabrina never failed to surprise, but she was graceful.

"*Careful,*" a man's voice warned, the angry whisper carrying through the darkness.

"Do we have enough knives?" another whispered.

"*Keep your voice down*. We don't want to wake the servants. I don't want this business untidier than what it already is."

There was no mistaking the last speaker. Owen Campbell.

"It isn't our fault," a man said. "Everything has gone wrong this night. We should have been done with this.

"Shut up," Campbell ordered.

They were coming up the stairs. One of the steps squeaked when they placed weight on it. Mac waited. They were almost upon him.

A shadow crossed and rose up the stairs, then another and another. Three men. One seemed unusually big and burly, just like the man who had attacked Sabrina.

What were the chances there was more than one party of men up to mischief in the middle of the night in Aberfeldy?

They went single file to the earl of Tay's room, walking right past Mac hidden in the shadows, and entered without knocking. Light flooded out into the hall before the door. Mac pressed against the wall.

The men didn't notice him. They weren't looking for him. They were too intent upon their mission.

No greeting met them from the inside. Since none of them wore masks, Mac could see Owen Campbell clearly when he entered the room. He had even paused in the doorway and looked out into the hall, as if he sensed Mac's presence but didn't glimpse him.

Campbell turned back to the men in the room.

"Let us do this quickly but be neat about it. I don't want blood on any of you."

Those were not words Mac wanted to hear.

Campbell shut the door, and Mac stepped out in the hall, almost meeting Sabrina, who was running up the stairs, her step so light, he'd not heard her, preoccupied as he was with Campbell.

She started to give a startled yelp, but Mac clapped a hand over her mouth—and then realized making noise might be their only solution.

He could hear Campbell's low voice giving instructions in the earl's room. He prayed that meant they had not murdered whoever was in there with them.

"When I say the word," he told Sabrina, "I want you to scream. I want you to scream loud and keep screaming while you run for your life and wake the servants. Understand?"

She nodded, then held up her hands. The glint of brass caught his eye. She had secured what was becoming her favorite weapon of choice— andirons.

"Good girl," he said, taking the poker. It was brass and well balanced. She pressed the shovel into his hand as well.

"What is going on?" she asked.

"I'm not certain," he said. He moved to the earl's door and took position behind it. "Now scream."

No scream followed.

Sabrina stood as if she hadn't truly grasped what he wanted her to do. He motioned with his fireplace weapons that he expected her to scream. *This* second.

With a nod of understanding, she opened her mouth and uttered the most puny scream Mac had ever heard. It obviously wasn't in her nature to scream. He'd heard women carry on about mice with more zeal.

However, it did serve the trick.

From the other side of the door, Campbell's voice said, "What was that?"

Sabrina's eyes widened. She had recognized Campbell's voice.

The door to the earl's room opened. Light flowed into the hallway, highlighting Sabrina standing at the top of the stairs, her brows together as if she hadn't fully comprehended what was happening and, for a second, Mac could have cursed.

She was so reasonable. In the short time he'd known her, he'd learned that she wanted the "whys" and the "hows." Her analytical mind made her a good partner in solving the mystery of Gordana's death.

But right now, Mac needed noise.

The big man who had attacked her that evening stepped into the hall.

Sabrina opened her mouth in angry shock. But instead of screaming or running down the stairs, she came charging toward the man and shoved him against the wall for all she was worth.

Apparently, she had the element of surprise on her side. Or perhaps coming from such a well-lit room into the hallway's darkness had made it difficult for the brigand to see. Impressively, Sabrina hit him just right, using her whole body in her attack.

"What the bloody—" the brute started, before falling back and catching sight of Mac behind the door. "What—?" he shouted, but Mac wasn't going to let him warn the others before Sabrina was safe. He slammed the man's throat with his elbow, dropping the shovel in his exertion. However, he still held the poker.

"I said *run*," Mac ground out to Sabrina. She'd done her part. Now he needed her to be safe, but Sabrina decided what she needed to do was scream.

And scream she did. The halls rang with her scream.

Mac was sorry he'd ever thought her a puny screamer. Of course, one blow could not quell such a big man, and Mac found himself fighting with the brute over control of the poker.

As if that weren't enough, Owen Campbell came out in the hall with another of his henchmen, one who held a wicked-looking butcher knife.

Seeing Mac struggling with his man, Campbell ordered both of his men to, "Kill that bastard. And you," he said to someone inside the room, "shut her up."

A third man came running out of the room. He, too, held a knife and went after Sabrina.

Now she ran down the stairs, with Campbell's man in pursuit. If something happened to her, Mac would never forgive himself.

The strength of ten men filled him. Fear could do that.

He won the poker by kicking the giant in the groin. The man fell to the ground. Mac turned and slashed the air with his weapon, connecting with the head of the smaller man, who dropped his knife and fell to the floor, screaming louder than Sabrina had.

The giant lunged for the shovel Mac had dropped. Mac jumped for it as well. For a moment, both men pulled on the andiron—and then Mac let go.

Once again, the big man lost his balance. He was a clumsy oaf. He crashed to the floor, and Mac finished him off with crack over the noggin with the poker.

There was a crashing sound from downstairs.

"*Sabrina*." Anxious for her, Mac started for the staircase—but Owen Campbell blocked his path. He held the butcher knife.

"I believe Miss Davidson has had an accident," Campbell said.

Mac moved forward in a murderous rage. He'd rip the man's heart out with his bare hands, but then a voice called up.

"Everything is fine," Sabrina shouted. "I found some andirons down here. You don't need to worry about this one, Cormac. The servants will take care of him."

"God, I love that woman," Mac said. "Love her."

He looked to Campbell. "She is safe. And now, you are going to pay dearly."

The Scot's response was to throw the knife with all his strength at Mac.

Fortunately, Mac had anticipated it. A butcher

knife is a heavy thing. It is meant for hacking at meat, not flying swiftly through the air. Mac easily avoided the cleaver while batting it out of the way with his poker.

Footsteps charged up the stairs. Excited voices asked what was happening. Sabrina had roused the servants.

Campbell swore and ran into the earl's bedroom, slamming the door behind him.

Mac stormed after him. He yanked on the door. Campbell was holding it closed on the other side, but his strength was no match for Mac's anger.

Winning the battle over the door, Mac threw it open, ran into the room—and came to an abrupt halt.

He was shocked by what he saw. The earl of Tay, Richard Davidson, Ingold the butler, and even the good reverend were bound and gagged like trussed pigs. Two of the men were on the bed, the butler on the floor, and the earl was in a chair. He could tell they were happy to see him by the relief in their eyes.

Unfortunately, Mac's momentary lapse of attention gave Campbell enough time to grab his own andiron from the earl's hearth. He whipped it through the air, and Mac smiled.

He was going to enjoy this fight.

Campbell lunged at him.

Mac feinted, turned, and crunched Campbell's nose with a direct blow with his fist. The Scot groaned and stepped back.

"Take a moment," Mac told him. "I'm certain that smarts. After all, I'm a physician. I know how to heal, and I know a hundred ways to pound your body and cause excruciating pain. Really. This will not be a good fight for you."

Sabrina had appeared in the doorway. She had several servants with her.

"You are outnumbered," Mac pointed out. "You might want to give up."

"And what? Hang?" Campbell demanded, raising his poker.

"It is a possibility," Mac said with satisfaction, but Campbell had another trick in mind.

Because, instead of attacking Mac, he turned, and raising the poker, started to bring it down on the head of the man closest to him, Richard Davidson. He knew he was trapped but apparently wished to make someone pay in a fit of boiling rage.

Mac realized his intent. He leaped forward and was able to block the deadly blow with his own poker. Their weapons crossed. They stood toe to toe, and it was now a test of strength and wills. One knew his life was at stake; the other had a score to settle.

They wrestled back and forth.

Looking into his enemy's eyes, Mac said, "You can't win. Give it up, man."

Campbell's face turned red with exertion. Mac was the stronger of the two. He knew he would beat Campbell—and he did. Campbell's poker bent. He tried to flail Mac with it, but the two were too close to each other. Mac easily wrested the weapon from him and threw it across the room.

Owen Campbell was defenseless. Nor could he run. Even if he had made the distance past Mac, Sabrina and the household servants blocked his way out the door.

"You are done," Mac advised him.

But instead of crying quarter, Campbell looked at him, and said, "What did I do wrong? Why did she not want me?"

For a second, Mac didn't understand. "She?"

"Gordana. Why would she choose *you*?"

Campbell was the man Gordana had rightfully feared.

"There was nothing between us," Mac answered.

Campbell barked his disbelief. "I saw her go into your room. She refused me, numerous times, as if I didn't matter. She kept me dancing to her tune, then she went to you."

"She might have just come to talk. Or entered my room when I wasn't there to give you the impression that we were lovers. We weren't. And even if we were, you shouldn't have killed her for it," Mac said.

"I didn't mean to kill her. *She made me angry.* She would not listen to me." Campbell punched his fist into his hand to punctuate his words. "I told her what I wanted, what I had to offer. I am an important man. I could have given her anything she desired. She turned me down. She said she wanted *you*, a man who couldn't offer her the coin for a meal."

Mac had not put down the poker. He'd seen men in Campbell's state before. It was a madness that took hold of them. They were capable of anything.

"*I loved her*," Campbell shouted, the words etched in pain. Mac understood. Years ago, he'd cried these same words to his brother over Moira, and now he knew the answer.

"She didn't love you," Mac said, as kindly as he could. "You can't have what doesn't want to be yours."

Campbell's shoulders dropped. "I can't have her now that she is dead, either. I didn't mean to hurt her. I forgot myself."

"I believe you—" Mac started, but Campbell wasn't listening to him.

Instead, he spun around and, before Mac could grasp his intent, threw himself through the window behind him. He crashed through the glass panes, breaking the wood framing, and hurling his body out into air.

Mac charged forward as if he could stop him, but Campbell was already gone. He fell heavily to the ground. Mac stared out the window at the figure sprawled on the drive. Even from here, he could see that the man was dead.

Several servants ran up behind him to peer at the body. Others began untying the earl.

Sabrina ran to Mac.

Her arms went around him, and she hugged him tighter than he'd ever been held before.

"I am so happy you are alive," she said. "So happy. And you are safe, Cormac. Safe. Everyone knows now that you didn't kill that girl. They can't hang you."

Mac nodded, momentarily overcome by both the suddenness of Campbell's action as well as the realization that he was free.

He was free.

The gag was removed from the earl's mouth. "He was going to murder us," Tay said, his voice hoarse with excitement. "He wanted to butcher us and blame Enright. Tricked me he did. Told me he wanted to talk, then he set about that grisly business."

"Why *hadn't* he murdered you?" Mac asked. "When we came to the house, you were already tied."

"His men had thought to use the knives in the kitchen. *My* knives. Campbell would have none of it. He feared a servant might discover them if they went down to Annefield's kitchen. He was angry they hadn't been prepared and that they hadn't brought Sabrina or you to him. They were gone an hour, leaving us tied up. We heard them plotting everything. Campbell said people would believe you were out for revenge." He took a deep breath and released it. "I need a drink."

Mac gently released Sabrina's hold and walked to Richard Davidson, who had almost had his brains bashed in. Mac removed the gag from the man's mouth.

"Will you tell the truth?" he asked the magistrate.

Sabrina's father looked at her, at his brother, and then to the floor. "Yes. Just untie me."

Chapter Twenty

he truth.

Those words were music to Sabrina's ears.

Mac began untying the reverend and the earl. A footman returned with the understatement that it appeared as if Mr. Campbell was dead. He also assured everyone that the men who had come with Owen Campbell were securely locked in the earl's library to await the magistrate's decision on what to do with them.

"Whisky," the earl said. "That is what needs to be done now. Fetch a tray—"

"And make it tea," Sabrina said, countermanding the earl's order. "No whisky for you, Uncle, until we hear the story. Good, black tea, and something to eat if you have it." She herself was starved, and she was certain Cormac was as well. The footman bowed and left the room.

Mac seemed concerned over the Reverend Kinnion. The wound he had received the night of his escape was not healing as well as one could wish it, and he was slightly feverish.

"He has been that way for some time," her father said.

"Where have you both been?" Sabrina asked.

"Hiding. In the attic."

Mac had Sabrina ask the servants for some black powder and clean rags.

"He sounds as if he is a physician," her father said.

"That he is," Sabrina said.

"Then he isn't an earl?" her uncle asked. "He said he was an earl when he called."

"He is also an earl," Sabrina was happy to inform them. "Lord Ballin."

"One with less money than the earl of Tay," Cormac muttered as he checked the reverend's eyes.

"Being an aristocrat is difficult nowadays," her uncle agreed.

"Will Kinnion be all right?" her father asked.

To everyone's relief, Cormac nodded. "We need to stop the infection, but the gunpowder should do that." He faced the others. "What happened?" he asked. "How did this all come about? And let me warn you, we already know a good portion of it."

"We found the gambling marker for what you owed Owen Campbell, Father," Sabrina said.

Her father groaned. "The thing has been the bane of my life." He looked to his brother. "It is his fault."

"I didn't ask you to gamble," the earl said.

"I was trying to win back what you'd lost," her father said. He looked to Sabrina. "He's cost us everything. I didn't realize how bad it was. I thought Aileen or Tara had some control over him—"

"My daughters don't lead me around by my nose," the earl protested.

"We'd be better off if they did," her father said.

A knock on the door signaled that the servants had arrived with the items Cormac needed. Mac made quick work of doctoring the hapless clergyman while servants appeared with trays of food. After he had been untied, Ingold had wanted to oversee the servants, but Sabrina made him stay where he was. He'd suffered like her father and her uncle. He needed a moment to regroup.

Once the servants were gone, and everyone had food, she pressed for more information. "So, you owed Owen Campbell money that we didn't have," she said to her father.

"And I wanted to marry Lilly—"

The earl interrupted with a sharp bark of laughter. "I don't know why. You don't have to marry her."

"Shut your mouth," his brother said.

Sabrina stared in surprise at her father. Everyone did. He never talked back to the earl.

But he had this time. "I'm done with your nonsense. I don't care any more if you take us all down, but you will not speak of Lilly that way. She's a good woman, something you wouldn't recognize unless it came in a whisky keg."

"You've been courting her longer than I suspected," Sabrina said quietly.

To her surprise, tears filled her father's eyes. "I'd had my eye on her, especially after this one tossed her aside the way he did, but I'd been afraid to approach her. Lilly has money. It hurts a man's pride for the woman to have more. When Tay told me how much he'd lost, I knew we were ruined. I thought to win some of it back. Campbell knew my plan and advanced me some funds. I believed I could use my intelligence and win. However, I lost my own blunt and didn't know how I was going to repay Campbell."

"Until he asked you to witness against me," Mac surmised.

Sabrina felt her heart ache as her father wrestled with what he'd done before slowly nodding. "Yes, he asked me to perjure myself. I was in Edinburgh the night of the murder, but I didn't see you with that girl or see you hit her. She was already dead when Campbell came to me. I'd spoken to him earlier about the marker. I'd begged him to give me time to pay it. I was afraid of going bankrupt, which he promised would happen. Then, a few hours later, he came to me and said he'd give me the marker if I served as a witness against you."

"Was the marker the only thing Campbell offered?" Mac asked.

"No, he returned most of the land he'd purchased from Tay. Some of it is lost. My brother has sold bits and pieces of it all over England. He's sold most of his soul as well."

"Here now," the earl said. He set his teacup into the saucer he held with one hand. "It's mine to do with as I wish."

"Of course," his brother answered. "More the fool we."

"So, who planned the escape?" Sabrina asked.

"I did," her father said. "My conscience was heavy with what was going to happen. You heard

Campbell. He was in love with the girl, mad for her, but she didn't notice him, and you can imagine what that did to a man with his conceit. From what I understand, he offered to keep her. He told me he poured out his heart. Of course, she refused him. She may have said something about the Irishman, and Campbell hit her. He didn't stop hitting her until she was dead. He was wild with grief. He claimed he hadn't known what he was doing. He is the one who had the idea of accusing you," he said to Cormac. "He'd also be punishing you for being a rival."

"He was not a good man to have as an enemy," Cormac said.

"No, he wasn't," her father agreed. "I found I couldn't be at peace with the hanging of an innocent soul. I truly hadn't believed you would receive a death sentence," he tried to explain. "In my testimony, I attempted to make a point of its being a crime of passion. Do you remember?"

Cormac frowned. "She was well liked, and passion is no excuse for murder."

"The law takes it into account," her father said, "but the judge didn't. At the most, I had assumed that you would be transported to Queensland. I didn't believe you would receive a hanging sentence. It was the papers' fault."

"Yes, the papers," Cormac echoed with disbelief.

"Well, if they hadn't called you the Irish Murderer or any of that nonsense, then no one would have paid attention, and all would be well."

"Actually, it wouldn't be well," Cormac pointed out. "I'd be on the other side of the world."

Her father made a dismissive sound. "It is better than hanging."

Sabrina had an urge to box her father's arrogant ears. Her gaze met Cormac's. Thank heavens, there was a glint of humor in his eyes. She couldn't believe he was enjoying himself. Then again, he'd just been handed a reprieve from death.

"When they sentenced you to hang," her father said, continuing his story, "I couldn't live with myself. I wrote what friends I had in London, trying to convince them to not approve the death warrant. You see where that took me."

"Well, I appreciate the effort," Cormac answered dryly. "However, I truly valued your sending Mr. Kinnion to my cell."

"That was a disaster," her father said. "I had bribed the guards to help with the escape. Everything was set. However, they cheated me. They were planning to recapture you and make themselves the heroes of the day. It was all a game to them. Ingold saw one of the guards take aim at Kinnion."

"I thought the guard was there to help see the escape through," Ingold admitted. "But then he shot Mr. Kinnion before I realized what was happening and could stop him. I believe he thought the reverend was you," he added sheepishly.

"It is a wonder I am alive at all," Cormac observed.

"Fortunately, the guard was not a good shot and I gave him a good solid knock in the head. Mr. Kinnion and I had a harrowing time escaping Edinburgh ourselves. Of course, once the guards discovered that the reverend wasn't their prisoner, no one cared to keep us. They were afraid we'd let word of the bribe slip."

"Your escape cost me a fortune," her father complained. "You can imagine my fury over hearing the money had gone for naught."

Money they didn't have, Sabrina realized . . . but this time, the thought didn't create a tightness in her chest. She took a step toward Cormac, startled by a new realization. *She didn't feel responsible for her father.* It was a heady thing to release years of what had been an unhealthy habit.

"The one lucky thing," her father was saying, "is that the bullet meant for Enright—"

"Ballin," Cormac said, interrupting him.

"What?" her father questioned.

"Enright is my family name, but I have the title Ballin. Lord Ballin," he reminded them. "I've denied it for too long. But it is my heritage and my right."

"Another penniless earl," her uncle opined. "We are a growing company."

Cormac didn't even spare him a glance. Instead, he addressed the Reverend Kinnion. "You are fortunate you were not killed."

"Yes, fortunate," the Reverend Kinnion echoed weakly.

"*I* had nothing to do with any of this," the earl of Tay said. "Nothing. May I have a drink now?"

"*No,*" Sabrina and her father said in unison.

"Very well," the earl responded, and launched into his own version of events. "Ingold brought Kinnion here. I hid him. I was going to say something to Richard, but before I had the opportunity, my brother arrived, telling me about the botched escape. So I hid both of them."

"How long were you going to hide them?" Cormac asked.

Her uncle frowned and scratched his chin. "At least until Owen calmed down. He was not happy you didn't hang. Until your neck was stretched or you had a bullet in your back, he feared someone might realize he'd killed that girl. Funny what men will do for a woman, isn't it?" The earl clanked his cup on his saucer as if pointing out it was empty. Sabrina ignored him.

Instead, she said, "I was very worried when you left without a word, Father. I thought you were with Mrs. Bossley. She thought you were with me. Can you imagine what would have happened if you'd had an accident, and neither one of us knew where you were?"

Her father didn't take the chiding well. "I was trying to save my neck."

"How did Campbell know you were all here?" Cormac asked.

"He didn't," the earl said. "That is the damn funny thing of it. He came here tonight to murder me, then he found the others. So he decided to finish us all off. He didn't want any witnesses. You know, murdering that chit really was a crime of passion. He probably could have been excused for doing it."

Sabrina didn't know how to justify such a comment. She gave her uncle her back. "Mr. Campbell sent his men for Cormac," Sabrina said. "Our house is in complete disarray."

Her father shrugged. "It is small matter, considering." And he was right. "I feel a fool."

No one argued with him, not even his brother.

"Well now," Cormac said, "the time has come to undo it all. I expect you gentlemen to confess to the Edinburgh court."

There was a moment of stunned silence.

The earl spoke. "We can't do that. Why, we would find ourselves in trouble."

Sabrina's temper rose, but the Reverend Kinnion saved her uncle from the tongue-lashing she had in mind as he said, "Absolutely. It must be done. Confession is good for the soul. I'm finished with this sort of adventure."

She looked to her father. "Sir?" she prodded.

"We have no choice," he admitted. "I pray they understand. At least now I don't need to worry about paying off Campbell."

"Ah, there is that," the earl agreed, and repeated with more enthusiasm, "There *is* that. How lucky can we be? I'd like to drink to our luck. We should celebrate it."

Everyone ignored him.

"Will I be in much trouble?" the Reverend Kinnion asked. "I'm certain the bishop will not be happy."

"Don't worry about the bishop," Sabrina said. "You have a wife who will be overjoyed to have you home. And as for you," she said, reaching for Cormac's hand, "a new life is beginning for you. One where you will wear your title proudly."

He nodded and, for a second, appeared almost overcome. She could understand why. He was free. He'd wanted freedom, and now he had it.

And then he surprised her by lacing his fingers with hers. He looked down into her eyes, his serious, somber. There was a moment of hesitation, as if he was about to do something over which he was uncertain.

He spoke. "Sabrina Davidson, will you be my lady? Will you marry me?"

For a second, Sabrina was unsure she'd heard him correctly. "You are asking for my hand?"

Cormac nodded. "If you will have me. I've little to my name, but I have skills, and I want to build a life with you—"

"Is this just because of what has happened between us?" she asked, needing to know if his feelings were true or if he was doing what was honorable or what he believed was expected.

But before he could answer, her father's harsh voice broke in. "Take your hands off my daughter. "I'll be damned to hell before I allow her to marry an Irishman. Earl or no."

Chapter Twenty-One

$\mathcal{M}$ac couldn't remember a time when words had ignited his anger into a rage. He was tired and covered with bruises from saving these men's worthless hides.

He hadn't even considered asking Davidson for his daughter's hand because Sabrina was *his*. They belonged to one another, and he'd run through the man who would say him nay.

But then there was the voice of doubt. He'd never loved Moira as much as he did Sabrina. She was fire to Moira's ice. However, what if she agreed with her father? What if she obeyed him—?

"I'm going with him, Father." She faced her parent, her head high, her stance determined. "I love him. I don't want to live my life without him."

Mac could have fallen to his knees in gratitude. Her love was not false. And it had to be love and love alone she felt because he had nothing else to offer her.

He swept her into his arms. Her eyes shone with the truth of her love. "You are so beautiful," he said. "So incredibly wonderful. And I love you, Sabrina Davidson. Do you hear me? *I love you*."

And then he kissed her with all the passion of his being.

She kissed him back. Thoroughly.

Their kiss broke, and Mac had to say, "You are becoming very good at this."

"I pray to become better," she answered, and he laughed. No matter what challenges were in his future, he could overcome all with this intelligent, vibrant woman by his side.

Richard Davidson stood. He blocked the door. "You will not leave with him," he instructed his daughter. "I forbid it."

"You can't stop me from doing what I want," Sabrina answered, as simple as that. "You would have to hold me prisoner to keep me from marrying him, and sooner or later, I would escape. And don't pretend you need me, Father. You'll have the Widow Bossley. She will make you a good wife."

"This man is not good enough for you, Sabrina."

She laughed at that, the sound bitter. "Why, Father? Is he too honest for you? Has he not told enough lies? Gambled enough? Drunk enough? Or is it that he doesn't have money? Yes, that is it, isn't it? Need I remind you, *I* don't have a dowry?"

A look of confusion crossed her father's face, as if he was surprised by her resentment, and she *was* angry. Mac understood why. She'd given her father his due, but now, she wanted a life of her own.

The magistrate opened his hands, a conciliatory gesture, an invitation to understanding. "I just want what is right for you."

"*He's* right for me," she answered. "He has my love. Should that not be enough?"

"There is more to the world, Sabrina, than simple love," her father said.

"I disagree with that," she answered. "Furthermore, Cormac and I have more than most. He has a profession and a title. Lord Ballin. It is worth as much as the earl of Tay."

"Mine is an old and honored title," the earl declared.

"As is mine," Mac said.

"In *Ireland*," Tay returned, and Mac enjoyed the mental image of shoving the man's head in a vat of the whisky he drank.

But it was Sabrina who spoke. "I once believed that the family title gave me a position of importance and meant that I had to hold myself to a higher standard, to keep myself apart from others. However, now I know titles mean very little. The measure of a man is what he offers others. Consider my cousin Aileen's husband, Mr. Stephens. He is a bastard son. Granted, his father is a duke, but I admire that Mr. Stephens has made his own way in the world. And look at Tara's Laird Breccan. I've heard you mock him, Father, because he believes in the old ways, the clan ways. He takes care of his people while the two of you"—she nodded to her father and uncle—"think only of yourselves. You've ruined Annefield," Sabrina said to Tay. "What was once a proud estate will soon be up for auction. And you, Father, you dare to tell me what I can and can't do? Whom I should and shouldn't love? You, who had so little respect for me that you kept secrets? I believe you are both a disgrace."

"But this man has *nothing*," her father said, as if needing to pound in the point.

"He has *me*," she answered. "I'm not *nothing*."

She turned to Mac, as if needing reassurance. "You do want me, don't you?"

"With all my heart, forever and always."

Tears came to Sabrina's eyes. "I warn you, I won't settle for anything less than being the proud wife of an Irish lord. I love you, Cormac Enright, and if you can forgive the fact that I am related to these two men who have given up all semblance of the honor they claim they have, then I will proudly stand behind you as your wife."

"*Beside* me," Mac corrected Sabrina, taking her hand. "I want you always by my side. We can conquer this world together."

"Then let us marry this day. This very moment." She searched his eyes.

"Shouldn't the banns be announced?" the earl of Tay asked.

"*Yes*," her father answered. "Three times. The banns *must* be announced."

"Not in Scotland," Mac answered. "You know that is not necessary, Davidson. Mr. Kinnion, will you marry me to this woman?"

Both Davidson and the earl turned to the clergyman still sitting on the bed. "You will not, Kinnion," Davidson said.

The reverend looked from one benefactor to the

other, then, to Cormac's surprise, he said, "Aye, I'll marry the two of you."

Sabrina faced Cormac, her blue eyes triumphant.

"I can't watch this," her father said. "I will not accept this marriage. Do you understand? Don't come to me when you realize what you've done. My door will be closed to you." He then walked from the room.

Tay watched him a moment, then left as well. He could be heard calling for whisky as he started down the stairs.

For a long moment, there was silence in the room.

Mac spoke. "I'm sorry," he said to Sabrina.

"I'm not," she said. "Father will be fine. He will have Mrs. Bossley, and she'll nurse his wounded vanity, but I can live without him. However, I cannot live without you."

"Which is what marriage is about," the Reverend Kinnion said. "I don't have my prayer book. Of course, that doesn't matter, I lost my glasses— but this is one sacrament I know by heart. Lord Ballin, I'm glad I played a part, however small, in delivering you from injustice. You are making a good choice, Miss Davidson."

"I agree," she said. "Now, please, sir, marry us."

The ceremony that followed was swift but heartfelt.

Ingold and a few of the other servants served as witnesses. There was no ring. Mac had nothing but himself to offer her, and that was all she wanted.

When they were done with their vows, he sealed his pledge with a kiss—and the realization that he was no longer alone in life.

The servants wished them well as they left the house.

The moon was high in the sky. It was a good night to marry. They walked across the yard, hand in hand toward where Dumpling had finished his hay and slept peacefully, one hoof cocked.

"What do we do now?" Sabrina asked.

"What would you like to do?"

"I need to collect Rolf. We can bring him wherever we go, can't we?" Sabrina asked.

"Of course. He's family."

They drove to her house. Davidson was not there, and that was just as well.

Sabrina gathered her things. She took only her clothes. Cormac was more practical. He raided the kitchen for Mrs. Patton's venison and some bread and cheese. He also took the blanket off Sabrina's bed. They might need it if they slept on the ground. They filled the pony cart.

"We'll be doing some walking," he warned.

"That's fine," she said. "But someday, I will want you to buy a lovely gray mare, and I shall canter around like a fine lady."

"You are a fine lady," he assured her. "You are *my* lady." He gave her a kiss and insisted that she sit in the cart while he walked.

She wasn't happy about that decision and, of course, argued, which is why they were still standing in the yard when Mrs. Bossley, wearing her maroon cape, pulled up in her rig. Dawn was just filling the sky.

"I came to say good-bye," she said. "Your father told me what happened."

"Where is he?" Sabrina asked.

"Asleep. In my bed."

"Are you certain you want him?" Sabrina said.

Mrs. Bossley's response was to laugh, a sign of the respect she had for Sabrina. "I do, and I'll marry him. We manage fine together. But I wanted you to have this." She pressed a heavy leather coin purse into Cormac's hand. "It is a wedding present."

Mac put his arm around Sabrina's shoulders.

"We can't take your money," he said, ready to offer it back.

"Of course you can," Mrs. Bossley informed him. "I have plenty. The two of you need a start in life. And someday, Richard will come around. I've already told him he must do what is expected to clear your name. He wrote this." She pulled from a pocket of her cape a letter. "It is his explanation to the court. I shall see that he travels to Edinburgh in the next few days."

"Thank you," Mac said.

She waved a dismissive hand. "He wanted to do it. He is tired now and feeling very low, but he is a good man. He will be true to his word and help clear your name. He'll also forgive you someday for defying him," she said to Sabrina. "He will regret his temper and make his peace with you. Men can be such hypocrites when they have their backs up."

With those words, she turned her gig around and drove off.

"I don't know if I will accept his apology if it ever comes," Sabrina said.

Mac took her hand. "I will ask that you do," he told her. He stood a moment, looking in the direction of the rising sun, where the sky was filled with the rose hues of dawn, then looked down at the letter he held. "He was a brave man to write this. Don't judge him harshly. I don't."

And he didn't. The man he had once been, the one who had nursed a grudge against his brother, had been transformed by love. He now understood that Lorcan had no choice but to be true to the love he and Moira had.

The one who had betrayed them had been Mac, with his temper. His spite had cost him so much, but he knew that it had not touched Lorcan and Moira. They had been happy together.

And now he was ready to be the man he should be—the one who loved and loved well.

"Are you ready to go, sir?" Sabrina asked. "Are you ready to take me out of this valley?"

He turned. Sabrina was in the cart, with Rolf sitting on the bench by her side. Strands of her hair had escaped her braid and curled around her face. Her blues were alive with excitement and her cheeks rosy from the morning chill. She was beautiful to him. Absolutely perfect . . . save for one small matter.

"One moment," he said, crossing to her. He leaned forward and kissed her thoroughly and completely. "Now I'm ready." She laughed, her happiness filling her heart.

With the snap of the reins, they set off into the world.

*A*nd so . . .

*S*abrina's father was true to his word, as Mrs. Bossley had predicted—or had orchestrated.

At great sacrifice to himself, he admitted to the Edinburgh court that he had lied in his testimony. Cormac's name was cleared.

To Sabrina's surprise, Cormac decided they should stay in Edinburgh. The city was to his liking.

She and Rolf, and even Dumpling, had some difficulty adjusting. Everything was noisy, but in time, she learned to enjoy the variety of the city.

Cormac began a practice as a surgeon. Because of his experiences doctoring on the battlefield, he had learned techniques that were of interest to the other doctors in Edinburgh. Soon, he and Sabrina had many friends, and Cormac began earning a good living.

More important, he was very happy.

His surgery was two rooms on the ground floor of their house. She often assisted him when necessary. Sometimes, Sabrina would overhear him whistling. The sound always made her smile.

Sabrina did not talk to her father. She was not as forgiving as Mrs. Bossley or even Cormac. She was so in love with her husband, she could not imagine her life without him. What her father and uncle had conspired to do in the name of money was unacceptable to her. She didn't wish her father ill, but she would not search him out either, and she found that the decision gave her peace.

In time, perhaps, their relationship would not be so strained, but Sabrina didn't have strong feelings one way or the other, and until she did, she would live her own life.

She heard from her cousins. After being caught up in the whirl of London, Aileen and her husband, Blake Stephens, had decided to return to Scotland. Aileen was now pregnant and wanted her baby born at Annefield.

However, they were not fools. She and Blake purchased a fine estate along the River Tay, where they would stay instead of relying on the earl.

Meanwhile, Tara had given birth to a baby girl and all said that her husband Breccan, a brawny man who had once had such a temper he'd been known as the "Beast of Aberfeldy" was at the beck and call of both wife and tiny daughter. Sa-

brina had laughed aloud with happiness the first
time she'd seen the huge, muscular Breccan holding his wee babe, Elizabeth. Lizbeth they called
her, named after Tara's late mother. Tara herself
had turned into the most generous of women. Sabrina and Tara now corresponded often and were
growing close.

However, as for Sabrina . . . she felt a bit of discontent. Once their house was set up, she found
herself at loose ends.

Motherhood would fill her time . . . perhaps. She
enjoyed helping in the surgery . . . but wondered
if there was something else she should be doing.
She adored her husband and was always ready to
show him her adoration . . . but try as she might,
one couldn't make love every hour of the day.

She began to wonder if there wasn't something
else for her and often said as much to Cormac.

One night, as he held her in his arms, he teased
her about the way she enjoyed reading the papers
for stories of crimes. "It seems to be one of your
favorite interests."

That was true. Sabrina enjoyed a good mystery
and often wished she knew more of the details
behind the stories she read. It helped to ease her
boredom. She'd also thought back to when she'd

been searching for her father and Mr. Kinnion. Yes, Cormac's presence had made that time important and exciting, but she'd also enjoyed the puzzle of unraveling the mystery.

When a strongbox was found missing at the local milliners, Sabrina had reasoned out who had taken it based upon clues she'd learned one afternoon spent trying on hats. She'd caught the apprentice in his lie. The milliner had been so thankful for Sabrina's help, he'd created a special bonnet just for her.

A week later, upon hearing a tale of a missing boy, Sabrina had asked a few discreet questions and learned of the lad's last movements. She'd taken Rolf to that section of the city, and with the hound's keen nose, they'd found the boy, trapped in a well that someone had covered. The lad had thought to hide there and had been too clever for his own good. Sabrina, Lady Ballin, was hailed as a heroine for saving his life.

Then, a few days later, while Sabrina was enjoying her afternoon cup of tea, Cormac appeared in the doorway. "I have a surprise for you," he said.

Sabrina liked surprises. "What is it?"

Cormac held out his hand. "Come." He took her downstairs. "Now, close your eyes."

"Why?"

"Please, wife, don't argue."

"But I argue so well," Sabrina protested.

"You do," he agreed. "Now, close them."

She did as he asked and he led her outside. He turned her so that she faced the house they rented. "Open them," he whispered in her ear.

Sabrina wasn't certain what to expect. She didn't know if he'd had the door painted or placed some other embellishment on the house.

For a moment, she didn't see what he'd done.

The entrance of their home also served as the doorway for his surgery. There was a sign beside the door with the name Ballin and the picture of a surgeon's knife and forceps.

Below this sign was another. It said, DISCREET INVESTIGATIONS AND INQUIRIES. The symbol was crossed andirons.

"What is this?" Sabrina asked.

"A challenge for you," he said. "I know you have had too much time on your hands. The city offers too many comforts for a country lass like yourself. One of my patients, Lady Dinwiddie, suggested that such a service would be of benefit to people of her class. She suggested that having someone with your sense of discretion could be of service to someone like herself. She was very impressed with the tale of how you found that lad.

At first, Sabrina didn't know if she liked the idea. She considered it a moment. "Discreet Investigations and Inquiries." She looked at her husband. "Exactly what does that mean?"

"It can mean whatever we wish."

"Would you help?"

"When I could. I would not like your running off alone, like you did the day you searched for the boy—"

"I had Rolf with me."

"I would prefer you had *me* with you. Nor do I believe you should have all the fun."

Sabrina looked back at the sign, and the sense of ennui that had plagued her lifted. He was giving her permission to do whatever she wished. It was a wonderful gift. She ran her fingers over the sign plaque.

"I like this," she said. "I do. But I won't push it. I mean, I have responsibilities here."

"You do," her husband agreed, opening the door for her to go inside.

"I can't go traipsing all over the place the way I did looking for that boy." She started up the stairs to their living quarters.

"Or to find that strongbox," he agreed.

"Yes," she said thoughtfully. "However, it would be nice if those who had inquiries to be made would come to me instead of my having to search them out."

"I thought you would find it easier," he murmured.

"And it would be a service," Sabrina allowed.

"It definitely helps those who need help."

She stopped at the top of the stairs and faced him. "Do you realize, I'm excited. This is the most intriguing thing anyone has ever done for me."

Cormac smiled. "I thought you would be pleased."

"And you will help?"

"I will insist upon it."

Her mind danced with possibilities, but then she said, "Who will need such a service? Truly? I mean it is a fine idea, but . . ." She let her voice trail off, aware of a strong disappointment.

"We'll see," her husband answered, and placed a kiss on her cheek. He started to return to his surgery, but Sabrina couldn't let him go without a proper kiss, which led to the bedroom, where they celebrated her new venture with enthusiasm.

However, he had planted a seed, one Sabrina hoped would bear fruit. Whatever happened with

"Discreet Inquiries and Investigations," it was a lovely thought that she was married to a man who was so aware of her, he would allow her to contemplate such a thing.

*T*he next day, Sabrina was in her husband's surgery, writing accounts in the ledger, when a woman of middling years and a sad, worried countenance entered the office.

"Excuse me," she said to Sabrina, "I saw the sign on the door. Is this the place where one can find help?"

For a second, Sabrina couldn't think of what she'd meant. She'd almost forgotten the existence of the sign.

"Discreet Inquiries," the woman repeated to prod her memory.

"Yes, yes, it is," Sabrina answered, coming to her feet.

"I need help," the woman said. "And I don't know where to turn. Lady Dinwiddie suggested I speak to you."

From the other room, Cormac had heard the woman. He came to the doorway.

Sabrina glanced at him, wondering if he had

put this woman up to making this call. It would so like him to do anything to please her, including hiring an actress to pretend to be in distress.

"I read how you found that lad in the well," the woman asked, as if she, too, wanted to ensure that Sabrina was genuine in her intentions.

"I did."

The relief that crossed the woman's face could not be feigned. She pulled a chair over to where Sabrina sat. Sinking down into it, she said, "Then please help me. My baby's missing, and I am half-mad with worry. Perhaps you have heard of her? Lacy Fletcher."

Everyone knew of the missing child. Six months earlier, the baby had been in the care of her nanny when both of them had disappeared. Mr. Fletcher was a well-respected academician from a highly respected family. Mrs. Fletcher had been an heiress. Her money came from her father's shipbuilding firm. "Mrs. Fletcher?" Sabrina guessed.

"Yes, I am, and I'm desperate, my lady," Mrs. Fletcher said. "I will pay any price to find my child. My father has hired men to search, but they have discovered nothing."

This was no ruse.

Sabrina glanced at her husband, and her heart filled with a love she could never have imagined.

She'd not known that a man could love her enough to let her pursue what made her happy.

His was an unconventional solution but one that pleased her. He would support her in this endeavor. He would let her be the woman she wanted to be.

And that was a priceless gift.

Sabrina stood. "Please, let us go upstairs where we can be private, Mrs. Fletcher. Would you enjoy a cup of strong, black tea? While we share a pot, you can tell me everything you know about your child's disappearance."

*G*ive in to your Impulses!

These unforgettable stories only take a second to buy and give you hours of reading pleasure!

Go to *www.AvonImpulse.com* and see what we have to offer.

Available wherever e-books are sold.

AVONIMPULSE

IMP 0811